Burn Rate

Zeb Carter Series, Book 3

By

Ty Patterson

Published by Three Aces Publishing
Visit the author site: http://www.typatterson.com

Original Cover Design: Nathan Wampler
Digital Formatting: Tugboat Design

Books by Ty Patterson

Warriors Series Shorts

This is a series of novellas that link to the Warriors Series thrillers

Zulu Hour, Book 1
The Shadow, Book 2
The Man From Congo, Book 3
The Texan, Book 4
The Heavies, Book 5
The Cab Driver, Book 6
Warriors Series Shorts, Boxset I, Books 1-3
Warriors Series Shorts, Boxset II, Books 4-6

Gemini Series

Dividing Zero, Book 1
Defending Cain, Book 2
I Am Missing, Book 3
Wrecking Team, Book 4

Zeb Carter Series

Zeb Carter, Book 1
The Peace Killers, Book 2
Burn Rate, Book 3

Warriors Series

The Warrior, Book 1
The Reluctant Warrior, Book 2
The Warrior Code, Book 3
The Warrior's Debt, Book 4
Flay, Book 5
Behind You, Book 6
Hunting You, Book 7
Zero, Book 8
Death Club, Book 9
Trigger Break, Book 10
Scorched Earth, Book 11
RUN!, Book 12
Warriors series Boxset, Books 1-4
Warriors series Boxset II, Books 5-8
Warriors series Boxset III, Books 1-8

Cade Stryker Series

The Last Gunfighter of Space, Book 1
The Thief Who Stole A Planet, Book 2

Sign up to Ty Patterson's mailing list and get *The Watcher*, a Zeb Carter novella, exclusive to newsletter subscribers. Join Ty Patterson's Facebook group of readers, at www.facebook.com/groups/324440917903074.

Check out Ty on Amazon, iTunes, Kobo, Nook and on his website www.typatterson.com.

Acknowledgments

No book is a single person's product. I am privileged that *Burn Rate* has benefited from the input of several great people.

Paula Artlip, Sheldon Levy, Molly Birch, David T. Blake, Tracy Boulet, Patricia Burke, Mark Campbell, Tricia Cullerton, Claire Forgacs, Dave Davis, Sylvia Foster, Cary Lory Becker, Charlie Carrick, Pat Ellis, Dori Barrett, Simon Alphonso, Dave Davis, V. Elizabeth Perry, Ann Finn, Pete Bennett, Eric Blackburn, Margaret Harvey, David Hay, Jim Lambert, Suzanne Jackson Mickelson, Tricia Terry Pellman, Jimmy Smith, Maria Stine, Theresa and Brad Werths, who are my beta readers and who helped shape my book, my launch team for supporting me, Donna Rich for her proofreading and Doreen Martens for her editing.

Special thanks to Pat Ellis, Crisis Intervention Coordinator/Chaplain, Puget Sound Regional Fire Authority, and Rusty Olsen, CFI, CFEI, Fire and Arson Investigator, Puget Sound Regional Fire Authority. Their advice on fires was invaluable, and any mistakes in the book are all mine.

Dedications

To Michelle Rose Dunn, Debbie Bruns Gallant, Tom Gallant and Cheri Gerhardt, for supporting me.

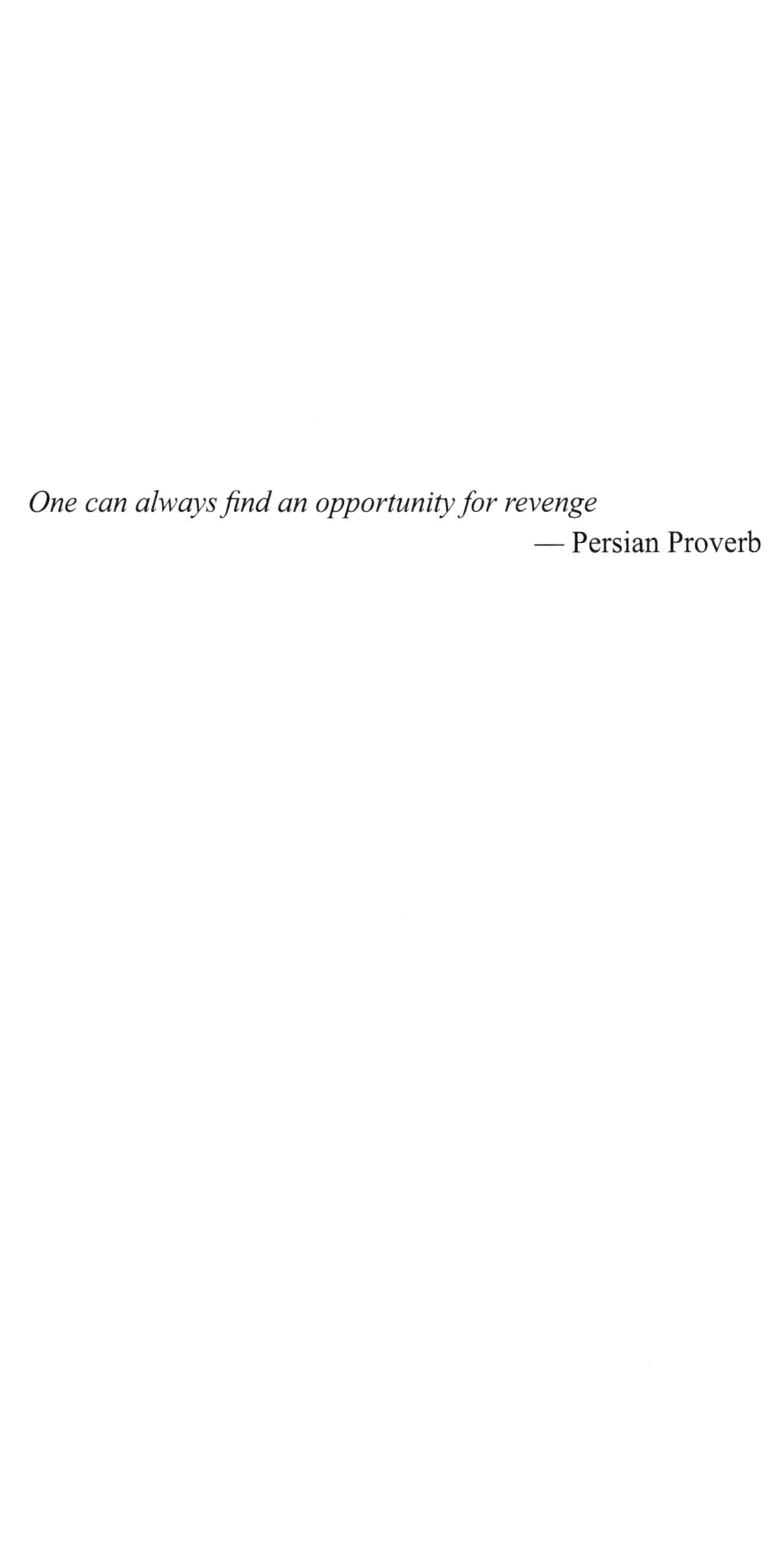

One can always find an opportunity for revenge

— Persian Proverb

Chapter 1

'Drive, Mister.' A gun pressed tight against the back of Zeb Carter's head.

He didn't move for a moment, stunned at the turn of events.

'Move,' the speaker gritted his teeth. He jammed the weapon harder. 'Didn't you hear what I said?'

It was just after noon. A New York afternoon in the summer. Bright sunlight on the sidewalks. Hordes of chattering tourists, cameras around their necks, following their tour guides dutifully. Office workers returning to their workplaces after hastily snatched meals. Skateboarders speeding through crowds in the daredevil way only they could manage.

Zeb had been out for lunch, as well, along with Meghan and Beth. A Vietnamese joint had opened up near their Columbus Avenue office, and the younger sister had talked them into trying it out.

And so, they had gone.

They had returned from Jerusalem a few months back, high from the events of their previous mission. Israel had recognized Palestine as an independent country, and the two nations were working on the finer details of a historic accord.

That single development had dramatically reduced terrorist incidents around the world. Zeb's warriors were benefiting from that lull. Nothing much was happening at the Agency.

'You want to join?' he asked the others, as he followed the sisters out.

'Nah,' Broker replied distractedly, focused on bettering his golf putt. Bear and Chloe, engrossed in something on their cell phones, didn't look up. Bwana and Roger were playing, aiming shots at a hoop on the wall. The two men waved them away.

Zeb went with the Petersen twins: he and sunshine and laughter. He had taken their SUV to the joint and parked it in an empty space.

It had happened on their return.

He had slid into the driver's seat, Meghan next to him at the front, Beth in the rear. Standard seating when the three of them were in a vehicle.

He saw the blur of motion from the corner of his eyes. Felt the rear door open and bodies slide in.

By the time it registered on him and the sisters, it was too late. A barrel was digging into the back of his head.

His eyes flicked to the rearview mirror. He was still stunned, anger growing in him at his carelessness.

I'm losing my edge. I wasn't paying attention to my surroundings, at possible threats.

He blinked when he took in the assailants. Two of them. Male and female. The former's weapon was on Zeb, the woman's on Beth.

They're kids! In their teens.

The boy looked to be sixteen, the girl a year or two younger.

Not that I am an expert on ages.

The gun at his head jabbed again. 'How many times do I have to tell you? You want to die?' the boy shouted. 'You,' he yelled at Meghan, 'don't turn back, or your friend dies.'

Zeb looked swiftly at the elder sister, who nodded imperceptibly. She, too, had caught the undertone of fear in the kid's voice.

He's scared. He isn't a seasoned carjacker. Could be his first such gig.

'Where to?' Zeb asked.

'Columbus Avenue. Near the Lincoln Center.'

He turned the key, flashed his indicator and joined the stream of traffic.

Do they know who we are? Are they aware of our office location?

It didn't seem likely. Zeb and his crew worked in a covert outfit that only a handful of people knew of. It was called the Agency and had only eight operatives. Its director reported only to the U.S. president and carried a vague job title. The organization went after terrorists, international criminals and threats to national security.

The two kids didn't fit that bill. They were smartly dressed, the boy in a t-shirt over jeans, neat haircut. The girl, her eyes wide, in a mid-calf dress. Both blond-haired, green eyes, well-shaped features. They looked like high school students.

Not scruffy, though. Preppy. Private school?

'Where exactly on Columbus Avenue?'

'I'll tell you when we get there,' the boy snarled.

There were ways Zeb could overpower his assailant. The gun was too close to his head. A swift move to the left or right and the barrel would be exposed. An elbow to the rear, break the kid's jaw, and the tables would be turned. Beth could easily overcome the girl.

He didn't do any of that, though. Neither did Beth. Meghan didn't react.

The three of them could read one another without having to speak. They wanted to see how this would play out. It didn't feel like a mugging or car theft.

Ahead, a light turned red. Traffic slowed. Zeb eased on the gas.

'Go!' the boy showered spittle on the back of Zeb's neck. 'I'll tell you when to stop.'

'You don't want me crashing into those vehicles,' Zeb explained reasonably. 'We'll draw attention. Cops might show up. I'm guessing you don't want that.'

'Please, mister,' the girl broke her silence. 'Drive as fast as you can.'

Her voice was breaking. *The two of them are close to breaking down. They're just barely holding it together.*

He looked in the mirror, at the girl, whose jaw was set tight. She stared straight ahead, didn't meet his eyes. Her gun was jammed in Beth's side.

The light changed. The snake of vehicles moved. Zeb accelerated. Overtook a cab. Honked to get a lumbering van to make way, got an upraised finger as they swept past.

New York. Attitude first, manners second.

Lincoln Center loomed in the distance. Their office building to their left. The kids didn't look at it as it slid behind them.

Nope, this isn't about us.

'Left, at West 62nd Street.'

Zeb turned on his blinker and navigated. He felt the boy's

breath on his neck. Could hear him breathing harshly, gulping as he swallowed. He spread out the fingers of his left hand.

A message to the twins.

Be ready.

A car nosed out of its parking space. He floored his SUV and squeezed into its place before another vehicle could.

'What are you doing?' the boy screamed. 'I asked you to drive.'

Zeb turned off the ignition and swung around in his seat.

'Shoot me.'

'What? Can't you see I have a gun?'

'Yes. Use it. Go ahead.'

The boy swallowed. His face turned red. The gun, a Glock, shook in his hand, its barrel pointing at Zeb's face.

'Mister,' the girl's voice trembled.

He and Meghan looked at her. Beth was watching as well.

'Please do as he says.' A tear rolled down the young woman's face. 'We need to go fast.'

'Why?'

'There's a gunman in our apartment,' she sobbed, her gun hand falling limply to her lap.

'If we don't take this vehicle to our building,' she shuddered, 'he'll kill Mom.'

Chapter 2

'Mister,' the boy pleaded, his eyes desperate, his Glock still up, 'Grace is right.'

Zeb looked at Meghan and Beth. They both nodded.

'Do you know us?' he asked the kids. 'Have you seen us before?'

'No, mister,' the boy replied, dully, 'that man sent us out. Asked us to return in fifteen minutes with a vehicle. We saw you climbing in your vehicle and grabbed our opportunity. We're running out of time.'

Zeb frowned. It didn't make sense. *Why would a gunman send these kids out for his getaway vehicle? Why would the two go a block away?'*

'Meg?'

'Yeah?'

'Get our creds out of the glove box.'

She turned to the front and reached forward.

'DON'T MOVE!' the boy shouted, veins throbbing on his forehead.

'Mister, please do as my brother says,' Grace, the girl, said anxiously.

'Relax,' Beth touched her shoulder. 'We can help.'

'YOU CAN! BY TAKING THIS VEHICLE TO OUR BUILDING,' the boy roared, firmly gripping his weapon.

'We're with the NYPD,' Meghan said, moving swiftly. She opened the glove compartment and withdrew three identity cards. 'Here. See for yourself.'

Each of the creds had their names, photographs and the NYPD's logos on them.

'You're cops?' the boy asked dumbly, staring at the creds.

'Something like that.'

'Travis,' Grace said urgently, 'he said no cops.'

'That's right—'

'Look at me,' Zeb commanded.

Grace and Travis looked at him, reacting instinctively to his tone.

'We can help. We are trained at this. I am Zeb Carter. This is Meghan. That's Beth, her sister, next to Grace.'

'Our mom will die, sir, if we don't move fast,' Travis's voice cracked, words rushed out of his mouth. 'That gunman needs this vehicle. He said he will shoot Mom if we don't return in fifteen minutes. We don't have time to talk. He said if any cops come—'

'Travis, is that gun loaded?' Zeb stopped him.

'Yes, sir. But—'

Zeb held his palm out. Travis hesitated for a moment and then handed over the Glock with an agonized cry. He buried his face in his hands and started crying.

'Grace?'

The girl gave up her weapon, too, tears streaming down her cheeks.

Zeb inspected the guns, removed the magazines, grunted,

slotted them back and tossed the weapons to the floorboards.

Not yet, he told the beast stirring inside him. *There's time for you, later.*

'Grace,' he addressed the girl, who seemed to be holding up better than her brother. 'We *will* get your mom back. Alive. I promise.'

She looked at him uncomprehendingly, dabbed at her face and sniffed hard. 'What? How?'

'We have done this before. I told you, we're experienced. Tell us everything that happened.'

'Travis,' she grabbed her brother's shoulder and shook him. 'TRAVIS,' she shook harder. 'We need help. We don't have a choice.'

The boy raised his head, took several deep, shuddering breaths and attempted to compose himself.

'We don't have time, Grace,' he said despairingly, 'I keep telling them that. They aren't listening.'

Zeb started the SUV and eased out. 'We have. That gunman needs a getaway vehicle badly, otherwise he wouldn't have sent you out. That fifteen minutes … that's just to put pressure on you.'

He might be wanting to kill the mother ... or molest her, once the kids are out.

That was a possibility he had to consider. 'Where's your apartment? Break it down for us as I drive.'

The teenagers explained, haltingly.

They were lounging in their living room with their mother, who had taken a day off from work. She had promised to go with them to a movie later in the day.

A knock on the door had sounded. Travis opened the door to face two men, one wielding a gun.

The strangers rushed into the apartment, shut the door and yelled at the family to stay quiet.

'Mom tried to reach for her phone,' Grace sniffled. 'That man slapped her so hard she fell. He taped her mouth and wrists and flung her on the couch. I screamed, Travis was shouting. He hit us and ordered us to stay quiet. The second man left the apartment. They had a vehicle waiting outside the building. He went to get it ready.'

'He was supposed to call when he brought it to the entrance,' Travis picked up. 'But he didn't. The gunman called him on his cell several times, but that second man didn't answer.'

'Then he sent us to find a vehicle.' Grace wiped her nose and leaned forward. 'Turn right on Amsterdam Avenue.'

Zeb turned.

'Carry on past those lights.'

'He gave you a cell?' Beth queried. 'How are you to communicate with him?'

'No cell,' Travis replied in a stronger voice. 'Like I said, he gave us these two guns and fifteen minutes. He asked us to knock on the door when we returned. He would shoot Mom if we brought the cops or tried any tricks.'

'I know what you're thinking,' Grace said bitterly in the ensuing silence. 'We should have used those guns on him. We thought about it. He was using Mom as a shield. He said any false moves and she would die.'

'Did you check those guns?' Zeb looked at her in the mirror.

'No, sir,' her hair flew around her face as shook her head. 'We were thinking of Mom. Nothing else.'

'And getting a vehicle,' Travis added. 'There, that red-bricked building.' He pointed to a highrise on their right. 'Our apartment is on the twelfth floor.'

Zeb scanned it. Nothing special about it; it was like thousands of such buildings in the city. Window-washers dangled from harnesses, scrubbing the glass sides. Traffic streamed by on the street, cabs honked, pedestrians walked on the sidewalk. Nothing unusual jumped out at him. He drove past the entrance, ignoring the kids' protests. 'You see that second man anywhere?'

They scanned the street to the left and right.

'No, sir,' Grace said, finally.

'What do they look like? What language did they speak?'

'They both were average height. Dark hair. Black or brown. I didn't pay much attention. Travis?'

'Nope, I didn't either. They spoke English, sir. They sounded American.'

'Names?'

'Names?' Grace asked, puzzled.

'Did they use each other's names?' Meghan clarified.

'No.'

'What were they wearing?'

'We weren't paying attention!' Grace yelled. 'Can you stop these questions? You said you would save Mom—'

'We will.' Meghan turned back to the front, sending a silent message to Zeb. *Now's not the time to ask more questions. They're close to breaking down.*

Zeb nodded, acknowledging silently.

He parked close to the entrance. 'Can he see us from above?'

'No, sir,' Grace replied. 'Our apartment overlooks the side street.'

He switched off the ignition and handed the key to her.

'Here's the plan.'

Chapter 3

'That will work?' Travis asked dubiously, when Zeb finished explaining.

'Yeah. Remember, he has your mom as a hostage. He's counting on you to be terrified, to not call the cops.'

He gave the Glocks back. 'Take them.' He looked searchingly at the teenagers. 'Act scared.'

'That won't be a problem, sir,' Grace tried a smile and failed. 'We are scared.'

'Go.'

The kids left the vehicle, looked back nervously at them, and walked towards the entrance when Meghan nodded reassuringly.

Zeb and the sisters exited the vehicle and followed them, several paces behind. *No concierge, no security,* Zeb thought, taking in the lobby automatically, his eyes sweeping.

'Can you hear us?' Beth spoke softly in her collar mic.

'Yeah,' Grace replied in their earbuds.

They'd outfitted the kids with miniature comms devices.

'Wait for our confirmation. Enter the hallway when we say we are ready.'

'Yes.'

The operatives headed to a door further away from the elevators. Stairways, the teenagers had explained. They started climbing, Zeb leading, Glock in hand.

That second man. He could still be about.

'We're in the elevator,' Grace murmured.

'Got that,' Meghan acknowledged.

The warriors started climbing faster.

The floors were separated by two flights of stairs, a landing in between. They didn't encounter anyone. They were on the fifth when Grace spoke again. 'We are here.'

'Go down, or up. We are yet to reach.'

They had reached the eighth floor when Grace checked in again, and when they arrived at the twelfth floor, the teenagers had completed two more aimless rides in the elevator.

Zeb cracked open the door to the hallway. Empty. He looked at the sisters. They had their Glocks in their hands, ready, a thin film of perspiration on their foreheads. Both were breathing easily. Twelve floors weren't a hard workout for any of them.

'GO!' he told the kids.

A wedge of light appeared to his left as the elevator doors opened. Travis stepped out. Grace followed. Neither of them looked in the direction of the stairways.

Good. They're sticking to the script.

Their apartment was a corner one, its door at right angles to the hallway. Fifty feet away from where they crouched.

Grace went in front and pressed the buzzer. Followed it with a knock. A minute passed.

The gunman's probably checking them out through the peephole.

A sliver of light appeared as the door opened. Faint voices, muffled, came through to them. Grace tossed her gun through the opening, collected Travis's and threw it inside, too.

The door opened wider. A shadowy form inside. The mother, her face pale, features indistinct. She disappeared from sight as the door shut.

Zeb waited a beat. The gunman might check through the peephole. See if the hallway remains clear.

He held his left palm up, fingers outstretched. Counted down by folding one digit at a time.

The three of them burst through the landing door when his small finger bent. They raced towards the apartment, Zeb in the middle, Meghan to his right, Beth to his left.

Thirty feet away. Their Glocks in front of them.

Now, twenty, then ten.

Their upper bodies swiveled, their right shoulders pointed forward.

They crashed into the door simultaneously.

It was made of wood, strong, well-built, but it couldn't withstand the concerted impact. It ripped apart at the lock with a tearing sound, swung inside and crashed against the wall.

First impressions registered on Zeb as they headed deeper into the apartment, crossing the small hallway at the entrance.

A couch ahead. Prints and photographs on the wall. Fire-place to the right. TV in a corner. Startled sounds. Travis and Grace, to the left, near a large window. A dining table behind them. The teenagers were white-faced, looking at them. A taller woman beside them, her mouth opening in a soundless scream.

A man next to her. Dark eyes, surprised. His hand rising.

Gun!

Zeb didn't know if he had shouted a warning. His body reacted instinctively. He dived behind the couch just as the assailant's weapon spat. He landed on his shoulder. Snapped a look. Beth and Meghan were both hugging the floor, Glocks trained on the shooter.

The man wasn't hanging around. He cursed loudly. Lunged towards the large window at the rear. Glass splintered under his weight as he flew out and disappeared.

'Did he just—' Meghan shouted in surprise.

Zeb leaped over the couch and approached the window cautiously. Cool air drifted inside. A curtain twitched at the side. He aimed his Glock over the sill and peered carefully.

There! The man was rappelling swiftly down the window-washers' ropes, his legs powering off the glass front of the building, giving him speed and flight.

The window cleaners swore and raged at him. The gunman didn't respond. He looked up once at Zeb and continued until he dropped out of sight.

'I bet you can't do that,' Meghan joined him.

'I don't even want to try,' he replied, with feeling. He shook his head, bemused at the manner of the assailant's escape.

'Zeb,' Beth nudged him, drawing his attention back to the apartment.

He turned around. The mother was sobbing, shuddering as she clutched Grace and Travis tight. He holstered his weapon. Meghan drew her cell phone and made a call. The cops. Beth went deeper in the living room and straightened an upturned chair.

The mother composed herself after a while. She wiped her face, blew her nose and faced the warriors.

'Mom,' Grace told her, 'these three helped us. We were

taking their car,' she broke it down quickly and introduced Zeb and the sisters.

'Maggie Colbert,' the mother managed a trembling smile. 'I …' A tear leaked down her face. 'I don't know what to say.'

'Did you know those men, ma'am?' Beth asked, as she cocked her head at her twin and sent a silent message.

Meghan nodded and disappeared in the direction of the kitchen.

'No. I never saw them before. You?' she asked her kids.

'Nope,' Travis shrugged his shoulders. 'We told them,' he jerked his head at their visitors.

'Did he—' Grace's hands flew to her mouth, her eyes wide.

Maggie Colbert figured out what her daughter was asking. She drew her close and hugged her. 'No. No. Not that. He removed my tape and asked me a few questions when you were gone. He hit me. But no, he didn't …'

She drew a long breath and planted a kiss on Grace's forehead.

Meghan returned, carrying a coffee tray. The heady aroma filled the room.

'I didn't know how you take it,' she smiled apologetically, 'so I made it dark and strong.' She poured the beverage in cups and handed them out.

Maggie Colbert settled heavily on a chair and took a sip. She closed her eyes briefly, and when she opened them, a semblance of control had returned to her face.

'He asked me about my research. … I am a professor,' she explained when her visitors looked blank. 'At Columbia University. My research is in the transport and disposal of hazardous material.'

Zeb's hair prickled.

'Hazardous material? Like?'

'Like explosives. And fissile material.'

Chapter 4

Reza Khalili was furious. He was raging. He landed on the sidewalk and looked up at the apartment he had escaped from. He didn't see anyone.

They will call the cops.

He tightened his jacket about himself, bent his head down and hurried down Amsterdam Avenue. The window-washers shouted at him, their voices lost in the sounds of traffic. No one paid any attention to him. This was New York. Everyone was hurrying to some place. Khalili didn't register on anyone's radar.

He saw a coffee shop ahead and ducked into it. Headed to the restroom and, once inside, removed his jacket and turned it inside-out. It now sported a different color. He shrugged into it and went to the mirror. Reached into a pocket and drew out a pair of colored contact lenses. Slipped them into his eyes.

He was now grey-eyed. He ruffled his short hair and headed out.

He stole a baseball cap that was lying unattended on a table, slipped it on his head and walked out.

He went to another café and bought a drink. The avenue

was flooded with cruisers when he came out with it. Cops raced inside the building. A crowd of onlookers gathered. A few people shouted questions at the police. Khalili sipped his drink, watched for a while and then headed for the Columbus Circle subway.

His anger had dissipated by the time he reached it. He was back to his cold, calculating self. He knew what he had to do.

He took the first train to Harlem and exited at 125th Street. Walked briskly for fifteen minutes until he came to a building that had seen better days. He climbed to the fifth floor, checking that he still had his gun with him. He had.

He knocked at the third apartment in the hallway, wrinkling his nose at the stink of urine, sweat and weed.

The door opened. Karim Rayegan, disheveled, scared, stood there nervously.

Khalili entered the apartment and shut the door behind him.

'What happened?' he asked coldly.

'You asked me to get the vehicle ready—'

'I know what I told you. Where did you disappear? I called you several times.'

'I was bringing round the car to the front. A patrol car was passing—'

'And you panicked and drove away. I knew it! The Man said this was your first job. I shouldn't have trusted you.'

'I am sorry.'

'Sorry?' Khalili yelled. 'Do you know what I went through? As it is, the Man's plan was rubbish. He wanted us to grab this woman and ask her about her research. Something she has invented. I told him that's not needed. But no, he wouldn't listen. On top of that, he thrusts you on me. I was this close,' he brought his thumb and forefinger together, 'to getting caught. Why didn't you answer your phone?'

Rayegan swallowed. 'I threw it away, in a sewer.'

'The car?'

'I left it in a long-term parking lot. I wiped it clean,' he added quickly when he saw his visitor's thunderous face.

Khalili paced the room, thinking swiftly. He would have to take control of this mission. No more working to the Man's plan. As for Rayegan?

He turned on his heel, drawing his gun smoothly, and shot his accomplice in the face.

He wiped the gun and dropped it over the body. Searched the apartment and found nothing to link him to the dead man.

He brought out his cell phone and made a call. It was early morning where the Man was, but Khalili didn't care about the time.

'The mission didn't go down,' he said as soon as the other person's voice came on. 'No, you listen!' He interrupted the other's questions and ran through the operation quickly.

'Your intel was wrong,' he said, angrily. 'You said Colbert would be alone. She wasn't. Her kids were with her. As for Rayegan? He didn't listen to any of my orders. I am lucky I got out of there alive.'

'Who were those three who came up with the kids?'

'I don't know. Should I have hung around to ask?' he asked, with barely concealed sarcasm.

'Were they police?'

'What difference does it make? The cops were arriving when I left the street.'

'You will have to—'

'This is what I will have to do. Stick to my own plan and

not take any input from you. You want the mission to succeed? You leave it to me. Don't interfere. I will come to you if I need anything.'

'Where's Rayegan? Give him the cell.'

'He can't talk,' Khalili said, coldly. 'I killed him. I don't need amateurs.'

'You can't do this alone.'

'I can. A lone killer has the highest probability of success in such a mission. You should know that.'

'There isn't a lot of time.'

'Don't I know it?'

'Remember—'

'Here you go with the threats,' Khalili ground out savagely. 'Yeah, I know you've got my folks.'

'Open that link I just sent you.'

The killer stopped pacing and looked at his phone. A link had appeared in a text message. He pressed it with a finger. It opened in a browser. A live video of a cell in which two people lay on beds. Even as he watched, a masked man entered and prodded them with an electric wand. There was no audio but Khalili could imagine the shrieking as the two forms jumped up, thrashed and tried to get away.

'Recognize your parents?'

'YOU DON'T HAVE TO DO THAT.'

'I know,' the Man replied, soothingly. 'Consider it to be an incentive. A reminder about our deal.'

'As if I could forget.'

'Complete the mission and you get them back.'

'How can I trust you?'

'You can't. But do you have a choice?'

The Man hung up and tossed the phone on his desk. It slid across the polished surface and came to rest against a thick file. Reza Khalili's. The best assassin in his organization. The killer had carried out several missions in Europe and in America. He had been killed in his final one, in an explosion. His body had never been found.

For two years, the Man, like everyone else, assumed that Khalili was dead. And then a stray piece of camera footage at an airline terminal in New York came to his attention. A man who looked suspiciously like the assassin. The Man pieced together the final mission. Concluded that the killer could be alive. If anyone could engineer his own death and assume a new life, it was Khalili.

He knew where the assassin's parents lived. It was a simple matter to grab them and torture them. The parents did not know anything. They, too, thought their son was dead.

The Man then placed a message on a realtor's website. 'This house *has* to be seen,' he posted. The estate agent's portal was what he used to communicate with Khalili.

A response came a month later.

'Not interested.'

The Man punched his fist in the air. Khalili was alive. No one else would respond to that message.

From that point on, it wasn't difficult to suck the assassin back into the game. After all, the Man was in a strong negotiating position. He had the killer's parents.

It didn't bother him that Rayegan was dead. He had been a sleeper agent in the U.S., and the Man thought he could help the assassin. It looked like he hadn't been up to Khalili's standards.

No one was. The assassin was unique. His kills were

legendary. He had taken out the British ambassador to the U.S. when the diplomat had been vacationing with his family in Italy. He had killed the Israeli public security minister. He could penetrate the toughest security and complete his assignment.

No intelligence agency knew what he looked like. There were rumors, of course, that the Man's organization had an ace killer, but Khalili had never been caught.

The Man nodded as if in confirmation. Khalili was the right man for the right job.

He looked at his calendar, at a date he had circled in red, three weeks away.

The G20 Summit. The leaders of the richest nations in the world would meet in New York. This time, the meeting would also have two special guests.

Reza Khalili's mission was to kill them all. The Man had spent months planning the operation. He had gotten Khalili into prime position. All they needed was the weapon, the means of killing. They had suffered a setback with what had gone down in New York.

However, the Man had immense confidence in Khalili. The killer would acquire a weapon.

And then, twenty-two world leaders would die in the greatest city in the world, in the most powerful country on the planet.

That would be the Man's revenge against Zeb Carter.

He picked up his phone and turned to the screen on his desk. It showed the cell and its two occupants.

'Prod them again,' he ordered.

It didn't hurt to remind Khalili what was at stake.

Chapter 5

Khalili removed his phone's battery and crushed the device with his heel. The SIM card would go down a drain. He went to the apartment's kitchen and made tea for himself.

He poured it in a cup and went to the window in the living room. He looked below at the street as he sipped. The warm brew went down his throat and inside him, sweet, just the way he liked it. It soothed him and got him thinking.

Maggie Colbert's research had received wide publicity. She had come up with a way to transport certain explosives, some of the most dangerous in the world, in a manner that escaped detection.

That method hadn't been her objective. It had been a serendipitous outcome, and once the story broke, the Department of Defense had stepped in immediately. It recognized the implications and saw the potential for terrorists to misuse the technology.

Khalili didn't know what had transpired once the DoD moved in, but the result was apparent. There was no more coverage of the research. Columbia University clammed up, and Colbert declined any interviews.

The Man directed Khalili to kidnap the woman and interrogate her. Colbert's breakthrough would be invaluable in his mission. Getting explosives through the tightest security that would be present at the summit ... Khalili immediately saw the possibilities and made plans for the snatch.

Maggie Colbert had no security around her, despite her invention. It seemed improbable, but the killer saw it with his own eyes. The university professor went about her business with no protection detail.

Khalili checked out her building and worked out entry and exfil arrangements. And then the Man sent Rayegan to help.

That was when it all started to fall apart.

The accomplice insisted on coming along with Khalili on his surveillance runs. He came up with the killer to Colbert's apartment on the day of the snatch.

I should have killed him earlier, Khalili thought, kicking the body. He wiped the kitchen cabinets and the windowsill.

His thoughts went to the video the Man had showed. His knuckles whitened. A red mist descended over him.

He thought he had broken free from the Man. He had lived for two years in the U.S. as a free man. And then the devious spymaster found him.

Khalili disliked the Man intensely, but despite that, he was tempted when he heard about the mission.

He didn't know about the spymaster's history with Zeb Carter. He didn't even know of the American's existence.

However, he shared the spymaster's dream of delivering one big blow to the Great Satan. An act that would reverberate around the world.

The Man's operation fit that bill.

Khalili wasn't a suicidal terrorist. He scorned those who

blew themselves up. He wasn't some ideology-driven crazed killer. Yes, he wanted to attack the U.S., but that was only because he had seen for himself what that country had done in the Middle East.

Khalili had operated in the war zones of Iraq and Syria. He had killed American and British soldiers. To him, the U.S. was an enemy and had to be treated accordingly. It was as simple as that. Jihad? That wasn't for Reza Khalili.

The Man … Khalili's pulse throbbed when he thought of the master manipulator. He was sure the spymaster had no intention of letting his parents live.

I will kill him, he thought, *when this mission is over.*

It wouldn't be easy. The spymaster was one of the best-protected men in the world. His organization had enormous power in his country. He had spies all over his nation.

Khalili would have to infiltrate that country and find a way to get close to the Man.

No, it will not be easy. But I will do it. Even if I die in the process.

That was the only mission he would sacrifice himself for, not the G20 one. And with that, his mind turned to the New York operation.

No more Colbert, he decided. She was too hot. He would have to find other means to carry out his killing.

He wasn't bothered that the professor and her kids had seen him. He checked himself in a broken mirror in Rayegan's bathroom.

He saw a six-foot-tall, lean man. Closely cropped dark hair. Clean-shaven. Dark eyes, now grey because of the contacts. There were thousands of men like him in New York. Millions in the country.

He spoke English with an American accent. He had several U.S. passports. He had several bullet-proof backstories.

He stepped out of the apartment and went down to the street. He donned a pair of shades and looked around casually. No one was interested in him.

He headed to the nearest subway. The most dangerous assassin the U.S. had known, planning the biggest kill in the world.

Chapter 6

Zeb and his team went to OnePP, the NYPD headquarters, that afternoon.

They had hung around at Maggie Colbert's apartment until the cops had shown up. They had given statements, as had the researcher and her children.

The cops arranged for the Colberts to sit for computer sketches of the perps. Zeb knew that wouldn't help. *Someone who can execute such an escape isn't an amateur.*

He parked his SUV in the building's lot and climbed out, the twins with him. Bwana, Roger, Bear, Chloe and Broker got out of two other vehicles.

'Any idea why he wants us all?' Broker led the way inside. He produced his credentials to security, who made a call, and they were waved through.

They still had to pass through metal detectors, which pinged at their weapons.

'You realize you're in the safest building in the city?' a cop asked sardonically.

'It is, now that we're here,' Bwana sniffed haughtily.

'Three of you, and yet you couldn't apprehend him?'

Police Commissioner Bruce Rolando goaded when they arrived in his office.

The head of New York's finest was a good friend. Zeb and his crew had helped his cops crack several cases over the years. They let the NYPD take credit, which earned them the cops' respect.

Rolando knew very few details about the Agency. He was aware it was a black-ops unit and that its director had significant juice in DC. He didn't know the specifics of any mission his visitors had carried out, however. He wasn't interested in knowing, either. He was just thankful that his visitors, some of the most lethal people he had met, were on his side.

'Let's see if the NYPD does better,' Bear growled.

The commissioner put up two fingers in a peace sign and waited for an aide to serve beverages.

'How did the kids react?' he asked when his assistant left. 'About their guns?'

'Shocked,' Zeb replied. The Glocks' magazines were empty when he had inspected them in the vehicle. He hadn't told them then, not knowing how they would have reacted. 'Horrified. Grace suspected that man intended to kill them all.'

'Any luck with tracing them?' Meghan emptied her cup and placed it back on the table.

'No,' Rolando growled. 'Serial numbers filed off. We got his prints on them and in several places in the apartment, but neither man is in the system. Officers are canvassing the streets, but I don't think they'll get anywhere. Those men have disappeared.'

'They were interested in Maggie Colbert's research?' Broker frowned.

'Yes, that man was questioning her about it. I think their plan was to take the family somewhere else, where they could question her at their leisure.'

'And kill them,' Chloe concluded.

'Yeah, that's our working theory.'

'Why didn't they interrogate her in her apartment?' Beth swept her hair back impatiently, her green eyes narrowed in thought.

'Because Colbert became a minor celebrity,' Zeb said slowly, 'after news of her research broke and the DoD got involved. They couldn't risk staying in her building. Not for long.'

'What was in that research?' Bwana's t-shirt came close to ripping apart when he crossed his forearms across his chest.

'You know as much as me,' Rolando shrugged. 'She was looking into ways to move hazardous material safely. A byproduct is that she found out how such material can be carried undetected by today's technology.'

'Any explosive? I heard something about spent nuclear fuel.'

'The DoD isn't telling. That research belongs to them now. Maggie Colbert, her research team and the university are sworn to silence.'

'Bruce,' Zeb cut in impatiently. 'Why are we here?'

The commissioner sighed and rocked in his chair. 'The NYPD is locked out. The FBI has taken over.'

No one moved for a while. Sounds of traffic seeped in despite the thick windows and paneling on the walls.

'This is your city. An attempted abduction happened here. Maybe an attempted murder, too. You were first on the scene.

And they've taken charge?' Bear rumbled, his face dark above his thick beard.

'Correct. This case has links to terrorism, to federal cases they are investigating, national security—they threw the book at us. I received the call from the director an hour ago. The mayor followed up and said he hoped I understood.' His knuckles tightened on the paperweight he was playing with.

'That happens, Bruce,' Zeb replied calmly. 'What do you want from us?'

'I have to spell it out for you?' Rolando raged. 'I want you to investigate. You'll have all my resources at your disposal. I do not like the FBI stomping on my turf.'

'This isn't the kind of operation we get involved in.'

'You already are. You're forgetting, Travis and Grace pointed weapons at you.'

Zeb kept quiet. He felt his team's eyes on him. He was aware Beth and Meghan wished to take on the case. *Heck, I do too. I don't like the idea of that gunman out there, loose. Who knows what he's planning. But—.*

'I spoke to Clare.' The commissioner dropped his bombshell. 'She wants you to get involved.'

'Clare?' Zeb sucked his breath sharply. 'You spoke to her?'

He checked his cell. No missed call or message. He looked at Meghan, then at Beth. They were blank-faced. Broker seemed to be smothering a smile. Bear wasn't smothering anything. He was grinning widely.

'Y'all knew?'

'Call her, Zeb,' the commissioner suggested.

Zeb called.

'Ma'am—' he began.

'I figured Bruce should be the one to tell you.'

'Why, ma'am?'

'You know the biggest game in town? In the country, in fact?'

Game? Zeb scrunched his eyebrows in confusion. And then his face cleared.

'The G20 Summit.'

'Yes. This is of interest to us as well. For the Agency. I'm greenlighting your team.'

'Zeb,' she stopped him before he hung up.

'Yeah?'

'You understand … why I did it this way.'

Zeb nodded, joining the dots. Clare, as director, had to manage the politics that came along with her job. Supporting the NYPD would earn the Agency brownie points. To be redeemed down the line.

'Yes, ma'am. Anything on the research?'

'Not yet. The DoD are stonewalling. I might have to go to the President.'

'I thought inter-agency cooperation was a thing.'

'So did I,' she replied, drily.

He ended the call, lost in thought, unaware that everyone was regarding him quizzically.

G20. Research. Explosives that can't be detected. How did I miss the connection? That dude could be a burglar. Or a terrorist. With that summit just weeks away, treating him as a possible terrorist is the safer option.

'You're still in shock?' Beth nudged him.

'No,' he stood up. 'We'll do it. It's an Agency operation.'

'No hard feelings?' Rolando stuck his hand out. 'At my going behind your back?'

Zeb grinned and shook it. Bruce, Broker and he went a

long way back. 'Nope. You'll share everything you have?'

'It's already with us.' Beth jumped up and patted her bag, referring to her screen. 'The commissioner sent it when he called us.'

'You knew, all of you, didn't you?'

'Yeah. Clare called us. She couldn't get hold of you. I told her we'd let Bruce tell you. We wanted to see your face.'

Chloe chuckled at the expression on his face. 'Zeb,' she shook her head, 'you're so easy to play.'

And that summed it up.

'We need to know what the Feds have got,' Meghan said, stopping them with an upraised finger.

All eyes turned to Broker, who went, 'Whoa! Why those looks at me?'

'You know why,' Meghan smirked.

Sarah Burke, Broker's girlfriend, was now Assistant Director at the FBI. The two had met during an Agency mission and, at the end of it, Broker was a tamed man.

'You want me to use my relationship?' His face darkened in anger.

'Yeah.'

'I'll take one for the team, in that case,' he said with a wink.

They left the commissioner after working out the details of sharing information, and when they reached street level, Zeb looked around as if seeing the city for the first time.

The summit was hard to miss. There were banners fluttering from lampposts, posters on the sides of buildings, large photographs of the visiting world leaders.

He shook his head, angry with himself. *I should have made the connection the moment I heard about Colbert's research.*

It could still be a random burglary. Or an act of espionage by another country. Or something simpler, related to her work, marriage, life. It could be anything.

He saw the man in his mind's eye. The way he leaped out of the window and went down the ropes. He was nimble, agile. He knew what he was doing.

Nope, the gunman wasn't a burglar.

'Let's get to work,' he told his team. 'We have a city to protect.'

Chapter 7

Meghan went to the large flipchart in their office the moment they entered it.

She wrote the date of the summit and circled it.

Beneath it, she wrote three words.

Who?

How?

Why?

She bit her lip for a while and then added a fourth.

What?

By the time she had underlined the first word, Beth had set up her screen to project on a blank wall.

'This is our perp,' she said, bringing up an image, 'a computer sketch created by the NYPD. After interviewing the Colberts. And there—' her fingers flew over her keyboard and various photographs appeared, '—are some likenesses if he wore disguises. The problem is—'

'There are any number of disguises he could adopt,' Chloe snorted. 'That was quick work by the cops.'

'It was. Commissioner Rolando lit a fire, that's why.' Another picture came up. 'This dude is the second man who mysteriously disappeared.'

'None of them are memorable.' Roger picked up the basketball and ran his fingers over its surface. 'You could walk past these guys on the street and you wouldn't give them a second glance. They are tanned and could pass for many ethnic groups. The Colberts said they had American accents, didn't they?'

'Yeah. What's more, Werner's come up blank, too.'

Werner, their supercomputer, housed a highly sophisticated AI program. It had access to several law enforcement databases in the country. It shared intel with the NSA and every black-ops outfit in the country, as well as several international intelligence agencies.

'We checked Columbia University's security cameras. No trace of the two men there. If they mounted surveillance on Maggie Colbert, they did it without showing themselves. There *is* a record of them entering her apartment building. But that doesn't lead us anywhere.'

'Interpol?' Zeb asked.

'We have asked them. They're yet to respond. The Brits, Mossad, the French, the Germans, none of them have our friends in their system.'

Meghan went back to the flipchart and started writing: Middle Eastern terrorists.

'Who else?' she turned to her audience.

'Heck,' Bear rumbled. 'It could be anyone. Zeb, we could be overreacting here.'

Zeb, who was in his usual position, lounging on his favorite couch, didn't respond immediately.

His eyes. There was no panic in them. They were cool. Confident. He knew exactly what he was doing.

'We aren't,' he replied. 'Meg, Neo-Nazi groups. Werner should have a record of all the active ones. Those who are capable of carrying out an attack.'

The older sister bobbed her head and added a line.

'Home-grown terrorists,' Bwana suggested. 'Anti-capitalist groups.'

'Let's not forget the cartels,' Broker chimed in.

The ideas came thick and fast, and in an hour's time, the flipchart was full of names.

'All right.' Meghan put down the marker. 'We'll put all these through Werner. It will sort them out, might throw up some new names and give us a list of likely candidates. We'll compare what we and other agencies have on those possibles. You know the drill.'

They did. They would break up into smaller units: Bear and Chloe. Bwana and Roger. Broker and Zeb. The sisters. Each team would take on some of the possibles. Standard operating procedure.

'What about the cops?' Beth turned to Zeb.

'Let's see how many candidates Werner comes back with. We'll then decide if we need Rolando's help. Bwana, Roger, didn't you have that snitch in that neo-Nazi group?'

'Yeah,' Bwana replied. 'Tucker. He's in White Freedom.'

'They're the largest separatist group, aren't they?' Meghan's brow furrowed.

'Yeah,' the large man's teeth gleamed sharply, in stark contrast to his ebony skin. 'You can guess what they're after, from their name. USA for white Americans. They started off in Texas originally but now have chapters in many states. One in New York state and another in New Jersey, too. They're increasing in popularity. They have slick messaging. Have funds. They buy TV spots. They're violent, but Wayne Bernier, their founder, keeps his hands clean. They have no love for President Morgan. They tried bombing one of his election rallies.'

'Bernier said that wasn't how White Freedom worked.' Meghan couldn't help grinning when she saw Roger's face. They all knew how the Texan felt about Bernier and the movement. 'That was the work of some stray members.'

'He would say that, wouldn't he?'

'Talk to Tucker,' Zeb said crisply. 'Find out what he knows. The rest of us,' he looked around, 'let's tap into our network. Our informants. We'll regroup every day. Share what we have found.'

'Which leaves us with just one matter.' Meghan looked suggestively at Broker, who threw his hands up in surrender and drew out his cell phone.

Broker's call to Assistant Director Sarah Burke went like this:

'Honey,' Broker said, resting his elegantly shod feet on his desk and looking out the picture window at the New York skyline, the very picture of insouciance. 'How's your day?'

Burke, in DC, held a finger up when an aide poked his head into her cubicle. The aide disappeared. Her face softened. 'Better, now that you called. Yours?'

'Busy.' Broker twirled a pen and glared at Meghan and Beth, who were trying to overhear. 'You know how it is. Fighting the bad guys. Keeping the country safe.'

Burke leaned back, a smile lighting up her face. 'I'm pretty sure those lines are somewhere in the FBI's manifesto.'

'If they are, I inserted them there.'

Broker was a hacker, one of his many skills. He had trained

the sisters once they joined the organization, and the three had gotten Werner to talk to several networks around the world.

Talk. It was a word the three of them used very loosely. It usually meant *hack*.

'Say, you looking into the Colberts?'

Burke looked suspiciously at her phone. 'That's why you called?'

'No, no,' Broker protested. 'I missed you—'

'Broker,' she snapped. 'Don't you think I know you well enough by now? You're on a fishing expedition.'

'Well, given that Zeb and the twins nearly died —'

'Save it! Nothing so dramatic happened.'

'It could have. You know what went down.'

Burke paused. The warriors were her friends. Meghan, Beth and Chloe were her besties. She was closer to them than any other female friend. She could be herself with them. She could let her hair down.

'How are they?' she asked softly.

Broker scowled at the twins, who had bored expressions on their faces. 'Annoying. Especially the sisters,' he said loudly. 'Acting superior. You know how they are.'

Burke giggled. An honest-to-goodness giggle. She knew how the Petersens loved to yank Broker's chain. 'So, they're good?'

'They are. You got anything on those perps?'

Burke's brows came together. She sat up straight. 'Broker,' she yelled furiously, 'you're on a mission, aren't you? An Agency one?'

'What if I am?' Broker huffed. 'The commissioner said you had frozen him out. That's no way for the FBI to act. Not with the G20 around the corner.'

'You know I can't tell you anything,' she seethed. 'That decision was taken by others, well above my paygrade.'

'Give us something, honey.'

She sighed and ran her fingers through her hair. The two seldom discussed work when they were together. She had an idea of what the Agency did and the kind of intel Broker had access to.

'Surely you must have hacked into our systems,' she said snidely.

'We did,' Broker admitted. 'There's nothing there.'

'That's because we have nothing on those men. No one knows who they are.'

'Terrorists?'

'That's our operating theory. And that's all I'll say.'

'You're coming down tonight?'

'Yeah. The usual flight.'

'I'll pick you up at the airport. I'll cook for us.'

'Don't bother. Your culinary abilities aren't as good as you think. We'll order takeout.'

Broker waggled his eyebrows suggestively, 'Netflix and—'

'Stop.'

'They've got nothing,' he announced when he ended the call.

'We knew that,' Beth snorted derisively. 'Looks like your girlfriend knows as much as we do. Maybe less.'

'I did my duty,' Broker replied grandly. 'I extracted the information from her.'

'Didn't sound like an extraction.' Meghan's eyes danced. 'She said you were a lousy cook, didn't she?'

'She did not.'

'Zeb,' Roger called out when the hilarity had died down. 'You think he'll go after Maggie Colbert again?'

'He might. It will be more difficult, however. Rolando's organized a protection detail for her. He's dispatched units to the university, too.'

Roger joined him at the window and the two watched traffic crawl on Columbus Avenue, below.

'He's out there somewhere,' Zeb said, half to himself. 'With his associate.'

Those two are in the wind, hidden among the eight million in the city.

Only they know what will go down in three weeks.

Chapter 8

Reza Khalili didn't know what would go down. Or rather, he didn't know how it would go down.

Assassinating the world leaders was still the plan. But how? With Colbert's research out of the picture, he would have to find a new way for the kill.

He rose the next day in his small apartment in Queens. He brushed his teeth, showered, poured milk in a bowl and filled it with cereal.

He sat at the dining table and breakfasted as he watched the news on his TV. His likeness came on screen, as did Rayegan's. He looked at it for a moment and shrugged. The cops, the FBI, the entire world could go looking for him. Khalili wouldn't look anything like the image flashed in millions of homes across the country.

The NYPD would find Rayegan's body, but even that would not get them anywhere.

He slurped loudly as he drank the milk from his bowl and wiped his lips with the back of a hand. He went to the sink, washed his hands and drank water.

He went to his bedroom and changed. When he emerged

from his apartment, he was wearing blue coveralls with *Javits* stenciled on his back. He picked up a yellow safety helmet and left his house.

'Yo, Mike,' Rusty, his foreman, greeted him when he arrived at the Javits Center. The conference and exhibition space was on the Hudson River, in Hell's Kitchen, between 34th and 40th Streets. It had close to two million square feet of space in all, and around seven hundred and sixty thousand square feet of exhibition space.

The center was organized on four levels, with exhibition halls and event rooms on each floor.

Mike Pollenberg, Reza Khalili's alias, worked on the first level. He was a technician employed by the convention center.

The real Pollenberg was dead. He was ash, after Khalili had burned him and scattered his remains far and wide.

Substituting himself for Pollenberg had required months of surveillance. 'It will take a year to put the plan in place,' he had told the Man, flatly, when the spymaster had outlined the mission.

'A year?'

'Yes. You think getting access to those world leaders is going to be easy?' he had snorted. 'That it will be like in the movies? I can sit in a hotel room and fire at them as they step out of their cars?'

The Man hadn't responded. Khalili didn't know it, but he had smiled in the darkness of his office. Khalili's comments had confirmed that the assassin hadn't lost his edge.

Getting close would be the biggest challenge, Khalili figured, once the Man agreed with his timeline. The NYPD would likely shut down traffic for entire blocks around Javits.

They would investigate every resident in neighboring apartment buildings, hotels and offices. They would stop anyone carrying anything that looked suspicious. There would be choppers, drones, electronic surveillance. The FBI would be present, as would the Secret Service.

No, there was no way he could use a sniper rifle. Planting explosives … now, that was a possibility, but they would have to escape detection. And getting them inside the center? What if he replaced one of the Javits' technicians?

Khalili had studied the workers at the center and had found that there were a select few who worked in the conference hall on the second level. That was where the summit leaders would meet and have a press conference.

Those employees had been extensively vetted by the NYPD as well as the FBI. Possibly the Secret Service as well. He didn't know which other agency was involved. Only they could enter the hall, but only after going through security checkpoints and a fingerprint scanner each day.

Khalili checked out each worker and found Mike Pollenberg resembled him. Same height, more or less the same weight. Short hair that was brown, green eyes. Fleshier face.

Pollenberg was an air-con equipment expert. Khalili knew nothing about air-conditioning. The killer was about to give up and look at another employee when he discovered the Javits man was a loner.

He didn't mingle with any of his co-workers. No family lived with him. He didn't date. He worked all day, then went home to his rental apartment in Brooklyn, where he drank a few beers and watched TV.

At least that's what Khalili figured he did, since the man never emerged from his building once he went inside.

Pollenberg's routine changed only on the weekends. Then, he went for an early morning run in his neighborhood. At lunchtime, he headed to Central Park. He bought food from a nearby truck, ate alone, read a book and napped occasionally.

He seemed to enjoy his solitary life.

I can learn air-conditioning. Whatever he does in his job, I, too, can acquire those skills, Khalili decided, and from that day, three months into his surveillance, Pollenberg's fate was decided.

The assassin was obsessive about his details. He studied his victim down to the smallest detail. How he walked. What he wore. Which car he drove. How he greeted his co-workers and restaurant servers.

He snuck into the man's apartment and placed tiny cameras and bugs. He stole several water tumblers and glass bottles from Pollenberg's home and lifted the man's prints.

Making molds from such prints was a highly specialized job, but Khalili was up to it. He had the tools and the experience. He labored over a table in his apartment that was covered with lenses, epoxy glues, adhesives, tweezers, cutters, rolls of thin, transparent sheets and a small furnace. Even with his expertise, it took him several attempts to get the molds right. And when he did, he stamped the prints onto sections of the sheets, which then went on his hands.

The assassin now had Pollenberg's fingerprints, as long as he wore those films on his digits.

In parallel, he enrolled in an industrial air-con maintenance course. It required three months of hard study. Khalili didn't mind it. He had been an engineer in his native country. He found he was a fast learner.

He made his move eight months after the Man had outlined the operation to him. By then, he was an expert at air-con equipment maintenance. He had even gone on a few jobs and had been well paid.

He walked just like the technician and even looked like him, courtesy of a highly realistic face mask that he had manufactured, based on the countless zoom, multiple-angle photographs and videos he had taken of Pollenberg.

The mask held the identity together. All those impersonation tricks that Hollywood productions showed … the world of spies knew all of them and had been using them long before movies discovered them.

Khalili's latex mask was carefully hand-painted and had hair work on it. It helped that Pollenberg's face carried a recent injury from a fall in the bathtub. No one liked to look at a bruised face for long.

The assassin was a pro at making masks. It was how he had survived in his business. He knew he could have made a very good living if he had made a business out of his skills. Killing people paid better, however. Much better.

He had impersonated the Javits man several times. In restaurants, in grocery stores, places the conference center's employees frequented.

No one questioned him. The mask worked.

One Friday night, he entered the technician's apartment as the man was slumbering in front of his TV. He smothered the Javits man with a pillow and held it down until his struggles died out. He waited in the still apartment until the night deepened and then rolled the body in a carpet he had brought with him.

He carried the heavy load to the elevator and out to a dark

van. He drove out to Staten Island, and there, in a remote spot few people knew of, he burned the body.

Reza Khalili took over Mike Pollenberg's life from that point on.

Chapter 9

'Anything more on him?' Zeb circled the dead body as he looked around the apartment.

They were in a fifth-floor apartment in Harlem, the next day. The gunman's accomplice lay at their feet. Shot in the face.

'Nothing.' Chang straightened his tie, and pointed at the Glock on the victim's chest. 'Murder weapon. Killer didn't take it with him. Serial number removed.'

Chang and his partner Pizaka, both senior NYPD detectives, had called Meghan. 'We got the second man,' Chang announced.

Zeb and the sisters arrived just as the forensic team was departing. They knew the two cops well. Chang and Pizaka were a two-man task force who took on high-profile cases and reported only to the commissioner.

Part of their success was thanks to the warriors. Zeb and his team cooperated with the two cops in any case that featured the city. That helped the detectives achieve a high closure rate.

'Who identified him?' Beth wrinkled her nose at the stench and bent down to have a closer look.

'Maggie Colbert and her kids.'

'They were positive?'

'Yeah. No doubt in their minds. This dude was the one who went to get the getaway vehicle.'

'Any chance they recognized the weapon?' Zeb asked.

Pizaka snorted. He was dressed immaculately, as always, in a pinstripe suit, glossy hair slicked back, a Windsor-knotted tie clipped to his shirt with an elegant pin. His shoes had been shined to a mirror polish. He looked like he had stepped out of a magazine cover. Except for his face, which carried a disgruntled look.

'You think they had a close look at the gun? With all that was happening?'

What's up with him? Beth mouthed at Chang.

No media, the cop whispered back.

The two partners had developed a reputation in the city. Pizaka was the media-friendly one. He actively courted the TV cameras and press reporters. Always had a news-bite for them. Had written a book that had become a bestseller.

Chang was his opposite. With his rumpled suit and disheveled hair, he looked like he had just gotten out of bed. He was content for his partner to take the lead with the reporters, and didn't mind that Pizaka got the limelight. Despite their different personalities, the two men were good friends and made a good pair.

Meghan bent over some scuff marks on the carpet that had been outlined by the forensic team.

'That's where we think he was standing.' Pizaka polished his already-gleaming shades and pushed them back over the bridge of his nose. 'The shooter. You can see his shoe marks, if you bend.'

Meghan crouched low as her sister joined her. The two women brought their heads to the carpet and nodded slowly when they saw the faint impressions over the layer of dust.

'We reckon our perp stood there and shot his partner,' Chang walked over to them and stood with his arm outstretched, pointing at the body. 'Cold-blooded. Prints going to the window, too.'

'We're running a ballistics match on the weapon,' he continued, 'but we aren't hopeful. We've got cops questioning other residents in the building to see if they knew the victim. A team's contacting the supervisor, to see who rented the apartment.'

'Aren't the FBI in charge?'

'We haven't told them, yet.' Chang grinned slyly. 'Commissioner said he'll inform them once we complete an initial investigation.'

Zeb tuned out as the sisters asked more questions. He stood over the body and looked at the spot the shooter had fired from. Less than ten feet. *An easy kill.* The remains of a phone were on the floor. No battery or SIM in it.

Our man's a pro. He'll leave nothing behind that can identify him.

He followed the sisters out of the apartment half an hour later, and donned his shades when they reached street level.

He waited a few beats, looking around casually, seeing nothing that pinged his radar. Beth gave him an impatient glance as she and her sister waited at their vehicle. He started. Stopped, when a voice called out.

'Zeb? Is that you?'

A man was sprawled on the sidewalk fifty yards away from the building's entrance. No one was giving him a second look. Pedestrians stepped around him as if he didn't exist.

'Eddie?' Zeb hurried to him, recognizing him. 'What's up, buddy? Why're you here?'

The homeless man was bleary-eyed, his clothes soiled. He stank of urine, alcohol and sweat. He lay on a flattened card-board box, his hands shaking.

'I'm sorry, Zeb,' the man grabbed his hand, tears welling in his eyes. 'I tried. But I couldn't resist.'

'Resist what?'

Eddie fumbled behind him and produced an empty bottle of alcohol. 'This. I'm sorry,' he clung to Zeb and sobbed, his frail body shaking.

He'd promised he'd stay sober the last time we met. Zeb held him close, ignoring the looks passersby gave him.

Who's he? Meghan came over and lipped silently.

A vet, Zeb responded.

The warriors had set up a fund that aided vets all over the country. It was administered by an independent trust and helped former soldiers set up small businesses, provided seed funding and also donated generously to various shelters.

Eddie, a former Marine, suffered from PTSD and alcoholism. He had struggled to adapt to life as a civilian and made the streets of the city his home. Zeb had come across him in a previous mission. Had tried to get him to go to a shelter, but the vet had refused.

'Keep an eye out for me on the streets,' Zeb had finally suggested.

'What for?'

'Anything out of the ordinary. Crime, suspicious-looking characters, burglary-in-progress.' He handed a card out, and thus Eddie had joined a growing army of street-informers that helped the Agency.

The vet had lapsed into a deep sleep by the time Zeb and the sisters carried him to their SUV. They drove him to the nearest shelter and checked him in.

It was when they were leaving that Meghan caught Zeb's sleeve.

'You noticed where he was lying?'

He shook his head. He hadn't paid much attention.

'He was on the sidewalk between the subway and the building's entrance. Prime view of all those who entered the building.'

'He could've seen our killer and the second man,' Beth broke in, excitedly. 'He could've overheard them. We should ask him, once he wakes up.'

'Good observation,' Zeb complimented them. 'Yeah, we'll return and question him when he's sober.'

They climbed into their SUV, unaware they were being watched.

Chapter 10

Khalili hunched lower in his cab as he observed the man and the two women. He recognized them immediately and wondered what had brought them to the building.

Behind him, the cab driver lay on the floor, unconscious, gagged and bound.

The assassin had decided to watch Rayegan's building after he finished work. He wanted to see if the body had been discovered.

Surveillance required a ride. Cabs were the most ubiquitous and anonymous vehicles in the city. The assassin found one parked just outside Javits.

'Off duty,' the driver protested when he slid inside. And then he stopped speaking when Khalili knocked him out.

On arriving, the assassin found NYPD cruisers at the dead man's building. *They've found it. I wonder what they'll make of it.*

He hung around for some time and watched idly. No cop came to him, nor gave him a second glance. He was keying the ignition when he saw the brown-haired man and the two women. He froze.

They're cops? It was possible.

He took their pictures on his cell phone and kept watching. They didn't talk to any police officer on the street, however. *They don't seem familiar with any cop.* The assassin observed as they stopped, turned back and went to the homeless man on the sidewalk.

His brow creased. Had that man been there when he and Rayegan approached the building? Khalili wasn't sure. He remembered the anger he had felt, then. Rage caused by his accomplice's amateurism. Rayegan had blurted the safe house's location—the place they were going to take the Colberts—as they headed to the building. Right there, on the street, for the entire world to hear. Khalili had shot him a murderous look and hissed at him to stay quiet.

I didn't notice that drunk. He could've been there. And if he was, he could have heard our conversation.

The killer gripped the wheel tightly and watched the three bundle the homeless man into their SUV and drive away.

He followed them cautiously, keeping three car lengths behind. He didn't have far to go, because in two blocks, the SUV's flasher indicated and it swept into a grey building's drive.

Khalili read the sign on the board. A shelter for the homeless.

He would have to return and take care of that drunk. He arrived at the decision without any debate. It didn't look like the man had spoken at any length to those three. However, if they were cops, or interested parties, they would return and question him. *I surely would, if I was in their place. No, that homeless man has to die.*

He checked out the building as he waited outside. It didn't

seem to have any great security. No guards, one solitary security camera at the entrance, nothing else that he could see.

It's a shelter, not a bank or a police station. It will probably have a reception and cameras down the halls and possibly in the rooms, to keep an eye on the residents. Nothing more complicated than that.

His surveillance targets returned, talking among themselves. Or rather the women did; the man just listened. He resumed tailing them, and this time the ride took longer. Straight down Columbus Avenue, paralleling Central Park, until the tail lights ahead flared red and the vehicle disappeared into a basement parking lot.

Khalili noted the building and continued driving.

He now had an address for the three. The next steps were to take out the drunk and to find who these three were.

I'll send their pictures to the Man. He has more resources. He can work out their identities.

Khalili had a bigger problem to solve.

How was he going to kill the leaders?

Chapter 11

Zeb drove down Columbus Avenue, his eyes alert. He checked his mirrors frequently, not paying attention to the twins.

Nope. He couldn't spot any tail.

I thought I felt something when we emerged from that dead man's building. Like someone was watching us.

He had checked out the surroundings when carrying Eddie towards their SUV but hadn't spotted any shadow.

Once in their building's parking lot, he inspected their ride. Nothing in the wheel wells or stuck to the undercarriage. No tracker.

'What's up?' Meghan raised an eyebrow when he wiped his hands on a rag and threw it in a trashcan.

'I thought someone was watching us. At that building.'

She pursed her lips, looked at the vehicle, then back at him. 'The killer?'

'Could be. Or it could be nothing. There might be security cameras on that street. We should ask Chang to get us footage.'

'We're way ahead of you, hotshot,' Beth smirked as she punched a button on the basement elevator for their office. 'He's arranging it for us.'

Bwana and Roger were in a bar in Plumsted Township, New Jersey, a ninety-minute ride from the city. The two had set out in the morning and were now seated at a corner table at the rear.

'You think he'll show?' Roger scanned the lunch-time crowd: mostly locals, who greeted one another and exchanged pleasantries with the bar staff. A few suits, a couple of families.

'He said he would.' Bwana perused the menu when the server came to their table. He ordered for himself as well as his friend. The two men sipped quietly when their orders arrived, comfortable in silence. Theirs was a friendship forged in distant wars, in the plains and the deserts of the Middle East and Afghanistan. Small talk to fill a gap wasn't required.

Tucker arrived an hour later. He was short with a thick head of blond hair and a beard that rivaled Bear's. He stood in the door for a moment, checked out the other customers, and headed their way when Bwana waved.

'You could get away?' Roger asked when the snitch sat down across from them and ordered a drink.

'Yeah.' Tucker bobbed his head. 'I told my boss I had to take a day off. He didn't mind.'

The informer worked in a gas station near Wharton State Forest, on State Route 206. He was manager of the facility, a job that gave him enough time to coordinate the meetings of the New Jersey chapter of White Freedom.

At one time, Tucker had a wife and a daughter. He had come up from his rural background by dint of hard work and had risen to the position of manager in the filling station. With a lovely family and a snug home, he was the poster boy for the American dream.

Until it had ended one day in a mugging gone wrong. The Tuckers had been visiting New York to show young Eleanor the bright lights. In a dark alley, a bunch of hoods had accosted them and demanded their possessions.

Tucker reached for his wallet. The thugs mistook his move and shot him and his family. He survived. His wife and daughter didn't.

That incident sent the snitch into a spiral of depression, and that was when he became aware of White Freedom. He found the group's propaganda attractive and, after an elaborate courting period, during which he had to *prove* himself by attacking a black family, he became a member of the neo-Nazi group.

That was three years ago, at a time when the group had no more than thirty members in the state. It now had close to a hundred, with Tucker the state chapter president. The local group organized monthly meetings in the Wharton State Forest, where they discussed recruitment, funding, activism and, in some cases, acts of violence.

One time, Tucker organized the robbery of an Indian-owned grocery store in Edison. The purpose of these acts wasn't to harm anyone. It was to convey the group's message, that the U.S. was for white Americans, and no other ethnic group was welcome.

The snitch planned his attack carefully. He checked out the store, noted its security cameras, and the times when traffic was lowest. After three months of surveillance, he executed the plan.

He, Mick, and Pete—they used only first names when on *mission*s—all put on dark clothing, gloved up, and donned masks over their faces.

They charged into the store, brandishing their guns, yelling at the tops of their voices. They demanded that the till be opened and money be handed over.

The first setback was when they discovered who was behind the counter. It was the owner's eight-year-old girl, who was managing the store while her dad took a bathroom break.

It was a setback only to Tucker, because Mick and Pete turned even more aggressive, thrusting their guns at her and screaming.

She started crying. Tucker flashed back to that night in New York. His stomach turned.

'Stop that,' he told Pete. 'She's scared. Stop yelling. Hand that money over, miss, quickly,' he told the girl as calmly as he could. He kept an eye on the rear of the store, from where the father could emerge.

They were working to a countdown. Not more than ten minutes in the store. They had already expended three.

'Hand it over, bitch!' Mick shouted.

The girl sobbed louder. Her hands shook as she tried to open the till.

Bile rose in Tucker's throat. This wasn't what he had signed up for. To scare young kids.

Just then, the rear door opened and the owner walked in. He was frail, white-haired, and walked with a stoop.

'Stop!' Pete trained his weapon on the new arrival. 'Raise your hands. Don't move. Tell your daughter to give us the money.'

The owner's face whitened. He raised his hands. 'Priya,' his voice trembled, 'do as they say, honey.'

The daughter cried louder. She finally got the till open. Reached into it to remove wads of bills.

Mick leaned forward and shoved her back. She fell to the floor.

'YOU!' the owner shouted and took a step forward.

'Stay there!' Pete snapped at him, his hand tightening on his weapon.

And then the door opened and Bwana and Roger walked in. The scene registered on them in an instant. Action followed the next. There was no need to confer. Three hoods against two trained operatives—it was hardly a contest.

Bwana surged forward, his right hand shooting out and upward. That snapped Mick's gun hand, sent the weapon flying to the ceiling. Bwana bodyslammed the hood and flung him against Pete and Tucker.

The three men went sprawling to the floor.

Priya screamed.

Roger and Bwana hesitated momentarily. Pete acted then.

He grabbed a crate of soda and flung it at the operatives, scrambled to his feet and shot out of the rear door. Mick followed, hot on his heels, as cans hit the warriors and exploded on the floor.

Tucker remained frozen, his eyes wide in shock, his mouth open, taken aback by the turn of events. His gun hung limply to his side.

'Let them go,' Roger told Bwana as he wiped fizz from his face. 'There might be more of them in the dark. You—' his Glock appeared and pointed at the White Freedom president. 'Drop your gun. Remove your hood and raise your hands. Slowly. Carefully. You don't want to die here.'

Tucker obeyed, and that was his first interaction with the warriors.

He's come a long way since that night, Roger thought as he assessed the gas station manager. That attempted robbery was a turning point for Tucker. He grew disillusioned with the neo-Nazi group, with its leadership and petty politics. It was as if scales fell from his eyes. He no longer empathized with their cause.

'I can be of more use to you,' he had told the warriors then, 'if you don't call the cops.'

Roger and Bwana gave him a searching look as if they could read his soul and asked the owner to hang up his phone.

'Talk,' Bwana growled.

'I'll be your inside man,' Tucker offered.

And that statement had set in motion a train of events that resulted in the Agency having an informer in the largest neo-Nazi group in the U.S.

The gas-station manager refused to be handled by anyone other than Bwana and Roger. 'No FBI, no cops. I will liaise only with you two.' He was firm.

And he delivered. He identified several White Freedom members who were cops, some of them in senior positions in police departments across the country. He revealed details on strikes the movement planned. Their armory, their sources of funding, their means of recruitment.

Not all of his intel was actionable by law enforcement organizations. The Agency acted, however. It wasn't constrained like the other bodies. It stopped several acts of violence and turned the perps over to the cops.

'You need to quit,' Bwana had told him when they had met earlier in the year. 'You can't keep snitching forever. The movement will suspect something. It will conduct an investigation.'

'They've already started,' Tucker said softly. 'All chapter presidents have been ordered to keep an eye on members. Watch their movements. We have hired private investigators.'

'Get out, man,' Roger leaned forward urgently. 'Get out while you've time. We can get you into WITSEC.'

'No,' Tucker's jaw firmed up. 'I'll continue as long as I can. I want to bring down Bernier.'

'They'll identify you!'

'I know.'

He met the operatives' eyes steadily. 'It's my penance,' he said softly.

Bwana threw his hands up in disgust and cursed.

And Tucker continued feeding them information.

'What brought you here?' The snitch took a healthy sip of his beer and wiped foam from his lips.

'These two.' Roger laid photographs on the table. 'They were involved in an abduction attempt in New York. Three days back. This dude,' he tapped one image, 'is dead.'

'What's so important about them?'

'Let's just say they are persons of interest.'

'I haven't seen them before.'

'They aren't in your movement?'

'Not in my chapter, for sure.' Tucker drank some more. 'But we are close to a hundred and fifty members now. I haven't met all of them.'

'Keep those. Let us know if you come across them.'

The informer slid the photos into his jacket and looked casually around.

'Something's brewing,' he said, his lips barely moving.

The operatives straightened.

'What?' The table creaked when Bwana rested his elbows on its surface.

'The movement's planning something. A big demonstration. Violent. We have been buying arms and explosives all over the country.'

'Where? When?'

'I don't know any details. No chapter president knows. Only Bernier and the council know.'

The council was a group of five, founding members who had started the movement along with Bernier. That body set the direction for White Freedom, which was then followed by all chapters.

'These weapons purchases.' Roger cracked his knuckles. 'We can do something about them.'

'The council's handling them directly. No one knows where they are stashed.'

Bwana traded looks with Roger. They could get Texas State Police or even FBI to raid White Freedom's Texas headquarters. *They won't store arms there*, Bwana thought. *It'll be too obvious. And that raid will speed up their hunt for the snitch.*

'Three weeks,' Tucker whispered. 'That's when it will go down.'

Chapter 12

'You've less than three weeks,' the Man said menacingly. 'You still haven't found a way to do it.'

His call had woken Khalili up the next day. He stared at the phone and reluctantly accepted the call. They had a system of informing each other their new numbers whenever they replaced burner phones.

He cupped the phone between his ear and shoulder and went about his morning. He was in Pollenberg's Brooklyn apartment, where he usually spent the nights.

The spymaster hadn't stopped talking by the time he sat down for his breakfast.

'You think I don't know?' Khalili replied savagely. 'I know what's at stake.'

'Your mother,' the Man said, his voice like a snake slithering in grass, 'she keeps calling for you. She calls your name when we are torturing her.'

The killer saw red. He hurled the phone against the wall. The bowl followed. He slammed his palm against the kitchen counter and screamed, veins popping in his forehead.

He stood motionless, breathing harshly, and when the mist

disappeared, cleaned up.

He washed his hands in the sink and went to his bedroom to change. Mike Pollenberg locked the door to his apartment and headed out to start his work day at Javits.

It came to him in the afternoon. He had joined Rafe Spinnelli, a co-worker, on a smoking break. It was normal for him to step out with his friends, even though he didn't indulge.

The two men chatted casually while Spinnelli reached into his pocket and brought out a cigarette. His other hand fumbled with a lighter, and when he sparked it to flame, Khalili stared.

Of course. I should have thought of that.

'Something wrong, bud?' Spinnelli sucked deeply, threw his head back and let it out.

'No, no. I just remembered. I had a dental appointment. I clean forgot about it.' He made a show of smacking his forehead with his palm and rushed away.

He gave the same excuse to Rusty and left for the day. He hurried to Hudson Park, grabbing a burger from a food truck. He found an empty bench, and there he sat, staring at nothing as he wolfed down his meal.

Children played, moms gossiped, but Khalili paid no attention to them. His mind was elsewhere. On a mission in Cairo, many years back, when he had been actively working in the Man's organization.

He had carried out one of his best missions: killing the Israeli ambassador as he watched a theater show.

The killer hadn't used a gun or explosive. That would have been impossible, given the security.

The diplomat and his family occupied a private box adorned with curtains. Drapes hung from walls of the theater.

Khalili had checked out the venue and had noticed the adornments. He smuggled aerosol cans into the theater and sprayed the box and as many wall-hangings as he could reach.

The spray contained a special solution: finely ground metal mixed with an accelerant. All it needed was a spark.

The killer provided that last ingredient when he stepped out of the show and made his way to the bathroom. He concealed a lighter in his palm and sparked it as he left through the door.

The curtains went up in flames with a *whoosh.* The fire spread rapidly to the balcony and penetrated the ambassador's box. Chaos erupted in the theater as the patrons tried to scramble to safety.

The ambassador's security detail rushed to help but were beaten back by the rush of panicked theater-goers. Their contingency planning fell apart under the crush of people. By the time firefighters arrived, the ambassador was dead. As were his family and several civilians.

Khalili didn't feel any regret at their deaths. Collateral damage. It happened on every mission.

He started when someone squealed. A little girl, pleading with her mommy to push her higher on the swing.

The assassin watched them absently for a moment.

The conference hall has curtains. Thick, floor-to-ceiling drapes. They are fifteen feet away behind the leaders' seating. There are more curtains to the side. Enough metal in the hall. I can weaken beams, get them to collapse.

He rose in excitement. A mother looked at him curiously, but he didn't notice her glance.

It could work. The FBI, NYPD, Secret Service, they'll all be looking for different threats. Explosives. Guns. They'll be looking for shooters. Their dogs won't be trained to detect fire hazards.

He crumpled the burger wrapper and tossed it into a nearby trashcan. He broke into a fast trot, going to the nearest subway, 34th Street Penn Station. It was three blocks away, but that gave him time to think.

He analyzed his idea from several angles. Security … he had already considered that. Making the fire happen. He had to work on that. He had to devise a triggering mechanism. What of the combustible agent itself?

He thought he knew.

A metal fire. Something that couldn't be put out by water, which was what most lay people reached for.

He glanced at his watch. He had time to go home, shower, and head out.

He had a date.

One that would end in a killing.

Chapter 13

'You aren't sharing!' Sarah Burke fumed at the warriors.

She had entered their office as they were gathered for their daily meeting. Bwana and Roger had recently returned from New Jersey, while Bear and Chloe had come back to the office after interviewing several of their informers.

They stood in a loose semi-circle with Meghan and Beth in the center, next to the flipchart. It was evening, sunlight filling their office with a golden glow.

Burke arrived without announcement. She was one of the few outsiders who had a keycard to their office and whose thumbprints were recognized by their security system.

She stood, hands on her hips, and glared at them, her gaze lingering longest on Zeb.

'Honey—'

'Don't honey me,' she snapped at Broker. 'I went to OnePP, and what did I find? Y'all had been to that Harlem apartment. You,' she pointed an accusing finger at her boyfriend, 'when were you planning on telling me?'

'Sharing.' Chloe crossed her arms across her chest and matched Burke for glares. 'Remind us again just how much you have told us? Where's your investigation gotten to?'

'That isn't—'

'It's one-way traffic, is it? We have to tell, but you don't show what you have.'

'Not that we agreed to share anything,' Beth sniggered. 'That sharing stuff, it's between the Feds and NYPD.'

Burke's eyes burned. Her mouth opened to reply when Zeb cut in.

'Take a seat. Help yourself to coffee.' He nodded at a pot and several cups on a side table.

Meghan gestured at her sister to hold her words when Beth made to protest. Silence fell for several moments until Burke moved to the table and poured a cup for herself.

'Jamaican Blue Mountain,' she said grudgingly. 'Beats what we get in the Hoover Building.'

She occupied a chair after shooting a murderous look at her boyfriend. Meghan resumed her briefing.

'As I was saying before we were rudely interrupted—' Bear chuckled in agreement. 'Werner has nothing on the perps. Facial recognition has nada. No domestic or international airport has anything on them.'

'We also got zilch.' Chloe didn't look in Burke's direction. They were friends … but this was work. And the FBI representative didn't have to come barging in like that, with attitude on top. 'We spoke to our network. Neither of these men seem to be in any terrorist or criminal network.'

'That our snitches know of,' Bear clarified.

'Zeb?' Meghan asked.

'I was on the phones. To Mossad, MI6, DGSE … no record of these dudes.'

'What about the Middle Eastern agencies?'

'I spoke to the Saudis, the Jordanians, Cairo … drew a blank there, too.'

'You hear what I hear?' Bwana looked at Roger.

'Yeah. Feels like they warmed their seats and got nowhere. Whereas you and I,' he said, adopting a righteous look, 'we did real work, buddy. Saving-the-world kind of work.'

'We'll give you a medal,' Meghan promised, 'once we know what you've got.'

'We spoke to Tucker.' Bwana's coffee mug looked tiny in his hands as he drank from it. 'He—'

'Who's Tucker?' Burke interrupted.

'He's an informer in White Freedom. We've cultivated him for a while—'

The FBI Assistant Director rose so fast that her coffee spilled on her trousers. She paid no heed. 'You've got a snitch? And you didn't tell us? Don't you know how long we've been trying to bring Bernier down?' she raged.

Roger made to speak and got a glare from Meghan. *Let her vent*, she messaged silently.

Burke vented for a full minute. Then she faltered when she found no Warrior challenged her.

'What?' she demanded hotly. 'You've got nothing to say?'

'You finished?' Meghan asked.

'You heard what I said.' The words didn't carry as much venom anymore. It was hard to stay angry when the other parties didn't react. Especially when one was wiping beverage off a trouser leg.

'Now, listen to us.' Meghan swiftly explained how Bwana and Roger had encountered Tucker. 'We had no interest in running an informer. We offered to hand him over to you folks. Or to the NYPD, even though he wasn't under their jurisdiction. You know what he said?'

'White Freedom has supporters in many police departments. Within the FBI, too,' Beth took over when her sister paused for breath. 'Bottom line, he didn't trust the cops or your people.'

'And he trusted those two?' Burke asked in disbelief, pointing at Bwana and Roger.

Meghan couldn't help chuckling. Bwana, large and menacing, and Roger, movie-star handsome, weren't everyone's idea of confidantes. 'I don't think he had much choice. He went with the only option he had.'

'All right, I'll buy that. But you still didn't cooperate with us. What happened to his intel?'

'Remember that raid in Dallas, a year back? When FBI and Dallas PD raided a warehouse and recovered arms and explosives? Turned out to be a White Freedom stash. That was Tucker's tip. We conveyed it to you, presented it as an anonymous tip.'

Meghan listed more instances, and by the time she had finished, all fight had gone out of Burke.

'I'm sorry—' she began.

'No need for that, Sarah,' Chloe cut her off. 'Let's get on with the briefing.'

Roger resumed from where Bwana had left off, breaking Tucker's revelations down succinctly. 'Nope, before you ask,' he told Burke, 'he doesn't know anything more. He'll let us know if he does.'

'That timing,' Bear offered, 'it's too close to the summit to be a coincidence.'

'Yeah.' Burke worried her bottom lip. 'Bernier has made noises about such events. He is an isolationist. *America for*

Americans. He isn't interested in globalism or world cooperation. It wouldn't be beyond his group to disrupt the G20 event. How do you want to play this?'

The last was directed at Zeb, who was observing silently.

'I guess you've got a lot on your plate?'

'That's an understatement.' Burke ran a hand through her hair, weariness showing in her face. 'This thing with the Colberts … we've gotten no further than you have, and there's some in the FBI who're asking whether that man is a genuine threat.'

'You run with Tucker's info. You have the manpower and resources to check out what Bernier might be planning. We'll stay on the Colbert gunman. Let the NYPD get back into the picture. Don't shut them out—'

'They shut us out! They told me about that second killing only when I visited them.'

'Burke.'

'Yeah. I get it,' she raised her palm in surrender.

'The cops will continue their investigation. Meghan and Beth will set up a daily debrief with the three parties. We've done this before. No reason why it won't work.'

'What about the Director?' Burke gnawed at a fingernail. 'It was his idea to take over from the NYPD.'

Bear swore under his breath. They had all heard of Travis Zastrow, a new appointee to head the FBI. He had risen up the ranks, was capable and had political ambitions.

'Clare will deal with him.'

'No blowback to you,' Zeb assured Burke, when a worried look crossed her face.

He glanced at his watch and grimaced. It was 8 pm. Their session had taken longer than he had anticipated.

'What?' Beth asked.

'Eddie. I was hoping to question him. It's late, now. He'll be asleep. I'll go in the morning.'

He would regret that decision.

Chapter 14

Eddie woke up at 10 pm, visited the bathroom, and tossed and turned in his bed when he returned.

Something was bothering him. Zeb. He knew there was something he had to tell his friend, but couldn't remember what. His memory often played tricks like that.

He mumbled under his breath and rose. Reached for the glass of water by his bed and drank it. His tongue still felt swollen, his mouth dry. He promised to give up drink for the millionth time and fell back on the mattress.

He tried to gather his scattered thoughts, shook his head violently when they refused to cooperate, and angrily turned off the night lamp.

He woke at 11 pm, when it came to him suddenly.

Of course. It was to tell Zeb about those two men. He knew what they had done to that nice lady and her kids in that building. He had overheard the cops. Those men, they had been arguing furiously. The one that got away, he had been telling the other to shut the hell up.

Eddie grabbed the notepad next to the glass of water. Searched for a pencil, got it. Started scribbling. An address in Queens. He yawned lustily. The pencil slipped from his fingers and fell to the floor. He searched half-heartedly. What was the hurry? He would tell Zeb in the morning.

He tossed the notepad to the table. He didn't see the page rip out and flutter down the gap between the bedside table and the wall.

Khalili arrived at the shelter at 2 am. New York never slept. However, it snoozed, and that time of the night, there wasn't much traffic.

He was driving another cab, an empty one that he had found a couple of blocks from his building. He parked several streets away and ghosted towards the shelter, a dark shadow blending into the night.

He scaled the shelter's iron gates, his hoodie pulled tight over his head, gloves over his hands, a backpack strapped to his chest.

He found an open window on the first floor and climbed inside. No alarm went off. He crept to the security desk. Two large men were slumbering in their chairs, a screen flickering in front of them. It had camera feeds on it.

The killer snorted beneath his breath. He went to the reception desk, searched for a logbook and found Eddie's room number.

Second floor.

He took the stairs and peered down the hallway. No guards. Cameras, however. Those weren't a problem. Not with the highly alert security people downstairs. His teeth flashed in a smile as he looked at the room numbers.

He came to Eddie's room. Tried the door handle gently. The door gave way. He slid inside and shut it behind him.

Stood motionless, listening.

The drunk was snoring so loud his sound could drown a chopper landing in the lawn.

This'll be easy.

Khalili went to the bed and, in the faint light from a window, looked down at Eddie. He was sprawled on his back, mouth open, drooling. The killer winced in distaste and carefully extracted the pillow from under the man's head.

He placed it over the drunk's face and it began.

The room had fallen silent when he finished. He searched for a pulse. None. He bent his head towards the drunk's mouth. No breath.

He turned on the bedside lamp and searched the room.

Eddie didn't have any possessions. No backpack, no bag of any kind. No cell phone. No weapons. A notepad had fallen to the floor. Khalili picked it up and inspected it. No writing on it. The killer returned it to the floor and searched the dead man.

Nothing in his pockets.

Threat erased.

Khalili vanished in the darkness of the city as silently as he had arrived.

Zeb got the call from Chang at 8 am the next day. He was alone in the office, making coffee for himself, when his phone buzzed.

'Get to the shelter, NOW!'

'It's about Eddie?'

But the cop had hung up.

Zeb finished his drink, grabbed his jacket and headed to the elevator just as the sisters entered the office.

'Where're you going?'

'The shelter. Chang called.' He jabbed a button and wasn't surprised when the twins turned back and joined him. They were like that.

'He say anything?'

'No.' Clipped response. His gut rolling. An unpleasant feeling in his belly. His radar pinging.

He drove out of their parking lot, finger on horn, scattering away traffic.

'Getting there alive will be great,' Meghan clutched the door handle.

He eased off on the gas. She was right.

His lips tightened when he saw the cruisers at the shelter.

'This can't be good,' Beth sucked her breath.

Meghan sprang out as soon as he parked. She raced to the entrance, Zeb and her sister following.

Her face was white when they arrived in Eddie's room.

'He's …' she nodded jerkily at the bed. Chang was in the room, as were Pizaka and several cops. A technician was taking photographs. Zeb and the sisters gloved up and approached the bed.

'How?' he asked Chang.

'Smothered.'

'You're sure?'

'Yeah. Pillow. That one,' the cop pointed. 'It's got bite marks. Saliva. Impressions of hands pressing down.'

'Any traces?' Meghan asked sharply.

'No,' Chang understood what she meant. The victim would struggle, scratch back, do everything possible to fight back. Sometimes, flakes of the killer's skin got caught in the victim's nails. 'There are trace fibers. Something dark. We'll investigate.'

'He was wearing something long-sleeved and was gloved,' Pizaka spoke from near the window. 'Room is clean so far. No traces of the killer.'

'Cameras?' Beth pointed to the hallway. 'There are several all over the place.'

'We got a hooded figure. No face. Dark clothing.'

'Security didn't spot him?'

'Security was sleeping.'

She cursed. Looked at Zeb, who was still looking down at Eddie.

'There's this,' Chang handed over a sheet of paper. 'It was behind that table.'

The sisters crowded and read over Zeb's shoulder.

Zeb. Eddie had scrawled the name. Underlined it.

Beneath it was another word.

Quee.

Just those letters. Nothing else.

'He was trying to leave a message,' Meghan breathed. 'Queens?'

'Sounds like that, doesn't it?'

'Suspects?'

Chang shifted on his feet, chewed his gum, 'We're talking to the staff, checking out if anyone had issues with Eddie. Cops are on the street too, interviewing other homeless people—'

'You know who did it,' Zeb looked up coldly.

'The Colbert gunman? Yeah, we're leaning in that direction,' the cop acknowledged, 'but you know how police work is. We gotta cross the T's and dot the I's.'

'We should've come yesterday,' Beth sighed. 'We should've questioned Eddie the moment he was sober. It looks like he saw or heard something involving those two men. Why else would he be killed? He was homeless. A vet. He was harmless. It can't be a coincidence, can it? He—'

She stopped when Meghan placed a hand on her shoulder. She sniffed loudly and wiped her eyes.

The beast raged in Zeb. It roared and urged him to act. His fists clenched. A vein throbbed in his neck. He waited for the darkness to recede, and when it did, a cold anger took its place.

'You'll send those feeds to us?' he asked emotionlessly.

'Yes,' Chang replied. 'As soon as we're done here. The cop knew about the veteran network. The intel from that source had helped the NYPD in several cases.

Eddie was in the wrong place at the wrong time. But the killer ... he made a mistake.

Zeb didn't know he had spoken aloud until he felt the sisters' eyes on him.

'Now, it's personal,' he said.

Chapter 15

The warriors watched the footage from the shelter. Several times. There wasn't much to see in the shaky, blurry two-minute clip.

The hooded figure appeared suddenly in the lobby. Approached the security desk. Spent a few seconds at the reception counter, then disappeared.

'He took the stairs,' Meghan explained. 'No cameras there.'

'He hasn't shown his face. Not once,' Chloe pointed out. Bwana, Bear and Roger were tight-lipped. They, too, knew Eddie. They, Chloe and Zeb had met the former Marine in Helmand, Afghanistan. A bond had been forged in the blood-soaked plains and valleys of that distant country.

The shadow appeared again in Eddie's hallway. It moved swiftly towards the room. Tried the door and disappeared inside. The clip ended.

'Gait analysis?' Broker queried.

'Werner's on it.' Beth turned off the wall projection and flicked dust off her screen. She darted a look at Zeb, who was lounging on his favorite couch, seemingly uninterested.

'We won't get anywhere with that,' Meghan said

dispiritedly. 'He knew about the cameras. That's why he had his head covered. Someone that smart will know about facial recognition, gait analysis, all the fancy tech we use. He isn't in the system. Besides, that clip isn't clear enough.'

'What about Eddie's message?' Broker played with a golf ball.

'That word,' the elder sister replied, disheartened. '*Queens*. We got nowhere with it. It's possible the killer has an apartment there. Or was planning to take the Colberts to some safehouse in the borough. Werner's algos are working. No hits so far.'

Broker nodded. He and the sisters had worked on the AI program. He knew how it worked. It would look into apartment ownership and tenancy, cross-referencing those with identification documents such as driving licenses. It would continually scan security camera footage.

They might get lucky if the killer was careless.

We can hope. There's not much else we can do, he thought, as he tossed the ball in the air and caught it. It wasn't hard to rent an apartment using fake credentials. *That's how the killer will do it. Fake everything.*

They had their first briefing call with the FBI and NYPD an hour later. Eddie's killing barely registered on the Feds.

To be fair to Sarah, she's juggling a million other things. Zeb shook himself out of his blue funk. *She knows we and the cops will look into it. That's why she's appearing uninterested.*

Chang and Pizaka brought them their first break that evening.

Khalili was ready by the evening. He hadn't gone to work that day. He had called in sick and had gone to the Home Depot in

East Elmhurst. He bought several tools and aerosol cans and headed to the workshop he had rented on 98th Street.

He had grabbed it as soon as he had seen the listing in a local newspaper. The rent was low, the place was an abandoned industrial area, and it was ideal for his plan.

The place was twenty minutes away from his Queens apartment, a brisk walk. He had his ball cap low over his head, shades on his eyes and headphones over his ears. He bobbed and swayed as he walked; to anyone watching, he was a man lost in music.

He checked out the street as he approached. No one around. The wrecked carcasses of cars lined the street. From one street away came the sound of clanging and hammering. Auto garages in that direction.

He raised the shutter to his workshop and rolled it down behind him. Turned on the light and inspected the premises. Dust hung thick in the stale air. An open space and machinery beyond. A crane above. A worktable with mechanical vices mounted on it. Hammers and saws and various tools scattered on the surface.

Khalili had intended to bring the Colberts to this place. He shrugged. That family was behind him, now. He placed his purchases on the table and went to the rear of the workshop. He rooted around until he found what he was looking for: several titanium flanges that had once been fitted to a boat.

He blew dust away and mounted one of them on the lathe. He worked for the next couple of hours, checking the outside of the workshop every once in a while. *The sound might attract attention.* He made a note to himself to mount security cameras and have a feed on a screen.

He gathered the finely ground powder, cut a small heap

and poured it on the ground. He lit it and jumped back when flames caught quickly.

It was about surface area. The metal, once in powder form, offered more surface area to oxidize. It sucked oxygen from the surrounding air, which fueled it. Water couldn't put it out, because it would take that element from water, too.

Khalili let the fire burn itself out and then inserted the remaining powder in the aerosol can, in a procedure he had practiced several times in the past.

By evening, he had his weapon.

Now, he had to test it.

Chapter 16

Pizaka entered their office at 7 pm. His suit had razor-sharp creases as if they were freshly ironed. His hair was slicked back and the inevitable shades were over his eyes, even though night had fallen and he was indoors.

'I come bearing good news,' he announced grandly.

The sisters looked up and then at each other. The cop was usually the bearer of ill tidings.

'Where's Chang?' Beth looked behind him. 'Oh, there you are.'

The second cop looked even more bedraggled than usual.

'Is that look deliberate? To show how hard you're working?' Meghan looked him up and down.

'We *have* been working tirelessly. Nonstop. Taxpayers need to get their money's worth.' He went past her, grabbed the coffee pot and poured a healthy share for himself.

He smacked his lips appreciatively after he had sipped, aware that eight pairs of eyes were focused on him and Pizaka.

Bwana sighed when the cop took his time. 'Chang, you know how high we are?'

'Fourteenth floor,' he said, when the cop took another sip

instead of answering. 'You can count for yourself as you go down. After I have thrown you out of the window.'

'Violence.' Chang finished his beverage and patted his lips delicately. 'That's all you folks know. That's why you'll never make good cops. You're like bulls in a china shop. Hammers searching for nails.' He held up his hands placatingly when Bwana rose threateningly.

'First, the bad news. We haven't identified the dead man. Or the killer.'

'New York's finest, huh? Tell us something we don't know,' Meghan taunted him.

'Sticks and stones,' Chang intoned, brushing away the insult. 'We've got a lead on the guns.'

He bowed silently, as if to rapturous applause after he dropped his bombshell.

'One of the guns,' Pizaka clarified, his lips twitching slightly when he sensed the thrill race through the room.

That lip movement from him was the equivalent of an average person rolling on the floor, guffawing. 'Ballistics match. The gun on the dead body was used in a gangbanger killing six months back.'

Elvin 'Vinnie' Godinez, twenty-eight-year-old street dealer, had been killed in Brooklyn, shot twice through the chest. The cops suspected the shooting was the outcome of an ongoing turf war between the Brooklyn Hoods and the Queens Tigers.

'The Hoods are a Hispanic gang,' Chang explained, 'while the Tigers are an equal-opportunity one. They have all races in them.'

'Who killed him? Our killer? Somehow, I don't see him as part of a street gang,' Beth's said, her hair swirling around her head as she shook it.

'We don't know. The case remains open. Cold case. Word on the street is that Willie McCree, the leader of the Tigers, killed him. We questioned him. He denied it. We didn't have anything else on him and had to let him go.'

'We ran through the list of the Tigers' members.' It was Pizaka's turn to help himself to coffee. He poured, drank and leaned against a desk. 'No one matches the Colbert shooter or his accomplice. We checked the Hoods, too, just to be sure. No luck there.'

'Our man isn't a gangbanger,' Roger drawled. 'He's a pro.'

'So where does that leave us?' Meghan asked in frustration.

The two cops exchanged a look. 'The Hoods,' Pizaka brushed invisible lint off the label of his jacket, 'aren't active anymore. The Tigers, though, are still going strong. Their gang is known to have a few houses in South Jamaica.'

'Why don't you question them again? Bring McCree in.'

'We sent a few patrol cars to his known hangouts. He wasn't there. We've left messages. No response.'

Beth snapped her fingers suddenly. 'You want us to find him and question him.'

'We wouldn't ask citizens to do that,' Pizaka replied indignantly.

'It would help, though,' Chang said slyly, 'if said citizens just happened to come across McCree and *overheard* his conversation.'

'We'll do it,' Bear straightened and hauled Chloe to her feet.

'No. Rog and I will go,' Bwana said, stopping him.

'Bwana,' Chloe smiled sweetly at him. 'McCree has to be questioned. Not killed.'

'Violence.' Chang shook his head pityingly. 'Hammers.' He ducked as a cushion sailed his way, then followed Pizaka out of the office.

Bear drove out of their parking lot, Chloe beside him, at 8:30 pm.

None of them knew where Khalili was or what he was planning.

Chapter 17

Reza Khalili was in his usual getup. Dark hoodie. Dark jeans. Gloves over his hands. A backpack, a ball cap, headphones over his ears.

He was in Times Square, which at nine pm was crowded. Tourists were snapping their cameras as if their lives depended on it. Street vendors tried to entice them with cheap trinkets. Office-goers lingered in doorways, chatting, preparing for the journey home.

Khalili was buzzing. Not with any drug or alcohol, but with anticipation. The aerosol was in his jacket pocket, a hand clutching it.

He scanned the scene, took in the crowd. Drifted away when a couple of cops walked through the square. He headed to the sidewalk which was lined with restaurants and cafes.

A couple stopped next to him, laughing. The woman held the man's face and kissed him. The man drew back and riffled through his pockets. Came out with a cigarette packet and a lighter.

The killer glanced around quickly. No one was paying

attention to them. No cops in sight. It was as if the three of them were in a bubble.

'Can I have that?' he gestured at the lighter and moved his hand in his jacket as if he was bringing out a cigarette, too.

The man nodded, a cig hanging between his lips. He sparked the device once. No reaction. He tried. Flame burst from the tiny nozzle.

Khalili acted.

He drew the aerosol out, spraying it even before it reached shoulder-height. The fine mist spread through the air, headed towards the couple and caught fire.

The assassin was moving away, head down, before the first scream reached him. He glanced back once and snorted when he saw onlookers trying to beat the fire with bottles of water.

Two people on fire.

Test passed.

Bear and Chloe caught it on the news just as they pulled up in a vacant spot in South Jamaica.

They didn't make anything of it. Random acts of violence weren't uncommon in New York.

Their destination was an apartment on top of a convenience store, a block away from Rockaway Boulevard. One street away from where they had parked.

The Tigers' building had a line of various outlets at ground level. A salon, a liquor shop, a Chinese takeout. Trashcans were on the pavement, some lying on their sides, their contents spilled. Cars were parked on the street, some with broken mirrors.

Some commentators called South Jamaica a ghetto. It was a working-class neighborhood with relatively lower median income compared to other parts of the city. Street gangs. Drug peddlers. Higher crime, though that was in decline.

Bear straightened his jacket and felt eyes on him.

Strangers will be noticed in this kind of neighborhood. Loud music blasted from the open windows of their target apartment. Voices shouted from within. A car passed, its windows down, packed with youths who yelled raucously, honked and drove on.

Chloe led the way, stepping over empty beer bottles and food wrappers. Her nose wrinkled at the stench as she navigated to the entrance and knocked. It was one of those doors that allowed entry to various apartments in the building. Bear pointed to a buzzer at the side.

She bent her head and peered at the apartment numbers and names. Shook her head when she couldn't read the faded writing. She pressed various buttons randomly and, when a surly voice came on, answered with 'Pizza.'

It worked. She shrugged when her partner chuckled softly. It was a routine that Hollywood and thousands of thrillers had made popular. *Looks like it still opens doors.*

She climbed the narrow staircase, Glock in hand, pointing downward. A child cried in some apartment, the sound coming to them faintly. Its mother's voice was muffled.

She reached the landing, turned right and headed to the door from where the music was sounding. More trash in the hallway. Stains on the walls.

She thumped the door with her fist. A peep door slid and a face appeared.

'McCree? Is he here?'

Thumping bass drowned any reply.

'Pizza!' she tried.

'Yo!' the man turned away.

The music lowered.

'Someone ordered pizza?'

Voices talked over one another, none of them making sense.

'Turn that shit off,' the hood barked. The beat got silenced. 'There's a white bit—'

Chloe slammed her shoulder against the door. It sprang back and caught the thug in his face. He stumbled, cried out, and collapsed when her elbow caught him in his face.

She took in the room swiftly. Eight men, several of them bare-chested. Some of them lounging on couches, smoking spliffs. Others drinking, jawing away.

Several weapons on a table. Handguns. A shotgun.

Two men moved towards the arsenal.

'Don't,' she said coldly, her Glock at shoulder height, covering them all.

A bearded hood rose slowly, his face darkening. 'Bitch,' he spat.

The next moment, his jaw broke when Chloe leaped forward and slashed her barrel across his face.

She moved so fast that no hood could react. She was back at the door, covering them, by the time their minds caught up with what their eyes had seen.

The gangbangers stood gaping, staring at the fallen man, who was moaning softly.

'I don't like bad language,' she said pleasantly, 'in case the message didn't get through.'

'I asked a question.' Her voice hardened. 'Where's McCree?'

'Who's asking?' a hood straightened, his eyes darting to the weapons on the table.

'I ask questions. You answer. That's how this works.'

The thug dived at the table, clawed at a Beretta. Fell back screaming when Chloe's round lodged in his shoulder.

Movement from an inside room. Another hood rushed forward, his eyes fierce, the Beretta in his hand pointed straight at the visitor.

Chloe was trapped. If she turned to face the new threat, the others would react.

'Go, Wes!' A thug crowed. 'That'll teach the bi–'

He fell to his knees, his eyes widening, clawing at the eight-inch blade that had pierced his shoulder.

'Language,' Bear admonished, entering the apartment as silently as a ghost. 'You!' he addressed the new threat. 'What's that? A Beretta? Seen anything like this? Know what it can do?' He raised the HK MP5 cradled in his left hand.

'Drop your gun,' he commanded.

'NOW!' he roared, when the gangbanger hesitated.

'Come forward.'

The hood shuffled inside the living room.

'There had better not be anyone else in any other rooms.'

'Do you know whose apartment this is?' Wes grated. 'You have any idea what we can do?'

Chloe took a long step forward and crashed her barrel into his temple. She surged to the side and grabbed the man she had shot. Jammed her Glock in his wound.

The thug screamed.

'I asked where McCree is. Nicely. Time for niceness is over.'

'Randall's!' the hood sobbed. 'That's where he is in the evenings.'

'What's that?'

'A bar,' he groaned.

'Bo! Shut it!' another gangbanger shouted. 'Don't tell them anything.'

He fell back when Chloe pinned him with flat eyes. She looked at each hood. Some seethed, some glowered, all stayed quiet.

'How many with him?' she asked Bo, gouging her weapon deeper when he didn't respond immediately.

'Four. God, stop,' Bo broke down, 'Only four. He'll be there now. For two more hours.'

'He won't. He'll run like a coward,' Chloe said contemptuously, getting to her feet. 'The moment you tell him about us, he'll flee. You're all the same. Tigers, huh? Tigers only when you are in a group. You turn to mice very fast when alone.'

'Willie ain't like that,' a hood at the back found his courage. 'He'll stay there. Go see for yourself.'

Chloe edged backwards to the door, her Glock still covering the gangbangers, who crowded together, poised to make a run.

'Don't try that.' Bear was enjoying himself. He produced a device and held it up for them to see. 'Recognize this?'

They did. They shrank back.

'Hey!' Wes cried in fear. 'There's no need for that. We cooperated.'

'Oh, I won't set it off,' Bear assured them, and chuckled when they seemed to sigh in relief.

'I will, if you don't stay put. I'll attach it outside, set it to explode if you follow us.'

He slammed the door and taped the grenade between the door and the jamb. Followed Chloe, who was darting down the stairs.

They hugged the line of stores once they got outside. That way, the gangbangers wouldn't spot them. They walked away swiftly, turned a corner and merged into the night.

'Tell me that was a dummy,' Chloe pleaded.

'It was.' Bear grinned in the dark. 'It worked, though. They'll stay inside for a while. Next stop—'

'Randall's.'

Chapter 18

Reza Khalili was unhappy. Yes, the test had worked. The aerosol had sprayed the titanium powder, which had lit most satisfactorily.

But he wanted more from his fire. He wanted it to spread rapidly, and he had to practice his delivery technique.

In Javits, he would be under pressure. He would have to come out of hiding from some place in the conference center, set fire to the drapes nearest to the leaders, and escape.

Speed was of the essence. Not just that of the fire, but also his movements.

He would have to practice again and again, until he had it down to perfection.

He watched the news for a while and smirked when the TV host said the attack was random and the perp remained unidentified. The victims, a Chinese couple, were in serious condition.

That soured the assassin's mood further. The fire had to kill. It couldn't leave behind injured, however grievous their burns were.

He would go to work the next day, start scouting for hiding

places, and in the evening, he would improvise on his weapon and practice.

Randall's was on Rockaway Boulevard, on the intersection with 135th Street. It was a white-painted building that appeared from the outside to have two floors. A small parking lot at the rear that was packed with vehicles. One entrance on the boulevard and another on the street. A service entrance was at the back, behind the parking lot.

Bear eased behind a pickup truck on the boulevard and followed Chloe to the bar. His HK was slung over his back, covered by a loose coat. He had his Glock in a shoulder holster, a blade strapped to his thigh and grenades in his pockets, real as well as dummies.

The knife he had left behind at the Tigers' apartment was a throwaway. No prints on it, since both he and Chloe were wearing flesh-colored gloves.

Meghan had sent them Randall's layout. A hallway on entry, a reception desk, and the bar immediately behind it. Tables spread out, which could be cleared to make room for dancing.

There were a few private rooms around the bar where high-rollers could play poker and dine away from the crush in the main room.

They knew how McCree looked. The NYPD had an extensive catalog on the gangbangers, and they could identify the hoods.

'Fast in, fast out?'

'Yeah,' Chloe answered.

The crowd would work in their favor. The Tigers wouldn't attempt anything in the presence of that many witnesses.

McCree's arrogance would help them, too.

'He thinks he's untouchable,' Chang had said while briefing them as they drove from the hoods' apartment to the bar. 'That thug was right. He won't escape even if they tell him you're coming.'

'Did they file a complaint?' Chloe had asked him.

That had sent the cop into a prolonged bout of laughter.

'The Tigers?' he wheezed finally. 'Lodging a report with us? That will be the day.'

Bear eyed the neon sign as they approached. Randall's. Blue. The apostrophe had slipped from its high position and was nearly a comma.

Chloe smiled brilliantly at the doorman, who opened the door with a flourish.

'We'll stick to the bar,' she told the receptionist and headed to the long counter.

They found seats for themselves and ordered a round. A scotch for Bear, a gin and tonic for Chloe. Sure, they were on a mission, but appearances had to be maintained. And who passed up on a scotch and G&T?

They left their seats half an hour later and discreetly explored the bar. The music was loud, now. A few brave patrons were dancing between the tables.

That way, Chloe lipped and nodded, in the direction of a dimly lit hallway between the bathrooms and the end of the bar.

Sound fell behind them as they headed deeper into the building. There were couches on the thick carpet, couples whispering sweet-nothings. A door. Bear tried it gently. The room was empty.

Another door. A bunch of women playing cards.

A turn, and there a hood stood guarding a door.

They recognized him. The thug sized them up as they went closer.

'Help you?' he asked.

'Yeah,' Bear replied and punched him in the gut.

Bear was six feet, four inches tall. He was large, muscled and moved like a panther. He had gentled his blow, but even that was sufficient to send the guard to his knees. A light tap to the temple and the thug fell unconscious.

Bear dragged him deeper down the hallway, caveman-style, and dumped him unceremoniously. It wouldn't matter if the man was discovered. They wouldn't be in Randall's for long.

Go, he nodded to Chloe, who was at the door.

She turned the handle and flung it open.

'Gentlemen,' she greeted the hoods.

Five men jerked their heads up. Cards in their hands, cigarettes in some lips, bottles and glasses nearby. Thick smoke in the room.

McCree, in a waistcoat over a printed shirt. A gun beside him.

The hoods scrambled straight. Their leader reached for his weapon.

Bear entered the room and tossed a grenade on the table.

The hoods froze for a moment.

Then dived out of the way, weapons forgotten.

Bear and Chloe took advantage of that.

They raced forward and grabbed McCree by the arms and hustled him out before any thug could react.

'Move. Don't make a sound,' Chloe hissed and jabbed her Glock in the thug's side.

McCree, dazed, bewildered, moved without protest. Bear searched the hallway and found a fire-detector in the ceiling.

He jumped high and sparked a lighter just beneath it.

Swore when nothing happened.

Tore a piece of his t-shirt, set it on fire and jammed it against the detector.

This time it worked.

The alarm sounded in the bar, a klaxon call drowning out every other sound.

Sounds alerted him. The hoods emerging from their room after realizing the grenade was a fake.

He fired his Glock over their heads and sent them dashing inside again. He fired a few more rounds into the ceiling. The shots, along with the fire alarm, set the crowd off. They stampeded towards the exits, milling around in a crush.

Precisely the effect he wanted.

Bear used his size to push through the mass of people and caught up with Chloe. 'He giving you any trouble?'

'Nah.' His partner shoved McCree forward, her Glock jammed tight against the small of his back. 'He's calling for help. Hoping someone will rescue him,' she shouted over the noise.

The hood yelled, as if on cue. No one responded. Everyone in the bar was intent on getting outside. Bear clamped a massive hand on McCree's shoulder and accelerated him forward.

'Go ahead.'

The hood swiveled his head and took one look at Bear, then at Chloe. He bit his lip, his face red with anger and humiliation.

They didn't hang around in the night once they were

outside. Bear cupped his palm over McCree's mouth and continued shoving him forward, while Chloe ran to their vehicle.

One moment to search the hood and remove an ankle-gun. Another to zip-tie him and toss him in the back of the SUV.

And then they were away.

'Who are you?' McCree yelled.

'Your nightmare,' Chloe answered.

Chapter 19

'Dude, how're you doing?'

The question caught Khalili by surprise. He pushed his shades back on his head and squinted at Rusty.

They were high up on a platform they had rigged in Javits, amidst piping and cables. Second-floor conference hall, right over the stage where the world leaders would be seated.

An air-con duct had developed a leak, and after inspecting it, Khalili decided several meters of pipe needed to be replaced. The foreman had agreed.

The assassin had then welded in place a new section and summoned his boss for an inspection.

'I'm good,' Khalili responded. 'Why do you ask?'

'You look distracted, buddy.' The foreman slapped him on his back. 'I asked you about the weld a couple of times, you didn't answer. Still thinking about that girl?'

The assassin's co-workers often gathered in a bar after work, grabbed a few drinks and let off some steam. Khalili never joined them. Over time, he'd given several excuses to avoid going along. The latest was that he was dating. Newly found love. His fellow workers knew he was a solitary person who lived alone. His news had been greeted with surprise and then loud encouragement. Ribald suggestions followed and hadn't stopped. Khalili grinned and bore it, often thinking of ways to kill the other workers.

'No, uh,' he put on a stammer and hoped he looked bashful. 'It's just that it's so new for me.'

'I know how it is, Mike,' the foreman said, slapping him on the back again. 'Heck, I didn't know how to talk to women after my divorce. Sheila, my second wife, did all the talking, however. Now, about that weld. Something wrong? You seemed to be staring at it.'

The killer froze for a second. He *had* been looking at the repaired section for a long time. It was facing the drapes to the left. If left unattended, the coolant would have sprayed on the curtains. He had wondered if there was some way to mix the powdered titanium with the coolant.

The air-con will definitely be inspected. Several times as we get closer to the summit. Nope. That won't work. I'll have to find some other way.

'Just wondering if it will pass inspection.' He put on an ingratiating smile and got another slap to the back.

'Why wouldn't it, buddy? You do good work. Hey, Joe,' the foreman said, leaning over the protective railings of the platform, 'start the gas. Let her rip. Let's see if this duct holds.'

Bear and Chloe had taken McCree to an abandoned industrial unit in Queens and tied him to a chair. They interrogated him under the light of a solitary bulb. The hood had raged at them and sworn to kill them. At that, Chloe had pointed her Glock at him.

'I've had enough of his whining. Shall I finish him?'

Bear stroked his beard thoughtfully. 'Nah. He isn't worth a bullet. Let me choke him.'

He advanced on the bound figure, who took one look at the large man and quailed.

'Anything,' he squealed. 'I'll tell you anything.'

'Huh!' Bear frowned. 'He's not that tough, is he?'

'They usually aren't. Not when they're alone.'

'I don't think he'll have anything worthwhile for us. Let me kill him. It won't take long.'

'WHAT DO YOU WANT?' McCree screamed. 'ASK ME. I'LL TELL YOU ANYTHING.'

'You killed Vinnie Godinez?'

'Vinnie?' the hood's eyes bulged. 'This is about him?'

His head rocked back when Bear slapped him.

'We ask questions. You answer. That's how this works. Did you kill him?'

'Yeah, yeah,' the thug blubbered, sweat and tears streaming down his face.

'He was encroaching on our turf. We warned him several times. Told his gang to back off. We beat him up but he still didn't listen.'

'What did you do with the gun?'

'What gun?'

McCree shrank when Bear flexed his biceps. 'I sold it, and two more guns.'

'Why? Who did you sell them to?'

'We didn't want the weapons on us, dude,' the gangster cried. 'Cops would have searched us.' Didn't the large man and the woman know how hoods worked?

'Who did you sell them to?'

'Angelo Eaton. He's our dealer.'

Chapter 20

While Khalili was inspecting the weld with his foreman, Zeb and the twins were driving to Camden.

The New Jersey town at one time had the highest crime rate in the country. Murder, drug trafficking, burglary, prostitution, mugging, rape— Camden had seen it all. Its median income was way below the national average. Bullet marks adorned the sides of buildings in its most violent neighborhoods.

Angelo Eaton, the Tigers' arms supplier, was based in Camden. He was known to the police as well as the FBI but had never been arrested.

'Stays clean enough to avoid being arrested,' Beth had sniffed when Werner spat out his details. 'Known to supply guns to gangs in the tri-state area and also to those farther away. Questioned several times by state police. Nothing came of it. The FBI even ran a sting operation but came away empty-handed.'

'He's smart.' Meghan lowered her window and closed her eyes, enjoying the rush of air against her face.

'Huh?' Zeb looked at her. The sisters hadn't spoken much during the drive. Beth was in boyfriend-texting mode, while the older sister snoozed.

'Eaton,' Meghan clarified. 'He's wily. Why would he tell us about the guns?'

'We'll ask him nicely.'

She smiled and glanced back at her sister, who was still hunched over her phone. 'What about McCree?'

'What about him?'

Bear and Chloe had left the hood in the industrial unit for several hours before making an anonymous call to the Tigers.

'Nothing else we could do. His confession—'

'Wasn't admissible to the cops. Obtained under duress.'

'Yeah.'

'Pizaka wasn't happy when we told him what went down.'

'Nope.'

'Neither was Burke.'

Zeb shrugged. 'We don't work the way they do. They'll just have to accept it.'

'All right,' Meghan trained her green eyes on him. 'Spit it out. How're you going to get Eaton to confess?'

'I really don't have a plan,' Zeb admitted. 'Let's play it by ear.'

She turned to the window when they entered the town. Zeb drove through the seedier parts of the city, first. Past dilapidated buildings, youths hanging around on the street, giving them dead-eye stares.

He then took them through regenerated neighborhoods. Homes, families, children playing in parks.

'We get it, Zeb,' Beth said, finally. 'There's no such thing as a bad town. Let's go to Eaton, now.'

The dealer was in downtown Camden, his store nestled between a deli and a shuttered shop.

Eaton's Arms, a signboard proudly proclaimed on the roof of the building. The dealer had an iron grille in front of the glass display at the entrance, in which several guns were laid out. A bell tinkled when they pushed through the door.

Zeb slowed when he took in the interior of the store. Several white, dark-skinned, and Hispanic- looking youths lingered over glass cases, talking loudly among themselves. All of them attired in what seemed to be the uniform of gang-bangers. Loose t-shirts. Jeans well below their waist. Ball caps. Tats visible.

He spotted the outline of weapons beneath their loose clothing and nodded imperceptibly when the sisters spread out casually, flanking him.

A few heads turned in their direction. Whispers and sniggers. A few leering glances at the sisters.

A balding, bespectacled man was behind the U-shaped counter, arms crossed, watching the hoods.

Eaton.

The dealer straightened when he felt Zeb's gaze.

'Help you?' he asked. 'You looking for any gun in particular?'

'I can show them *my* guns,' a thug looked at Meghan and smacked his lips.

Big mistake.

She took a long stride and backhanded him across the face. Followed it up with a full-palm slap. The hood's head rocked on his neck. His lips split. His eyes narrowed in pain and shock.

Anger followed.

'YOU—' he snarled and lunged forward.

Simultaneously, several gangbangers reached beneath

their shirts.

They froze when three Glocks appeared in the hands of the newcomers, pointed at them. Meghan's weapon aimed at Split-Lip.

'Your mommy didn't teach you manners?' she smiled sweetly, 'especially when women are around?'

'Do you know who we are?' a narrow-faced Hispanic thug hissed.

'Gangbangers?'

Narrow Face flushed dully. A muscle ticked on his face. His hand twitched towards his weapon. It stopped when a shotgun racked.

'Get out, Ramirez, and take your men with you. Cole started this. He should have kept his mouth shut. I've told you several times. This is a place of business. Not a bar.'

Ramirez, Narrow Face, made to protest.

'Out!'

The gangbanger slinked out, the rest of his men following him. Cole dabbed at his bleeding mouth, glared at Meghan and left.

'You aren't cops,' Eaton said coldly, his shotgun still up, pointing to one side. 'You're Feds? I've got nothing to say to you.'

'That's how you treat customers?'

'You aren't gun buyers,' the dealer replied flatly. 'Those moves, the way you produced those Glocks. Your looks, clean-cut. You aren't hoods. Only two kinds of people enter my establishment. Gangs and law enforcement. Whichever agency you're from, I have nothing to say to you.'

Beth went to the counter and leaned across it to look at a case hanging on the wall that contained a matched pair of flintlock pistols.

'Are those Henry pistols?' she asked incredulously, peering hard at the small writing beneath the case.

'Yes, ma'am,' Eaton replied, the angry look on his face dissolving, 'from their Nazareth factory. Those guns were made sometime in 1825. I have provenance documents.'

Meghan joined her sister, and the two stared at the display case for a while.

'You know your weapons. Very few can identify their make.'

'Our dad was a collector. He used to take us around the country as he tracked down old guns.'

'Those aren't for sale,' the gun dealer said proudly. 'They are part of my collection.'

'Is this from your collection, too?' Zeb brought out the Glock that had killed the accomplice.

Eaton looked at him and then at the gun. Hardness returned to his face. He took the gun, inspected it and tossed it back.

'There are thousands of such Glocks in the country,' he said scornfully. 'That one doesn't have its serial number. I don't trade in unidentifiable weapons.'

'Cut it out,' Zeb told him coldly. 'You are the biggest supplier of weapons to gangs. You deal only in untraceable guns.'

'I run full background checks on my customers,' the bald man snapped. 'None of them are criminals.'

A snort. Beth, who had a hard time keeping a straight face.

Eaton reddened. 'You folks need to leave. You're hindering my business.'

'This gun.' Zeb ignored him. 'Who did you sell it to?'

'I've never seen it in my life. I've had enough of this,' the dealer yelled. 'I'm calling the cops.'

'Go ahead. I'm sure they'd love to come to your rescue. The police and you have history, don't you?' Meghan taunted.

Eaton's lips tightened. His eyes narrowed. 'Who are you? Feds? You haven't shown any identification.'

'Nope.'

'State police?'

'No, sir.' Beth sighed. 'We are investigating a murder—'

'So, you *are* cops,' he accused.

'No. We are security consultants.' She handed out the firm's business card and introduced the three of them. 'The person killed is of interest to us. Intersects with an assignment.'

The gun dealer fingered the card suspiciously. 'You're from New York. NYPD allows you to operate like this?'

'We're a licensed investigative agency as well, sir. This gun—'

'Willie McCree sold it to you.' Meghan cut to the chase and waited for a reaction.

'Never heard of him,' the dealer replied promptly.

She brought out her cell phone and played an audio clip on it.

'We didn't want the weapons on us, dude,' the gangster cried. *'Cops would have searched us.'*

'Who did you sell them to?'

'Angelo Eaton. He's our dealer.'

'That's Willie McCree,' Meghan stopped the clip and pocketed her cell. 'Confessing to selling that Glock to you.'

'I don't recognize that voice—'

He jumped when Meghan slammed a palm on the counter. Guns rattled. Eaton's phone slid off the glass and fell to the floor.

'That Glock,' she spat, 'has links to terrorism. We don't have time to dance around with you, Mr. Eaton. McCree sold that gun to you six months back. After killing Vinnie Godinez, of the Brooklyn Hoods. That weapon then turned up in Harlem early this week. Placed over a dead body. How did it get there?'

'I don't know—'

'Mr. Eaton,' she snarled, 'we aren't the cops. We aren't the FBI. We're worse. We can shut you down, just like that.'

'We don't need to do that, sis.' Beth smirked. 'We'll just let his customers know that he's turned snitch. They'll deal with him their way.'

The gun dealer paled. He moistened his lips nervously. He came from behind the counter and shut the door. Turned over the OPEN sign in the window to CLOSED.

'Just who are you, really?' he asked.

'Who we said.' Meghan pointed to the business card impatiently. 'You can make calls to the NYPD and verify us.'

'To New Jersey State Police as well. To any federal law enforcement agency you might know, and I bet you know many,' Beth said sweetly.

Zeb cut off Eaton when the dealer made to protest.

'We aren't wearing any wires. You can search us. We aren't interested in your business or your dealings with gangs. All we want to know is how that Glock ended up in Harlem.'

The weapons supplier didn't move.

'Eaton,' Zeb said softly, 'Did you hear what Meghan said? That Glock is linked to a possible terrorist plot. If anything goes down, all bets are off. You'll disappear. Just like that. You—'

'I don't keep records,' the dealer blurted. 'No paperwork

is involved when I sell to the gangs. They're all cash deals.' He snatched the weapon from Zeb's hand and brandished it. 'See? No serial number. I have bought and sold many such Glocks in the last six months. Nothing stands out about this one. I remember McCree selling me a gun some months back. Wait up.'

He gave the weapon back, disappeared into a backroom and returned with a tray full of handguns. Glocks, Berettas, Walthers, many makes. 'All these have been sold to me by gangs. None of them have serial numbers. Hoods know I trade in cash only. A customer comes to me and asks for a Glock, I show him what stock I've got. Someone's looking for a Colt, I sell the one I have.'

'Obviously I sold McCree's Glock, if that's the one you have, to someone. I don't remember who. I get a lot of business. My inventory moves fast. Ramirez,' he jerked his head at the street, 'was interested in buying some Colts. Business that you drove away.'

'How do you take on new customers? They could be cops or federal agents in disguise.'

A crafty look crossed Eaton's face. 'They have to state who referred them. I make a call to that person, verify, and if the buyer has cash, we're in business.'

'Have you seen this man?' Beth showed him the killer's likeness.

Eaton glanced at it for several moments and then shook his head. 'There's a constant stream of traffic in my store. I don't remember everyone I deal with.'

'Look carefully.'

'I said I don't remember,' the dealer flared. 'Nothing about him stands out. Who is he?'

'This dude?' She ignored his question and produced the photograph of the dead man.

Eaton studied it for a while and shook his head. 'Don't think I saw him. Who are these men?'

'The first man shot the second man with the Glock you sold him.'

'That's not on me,' the dealer said furiously. 'Yeah, I sell guns. So what? I am not responsible for how people use them.'

'Was he a new customer or an existing one?'

'Don't remember.'

'Eaton,' Meghan growled, 'If you're holding back—'

'I'm not,' the weapons supplier yelled. 'What do I gain from doing that? You're from some black-ops agency. I know what you people are capable of. I've heard enough stories. I'm telling you everything I know.'

Meghan didn't engage with him. She cursed and looked at Zeb, who shook his head in defeat. This had always been a possibility, that Eaton had no leads on the men.

A dead end, he thought savagely.

The gun supplier read their body language.

'I have cameras,' he said helpfully.

Chapter 21

'Zeb Carter!' the Man screeched. 'How did you come across him?'

Khalili winced and held the phone away from his ear. It was evening. He was back in his apartment after work. That was where the tools of his lethal trade were. Pollenberg's place was clean. It had to be.

The assassin had gulped down a hastily made dinner and was working on the aerosol when the spymaster called.

'Zeb Carter?' He attached adhesive tape to the aerosol and held it in his palm. It stuck. 'Who's he?'

The Man breathed harshly for several moments before controlling himself. 'Those pictures you sent. That man is Zeb Carter. Those women are his associates. Beth and Meghan Petersen. Twins. The three of them work in a covert-ops outfit.'

Khalili looked up at that and focused his attention on the call.

'A very powerful one,' the spymaster continued. 'Not many know it exists. How did you get their photographs?'

'They're the ones in Colbert's apartment. They came with her kids.'

The Man swore loudly and for a long time. 'Eight million people in New York,' he said bitterly, 'and those kids had to find Carter.'

Khalili thought the spymaster was overreacting, but he didn't say so. *So what if this Carter is now involved? No one knows where I am or about my Pollenberg disguise. And they never will.*

'I know what you're thinking,' the Man carried on. 'Don't underestimate this American. He and his associates are the most dangerous operatives I have come across.'

'He's not my concern.' Khalili picked up the aerosol and strapped it to his left palm. He lowered his sleeve and adjusted it so that it covered the can. He tugged and pulled at the fabric until he was satisfied with how the cuff fell.

'You're right,' the Man agreed. 'But I'll send you his dossier. You need to know who else is hunting you. Have you figured out the kill device?'

'Working on it.'

Khalili hung up and picked up a lighter. He taped that to his right palm and practiced. Left hand coming up, forefinger squeezing the nozzle, right hand rising smoothly, thumb flicking the lighter.

He repeated the motions until he was confident he could carry off the moves. To an observer it would just look like he was raising his arms.

He grabbed his hoodie and stepped out of his apartment. It was killing time.

Khalili went to Times Square again and hung about in the milling crowd. The Chinese couple had succumbed to their injuries, but that didn't give the killer any joy. He had tweaked the aerosol and made the spray more potent. He lingered in front of a TV in a store window and followed the news for a while. The NYPD were pursuing all leads in regard to those burned tourists.

The assassin sniggered. He knew what *pursuing all leads* meant. The cops had none. They probably had some CCTV camera footage of a hooded figure setting the tourists alight, but hey, this was New York. Hoodies were commonplace.

Don't underestimate the cops.

He sobered immediately. It wouldn't do to be overconfident.

He decided not to attack in Times Square. There was a heightened police presence there now, and people would naturally be more wary.

He drifted to the side streets, checking out those with the least traffic. He found his target on West 43rd Street: a drunk searching through a trashcan for food. No one close to him. The nearest subway station was on 42nd Street.

Khalili looked around. Still no one close by. A couple on the other side of the street. An SUV heading away from them. He pulled his hoodie tight around his face, lowered his head and walked swiftly to the homeless man.

'Hey,' he called out softly.

The man looked up.

The killer's left hand flashed up, and a fine mist sprayed out and started settling on the drunk's face.

'What—' he stumbled back.

Flame jetted out from the killer's right palm. The powder caught fire. The man grunted and slapped at his face ineffectually as Khalili kept firing the spray, feeding the flames.

'LOOK!' someone shouted from behind him.

The assassin fled. He raced to the first turn and huddled in a recessed doorway. He ripped off his hoodie, reversed it and put it on. It now sported a bright red color. Screams and yells sounded from the street he had left.

A mother pushed past him, toddler in her arms. She looked at him curiously and turned away when he glared at her. The killer crossed the street and merged into the crowd, all the while keeping his hands down.

He shivered and trembled in reaction once he was back in his apartment. Whoever had shouted *look* had sounded close. He was lucky no one had given chase.

It worked. That's important. I'm sure that drunk's dead or is dying soon.

He now knew how to spray the curtains at Javits and light the fire.

He still had to work out how he would get close to the leaders during the summit, but at least he had his weapons.

He showered, changed into fresh clothes and headed out. To Pollenberg's place, where he would sleep.

Zeb was alone in their office when the local news station reported the burning man's death. He didn't think anything of it. A sound behind him.

Meghan, and Beth on her heels. Both in Tees and jeans, hair down. They plopped on the couch next to him. The elder sister sighed and popped her knuckles.

'Shall we play it?'

'Yeah.'

She plugged a flash drive into her screen and projected it to the wall. The storage device contained a month's worth of video from Eaton's store.

They knew when McCree had sold the weapon to the dealer.

'I tag all my guns,' the arms supplier had explained, showing them a weapon with a label tied to the trigger guard. 'No gun stays in my inventory for more than a week. I have a very fast turnover.'

'That tag,' Meghan spoke to herself as her fingers danced over the keys. McCree appeared on the wall, gesticulating as he negotiated a price with the dealer.

She wrote a piece of code, a unique key, and attached it to the Glock. She then commanded Werner to search for that weapon in the entire video segment.

Beth went to the kitchen to make them coffee while the supercomputer worked, and by the time she returned, her sister had frozen the clip.

'There,' Meghan exclaimed in satisfaction. 'That's the Glock. And that's our buyer.'

The customer had his back to the camera, a hoodie covering his head. He never looked up the whole time he was in the store.

'Go back,' Zeb told her. 'Let's see him arrive.'

She scrolled back and restarted the video. One moment Eaton was idly polishing the glass counters, the next, he was greeting the new arrival, whose head was bent.

'He knows there's a camera,' Beth said, sipping her coffee. 'Look at the way he moves. He doesn't raise his head.'

The two men spoke for a while and then Eaton went to a back room and returned with the Glock. The customer handled it, asked several questions, shaking his head occasionally.

'Negotiating.'

'Uh-huh,' Meghan agreed.

Eaton disappeared once again, and this time returned with two more guns.

'Are those …' Beth leaned forward, squinting.

'Yeah,' Meghan snapped her fingers in excitement. 'Two more Glocks. The ones he handed to Grace and Travis. He bought all three from Eaton.'

The two men traded words for several moments, with the dealer throwing his hands up every now and then. The hooded figure finally reached into a pocket and brought out a wad of bills. He handed them over to Eaton, who counted them. The dealer stuffed the notes in his pocket and shook hands with the buyer.

Money received. Guns exchanged. Deal done.

'How long was he in the store?' Zeb asked as the hooded man disappeared from view.

'Just over eighteen minutes.' Beth pointed to the counter ticking away at the bottom of the clip.

'He didn't look up once.'

'Which means he knew where the camera was.'

'Or was just being careful. Any cameras near Eaton's store?'

'On it.'

'Meg? How about—'

'Yeah,' the elder sister reached for her cell and dialed the dealer's number.

'How did you know what I was asking?'

'We're smart, Zeb. We can read your mind. Eaton?' she called out when the weapons supplier came on the line. 'It's Meghan—' She broke off when a torrent of words burst from the other end. 'Yeah, I know it's late. But that's when you do business, right? Night is when your customers come out of hiding.'

'Go to your computer,' her voice sharpened. 'To that file

you copied for us. We found something.'

She arched an eyebrow at her sister while she waited. Beth shook her head in disgust. *No cameras,* she mouthed. *I've got Werner looking, in any case.*

'Yeah,' Meghan turned to her cell. 'Hold on. I'm putting this on speaker. Beth and Zeb are with me. Can you hear us?'

'Yeah, though I wish I didn't have to,' Eaton grumbled. 'What do you want?'

'You've got that video clip on your screen?'

'Yes, what about it?'

'Fifth hour, thirty-six minutes. Play it from there.'

They heard the faint sounds of clicks and the dealer's breathing. 'Got it.'

'Watch and tell us what you remember.'

The dealer cleared his throat after a while. 'I wish I could tell you something, but I can't. This was six months back. Must have been a straightforward deal, otherwise I would have remembered.'

'You sold three Glocks to him, Eaton,' Meghan ground out in frustration.

'No big deal. I've sold dozens of weapons at a time.'

'Was he a new customer? Whose reference did he take?'

'Are you hard of hearing?' the Camden man snapped. 'I would've told you if I recollected anything. I don't. Stay away from my business and don't call me again.'

He hung up on them.

Zeb sighed and scratched his cheek. He rose and stretched, looked at the video on the wall. Frozen at the point where money was being exchanged.

Something about it struck him. He frowned.

'That clarity.'

'What of it?' Meghan stood next to him.

''That's unlike most CCTV feeds I've seen.'

'Because it's an HD camera, Zeb. Keep up with the times. Holy—' She broke off and darted towards Beth's keyboard.

'Move, slowpoke,' she shoved her sister to the side and fiddled with the controls.

She played the video again and fist-pumped in delight when a voice spoke on the video.

'I'm looking for a Glock.'

Chapter 22

'No name,' Meghan looped back the video and played it several times. 'He doesn't say who he is. Not once during his time in the store.'

It was 9 am the next day. They had played the clip a few times in the night and had watched it again in the morning. This time with sound.

They had made an elementary mistake when they had played it the first time. They had assumed the camera didn't record audio and had therefore muted their speakers.

'Eaton doesn't ask, either,' Beth chimed in. 'He asks for a reference, however.'

'What good does that do us?' Meghan chewed her lip in frustration. Because a cruiser had gone past, siren wailing, and had drowned out the buyer's reply. The dealer had evidently heard it, because he had disappeared to make a call and reappeared, smiling in satisfaction.

The sisters had tried to separate layers of sound but had failed. 'We could have done that if the clip was professionally recorded,' Beth explained to Zeb, who was watching silently, a distant expression on his face. 'But this camera is an off-the-shelf HD one. It records sound in one layer.'

The twins had hacked into Eaton's phone records and identified the number the dealer had called. It turned out to be a burner, no longer in use.

The majority of the video was the negotiation, which didn't lead them anywhere.

'Play that last part again,' Zeb requested.

Meghan scrolled forward to where the buyer was stuffing the weapons in his pockets. A ring sounded. He brought out a cell, looked at the screen.

'Mi—' he answered, headed out of the store, and that was the last they saw or heard of him on the clip.

'The way he answered that call,' Zeb mused. 'Assertive. Like he was stating his name.'

'Yeah,' Meghan agreed, 'But that syllable could be anything.'

'Mike?' Beth guessed. 'Michael? Miguel? Misha? Mickey? Miles?'

'It's him, however?'

'Confirmed,' Meghan assured Zeb. 'Werner's run gait analysis. It's him. We can run his voice with the Colberts too, if you wish, but I don't see a need.'

'Voice analysis?'

'Werner's onto it. Comparing it against databases we have. So far, no matches.'

'Did he kill Eddie?'

'No luck there. That other clip, the one in the shelter, was too short. It wasn't clear enough for Werner to run a comparison. But who else would kill Eddie?'

Zeb grabbed his headphones and wrapped them around his ears. He went to his screen and watched the store video for what felt like the millionth time.

Just who are you, dude? And what are you planning?

'Mike?'

Khalili jumped when Rusty came from behind him and tapped him on the shoulder.

'What're you doing here?' his boss frowned. 'I thought you'd be up there.' He pointed to the platform above them.

'I just wanted to get a feel for this place,' the killer grinned sheepishly as he looked around the stage in the conference hall. He had been fingering the curtains, examining the fabric, when he had been interrupted.

'You've seen this stage before. Several times.'

'Yeah, but the closer we get to the date, I can't help feeling excited,' he feigned embarrassment.

'I know the feeling. Here,' Rusty grabbed him by his forearm and led him to the center of the stage. 'See these lines on the floor?'

Khalili nodded when he saw the faint markings.

'That's where the seats will be placed. Long tables will be placed here,' the foreman pointed at more markings. 'This,' he spread his hands expansively, 'will be where the most powerful people in the world sit and address their audience.' He pointed to the rows of empty chairs in the vast hall.

''Can't wait,' the killer said, rubbing his hands enthusiastically. 'The atmosphere will be electric.'

Rusty looked at him quizzically. 'You and I, buddy, all of us,' he nodded at their co-workers, 'will be catching it on the box. At home, along with millions of other people.'

The assassin thought he had misheard. 'Come again?'

'You thought we would be here on the day, Mike? Really?'

The foreman laughed. 'Hey, Chuck.' He waved another technician over. 'Mike thinks we'll be here on summit day. That we can watch the proceedings from behind the curtains. Like this was high school.' He slapped his thigh and chuckled, shaking his head in disbelief.

His humor fled when he saw the expression on Khalili's face. 'Shucks, Mike. I forgot. It's your first big gig, isn't it? The rest of the crew have been through a few like these. Not on this scale, but close enough. No one,' he shook his head remorsefully, 'none of us will be here on that day. I thought I told you. The place will be crawling with Secret Service, Feds, cops. They don't want us around. Which is why we have got to make sure everything is working perfectly.' He looked up at the platform. 'We don't want any of those leaders to catch a cold, do we? And hey, the Feds are here tomorrow. Another security check on personnel. Be sure to show up.'

And with that, he left, laughing at Khalili's naivete.

The killer stood still. There was a roaring in his ears. His vision darkened. He hadn't anticipated this. All his research had indicated that he and many of the crew would be in the hall on event day. To address any mechanical issues that might crop up.

All my planning's wasted. He forced his body into motion when Chuck looked at him curiously.

'You all right, Mike? You look pale.'

'Yeah.' He clutched his brow. 'Something I ate the other night. It's not agreeing with me.'

He went to the bathroom, occupied a cubicle and sat on the toilet. He closed his eyes and breathed deeply.

Control.

He was the world's best assassin. Dealing with the

unexpected came with the job.

Control. Breathe in. Breathe out.

He felt balance returning to him, and with that, confidence returned.

Okay. So he would have to alter his plans. Find a way to burn the place down remotely.

It could be done.

He would do it.

Chapter 23

'How will you kill now?' the Man had raged the previous night when Khalili had returned from work and had broken the news to him.

'I'll find a way.'

'You said it would take a year to plan. What has that gotten you? The summit is less than two weeks away and you still don't—'

'If you thought it would be that easy, you could have used your other killers,' the assassin replied coldly. 'I have access to the conference hall. I'll figure out something.'

'You don't need me to remind you—'

'Enough with the threats,' the killer grated. 'They become useless if they're repeated too often. I know what you're capable of. Don't forget what *I* can do.'

Khalili recollected the conversation as he took the subway to work. He put the Man in a box and stowed it away in the deep recesses in his mind. He knew the spymaster could not be ignored that easily, but for now, he had to think of alternate means of assassinating.

Sniper rifle, remotely detonated explosive, car bomb,

grenade, rocket launcher, poison gas … nope, none of those would work. He had ruled those out for a reason.

Fire. That was still his best bet. However, how to start one when he wasn't present? He closed his eyes as the car rocked. It was packed with morning commuters, loud voices discussing the previous night's game. Many people on their phones, a few heads bobbing to music. His eyes opened when someone laughed. A woman opposite him was making her face up. She applied eyeliner and then lipstick. Used a small spray to perfume herself.

Spray. His titanium powder idea was a non-starter, now.

He shut his eyes again and started drifting to sleep. Random images came to him. Rusty's laughter. The tourists on fire. The weld.

Weld. He sat up straight. What if he could attach a canister? Time it to go off in twenty-four hours. Or whatever time period was needed.

Would the law-enforcement authorities inspect the ducting that high? He doubted it. Sure, there were sniffer dogs and electronic devices that could identify explosives. But metal hazard? Heck, the entire air-con ducting could combust.

Nope, there was no way the Feds or the Secret Service and whoever else was involved in security could detect a flammable metal.

With that decided, which substance to use?

Sodium. It came to his mind readily. It would burn in water. Something to do with reaction with oxygen, freeing up hydrogen and giving off heat. Chemistry that he had learned in school. Even if there were sniffers, either canine or electronic, there would be enough salt shakers in Javits to give false alarms.

He decided to watch science videos when he was back home. He would then figure out how to bring the metal into the conference hall and trigger it.

There remained the titanium powder. Some of it was still left in that industrial unit.

A smile swept his face. He would test it out one last time. Khalili didn't take pleasure from killing. It was his job. However, there was something about fire.

Yes, he would set fire one last time that night.

Fort Davis, Texas

They met at a large ranch in Fort Davis, well away from the populated towns and cities of Texas. The town was named after a fort built on the San Antonio-El Paso road, which in turn was named after a secretary of war.

The ranch was owned by a billionaire friend of Wayne Bernier, a generous donor to their cause. It sprawled over two hundred and fifty thousand acres and was one of the few very large ranches that actively carried out livestock operations.

The founder of the separatist movement stepped down from the Lear jet. He donned his shades, adjusted his hat and looked around. Rolling green carried all the way to the mountains in the distance. Moving specks of brown and black that were cattle. Cowboys, horse-mounted, in pursuit of a recalcitrant steer. A blue sky overhead, flecks of powdery clouds drifting across it.

Bernier breathed deeply. Texas. It was home. It was freedom. It was for Americans who could trace their ancestry back to the Civil War and way beyond it. People like him. White people like him. He would do anything to keep the state and his country for those of his kind.

He adjusted his hat again and walked to the SUV, where a driver awaited.

'Billy, you good?'

'Yes, sir.'

'The others?'

'They came yesterday, sir. Stayed in the ranch house.'

'Let's go.'

Billy drove a short distance to the ranch house, a sprawling structure situated geographically in the center of the estate. The SUV rolled up the driveway and stopped in front of large oak doors. A cowboy sprang forward, opened his door and escorted him inside. Bernier nodded in thanks and followed the man down a hallway, past a sitting room, an entertainment room, several chambers and into a meeting room.

Five men, casually attired, shirts and t-shirts tucked into jeans, rose when he entered. Bailey Wunsch, Markus Pagac, Brando Spinka, Merle Anderson and Chauncey Kiehn. They comprised the council, the executive body that ran White Freedom. Bernier presided over it, but as founder-president of the movement he could overrule any decision, any diktat that the body came up with.

He greeted them by their first names, backslapped and shook hands with them. Drinks were served and consumed and, after small talk, the serious business began.

'Where are we with the summit?' Bernier removed his shades and looked around the table.

'An American bank, a German automaker and a Silicon Valley tech company,' Pagac said, withdrawing a small notebook from a pocket and glancing at his notes. He mentioned their names. 'They have operations all over the world. They've—'

The founder waved him forward. Those firms were household names the world over. 'Why them?'

'Their CEOs and board members have been lobbying the president hard. They want to ease immigration laws. Access to foreign labor is their excuse. They say there aren't enough skills in the country. They're losing their competitive advantage, so they claim. You know the arguments.'

Everyone nodded. They had.

'Their New York offices are downtown. Nowhere near Javits. The day of the summit is a Sunday. No staff on premises. Thin security.'

'What will go down?' Bernier asked, even though he knew. They all knew, but it was necessary to go through the details, repeatedly, until they spotted all wrinkles and ironed them out.

'Those offices will be bombed by our people,' Pagac said bluntly. 'A call will be made to the NYPD subsequently. Anonymously. That those companies should change their ways. Take American workers. That these explosions are just the beginning.'

'Blowback?'

'None,' Pagac said confidently. 'We won't take credit. In fact, you'll arrange a press conference an hour later and denounce the bombs. You'll say that you disagree with those companies, but attacking their offices isn't the way to get them to change. We'll all be in Texas.'

'What about our members? Those who'll be involved?'

'We're using four members from the New Jersey chapter and four more from Dallas.' He offered names. 'All will travel to New York on Saturday. Aliases, disguises, alibis, everything is in place. They'll attach the explosives at night, set the timers and leave. We want to make a statement, nothing more. The bombs will be powerful enough to destroy the first floor.'

'Won't these devices be spotted?' said Kiehn, polishing his glasses with a piece of silk.

'We're confident they won't be. All these buildings have glass entrances, mirrored surfaces and several potted plants outside and around them. Our bombs will be hidden in the earthen pots. We'll have five bombs for each building.'

'Worst-case scenario, even if they are, the message has been sent,' Bernier shrugged.

'There's one more thing.' Pagac looked at them.

'What?'

'There could be cleaning crews in the building on Sunday.'

Bernier frowned. 'Those are Mexican, Filipino women usually, aren't they?'

'Black men and women as well.'

'Collateral damage.' The founder waved dismissively. 'No loss.'

Chapter 24

Fort Davis, Texas

The six men took a break for lunch, a sumptuous six-course meal served by white-jacketed waiters. Coffees followed and more small talk. None worried about being overhead or being spied on.

Their billionaire friend had security to rival the president's. Better, he frequently boasted. Counter-surveillance devices were carefully hidden in and around the house. It was frequently checked by an exclusive Texas firm, and an electronic blanket surrounded it, preventing any long-range audio surveillance. Several of the cowboys in the house and a perimeter surrounding it were security professionals. They wouldn't hesitate to open lethal fire if they spotted any intruders.

Bernier tapped against a glass tumbler to signal the end of lunch.

'Those eight men,' he resumed, 'they're all cleared?'

'Yeah,' Wunsch answered. 'Our PIs have given them a clean chit. None of them is our traitor. Of course, they don't know anything of what we're planning.' He shifted in his chair uneasily.

'Spit it out, Bailey,' Bernier sighed. 'What is it?'

'There will be nine men, actually,' his friend said apologetically. 'The eight will be led by a chapter head: Tucker. He's the smartest of all the chapter heads. He's not far from New York. He's proven himself. He's in the best position to lead this team. He, too, doesn't know anything, yet.'

A silence fell over the room.

Bernier knew the investigation into the members to find the snitch was nearing completion. However, its remit had been to check out foot soldiers only. The majority of the members reported to chapter presidents, who in turn were accountable to the council. A very flat organization.

At the last council meeting, a unanimous vote had been taken to look into the chapter presidents, too. Wunsch had hired a separate firm of investigators for that purpose, a Houston one whose CEO was a White Freedom sympathizer. That firm had swung into action promptly and had started tailing all the presidents. It hadn't delivered a report, however. Not yet.

All eyes turned towards Bernier, who played with his water tumbler as he thought. There were eight chapters around the country. Eight chapter presidents. Investigating them wouldn't take long. Tucker … he was a fast-rising star in the group and there had been discussion about admitting him to the council. If he turned out to be a snitch ... 'Light a fire under those investigators,' he rapped out at Wunsch.

'And if Tucker or anyone else turns out to be an informer?' Spinka ventured.

Bernier's lips tightened. 'We know what to do, then.'

Wunsch bobbed his head in acknowledgment, even as a chill raced through him. There was a small group of members within White Freedom who were the first to be investigated and cleared. They didn't socialize with other members. They kept to themselves and reported only to Bernier.

They dealt with straying members. Those who didn't toe the line. Those who had second thoughts about the movement. Members who might be inclined to snitch. Their methods were brutal, violent, and their encounters with any member were made transparent in the group. White Freedom had had a few snitches in its history, rats who had turned on the movement and had fed intel to the FBI.

This select group of members had dealt with informers effectively, by extinguishing their lives.

This group's name described what its members did.

It was called the enforcers.

Chapter 25

Khalili ventured out the next night. He had done his research well. A curtains and blinds store in Brooklyn was his destination. He had chosen that outlet because of the foot traffic it got. The shop wasn't crowded in the evening hours. It wasn't empty, either. The second reason was the security setup. There were three ceiling-mounted security cameras on the store's floor. From his initial surveillance run, the killer knew they were a cheap make that delivered not-very-sharp images to a central computer. That suited his purpose.

He had an aerosol can taped to his left wrist, its nozzle snuggled inside his palm. A lighter was attached to his right hand. The ever-present hoodie was over his face.

He kept his head down and entered the store. He ignored an oncoming salesman, projecting a cold vibe that made the eager employee back off.

He went to a sidewall and fingered the hanging curtains. His back to the cameras, no part of his face shown. Good tradecraft that was habit due to years of experience. He was the world's best assassin for a reason.

He went to another wall where there weren't other

customers. Did the fingering thing again. Looked sideways. No one near him. Glanced back. Store staff were busy with other patrons. No one was paying him any attention.

His left arm came up in a lightning move. The nozzle squeezed, and a barely detectable mist sprayed out. His right wrist came to his waist and sparked flame.

The curtains caught fire with a satisfying whump. Flames leapt across the wall, lighting up other fabric. A woman shrieked. Stray sparks flew in the air and settled on some patrons.

Khalili didn't stay to watch. He headed out rapidly, screams and yells fading with each step. His heart was pounding, his face was flushed, but he didn't look up as he executed a complicated maneuver of crossing side streets and alleys and reversing his hoodie.

By the time he reached the subway, his pulse had returned to normal, and his face had acquired its habitual cold mask.

He prepared his evening meal when he got home and turned on the local news station. A TV reporter was excitedly covering the fire. The store was reduced to a shell, the fire still going strong. Its stock had burned, and three customers were seriously injured when flaming drapery had fallen on them.

Firefighters and emergency services workers were in the background as they fought to control the conflagration.

The back of the store had rolls of fabric that had lit up, and the fire had spread fast and furious, the TV woman reported.

'It's unclear how this happened,' she said, her face glowing in the red and orange of the fire. 'The NYPD isn't ruling out arson, but a full investigation can begin only when the flames have been put out.'

Khalili watched from the safety of Pollenberg's apartment.

A crowd had gathered outside the store, gawkers and curious onlookers who surged at the perimeter the cops had laid out. The reporter interviewed several of them, none of whom had anything relevant to say. She tried cornering a few cops but was brushed off.

She signed off with a few cheerful words. She had her story. She had her ratings. New York City had another spectacle to entertain itself with.

Khalili washed his dishes, turned off the TV and sat in the darkness of the living room. Now that he was back to his rational self, he was troubled. Starting that fire was a needless risk, he admitted to himself. There was no need to expose himself in that manner.

Why did he behave that way? He had carried out several kills throughout the world. Why was he so uncharacteristic on this mission?

He debated with himself and then went to bed, unsatisfied.

The answer came to him when he woke in the night, caught between sleep and wakefulness, when time ceased to exist.

That sense of foreboding deep within him that he didn't acknowledge … maybe it was telling him something. Maybe he wanted to be found. He tried to analyze that thought, but sleep gripped him. And when he woke up, he had nothing on his mind other than starting a sodium fire in Javits.

Werner yawned and stretched. He tossed his book aside and looked around the Columbus Avenue office. Meg and Beth were there. The only two people in the universe that mattered. Well, the others mattered, too. Broker, Zeb, Bwana and Bear, who both looked like they could crush a computer like it was a can of soda, Roger, Chloe … of course, they were important.

But not in the way the twins were.

Werner turned into a puddle, figuratively of course, when the sisters caressed him and spoke to him via their commands. Werner would do anything for them. He removed his feet from his virtual desk and surveyed his world.

There was a time when he was dating a Swiss supercomputer. Dating was probably a strong word for the games of chess they played. It didn't matter anyhow. The lady had moved on. Werner had tried chatting with a British supercomputer, but that hadn't gone anywhere. He was intrigued by a smart, svelte one in Paris, in the DGSE headquarters, but she wasn't online. Probably at work.

Work. That reminded him. He dug up the news clip that had surfaced in the night.

Meghan had programmed him to look for that hooded figure in the vastness of New York.

Now, that was an almost impossible task, given the enormous dataset that the CCTV cameras scattered through the city contributed to. Werner had the assassin's gait, and his voice, from that gun dealer's store. Despite those, the task was insurmountable.

He was aware of the previous fires caused by a mysterious assailant. The cops had released brief footage of a hooded figure running away from the Times Square one. Some passerby had captured it on a cell phone. The appeal for information had resulted in a flood of calls, all of which turned out to be useless. A criminal arsonist, the NYPD had declared. That's who that man was. He seemed to get off on setting people on fire. An urban terrorist.

Local news channels speculated on the killer and online forums discussed him. Werner got no clues from any of those.

He had checked out that shaky clip as well. It was too short, however, to run any analysis.

But that store fire … Werner reached into his memory and brought up the news report. Watched it carefully. Nope, nothing there. He accessed the NYPD's systems. Of course, he had access to them. There were very few databases in the world Werner couldn't access. Very few. And for even those, Meg and Beth were constantly trying new approaches.

There: the NYPD's forensic team had the store's CCTV footage. Wait, what was that?

Werner felt virtual goosebumps as he watched the blurry video. A hooded figure entering the store. Fingering curtains and drapes. He leaned forward suddenly when the man, yeah, a male, no doubt, moved suddenly and flames started.

Werner fired several programs simultaneously. One sharpened the store's video. Another slowed motion. Now, he could see what the arsonist did. He could spot the tip of an aerosol can in the man's left palm. Clever. And that pale patch in the right … Werner ran a shape-comparison and in nano-seconds had his answer. A lighter.

Now, to compare this arsonist to the Times Square dude.

Werner grimaced. Thirty percent match. The Times Square clip was too short to make a more meaningful match. However, the hoodie looked similar, the way the men bowed their heads in both instances … all of that looked similar.

Two more video comparisons to go.

He ran the curtain store clip against the one from the homeless shelter. The one where Eddie had been killed.

He made a face when the algorithm didn't return any result. He had been expecting that. That shelter had gone for cheap cameras. Dim lighting at night hadn't helped.

He took a breath. Now for the big one.

He brought up the Angelo Eaton video, played it alongside the Brooklyn clip, and ran several algorithms.

Eighty percent match!

Werner danced a virtual jig. He threw his head back, air-guitared and howled at the sky.

And then he sent a message to the sisters. They were busy with some crossword puzzle thing that he could have solved for them without even taking a breath.

He would wait for their reaction. They were his … he stopped himself from going mushy. He would die for them. That would do.

Death. Hmmm. How did an AI program die? And on that, he retrieved his book and went back to reading Nietzsche.

Chapter 26

A text from Mark distracted Beth from the crossword. She raised her head, glanced at her cell and fired a reply.

'What?' she asked defensively when she saw her sister's expression.

'That moony look on your face when he calls or messages,' Meghan sniggered. 'So adolescent.'

'Meghan Petersen, just because you don't have a special—' She broke off, distracted by the flashing message on her screen.

She gasped, grabbed her twin's shoulder and pulled her towards the screen. Her fingers ran commands. The screen-saver disappeared and videos appeared, the gun dealer's, as well as another one. Both played, and when they ended, there was Werner's terse message.

Eighty percent match!

Meghan drew a sharp breath as the words registered. 'What's that second clip?'

Beth was typing even as she asked. 'Werner grabbed it from the NYPD's forensic department. Looks like the store had CCTV cameras. *ZEB!*'

An hour and a round of coffees later, the warriors were

still bunched around Beth's screen, the videos on loop.

'Why would he start fires?' the younger twin asked for what felt like the millionth time.

'Beats me,' Roger's nails scraped across his day-old stubble. 'It looked like he was a pro … but this fire. That's amateur play.'

'Not just this one,' Bear growled. 'It looks like he was the arsonist at the other two as well. Two Chinese tourists died. A homeless man, too.'

'Werner says there's only a thirty percent match with those too.'

'Thirty's good for us. The cops will need more,' Chloe reached over their shoulders and stopped the videos. 'We aren't the cops.'

'Someone's lost for words,' Beth looked pointedly in Zeb's direction, who was staring into the distance.

'He's astounded at our genius,' Meghan replied smugly and high-fived her sister.

'Zeb?' Beth shook him impatiently.

He stirred. 'Send that to Chang, Pizaka and Burke.'

'Done.'

'I've been thinking.'

'He's been thinking,' Beth intoned. 'Pray, enlighten us.'

'What if he's practicing?'

'Practicing what?'

'Setting fires.'

Chapter 27

A silence greeted his words. Broker tossed a golf ball in the air and caught it. Bwana chewed on gum furiously. Chloe's brow wrinkled. Roger scratched his jaw again. 'You mean like a new weapon?'

'Yeah.'

'You might be onto something,' Bwana sounded like barrels rolling on a wooden floor. 'It's what we would do if we were working with new, unfamiliar weapons.'

'Got it.' Meghan flicked her hair back impatiently. 'But why fire?'

Her green eyes swung towards Zeb. He didn't answer. *She's smart. She'll work it out.*

Meghan did, an instant later.

'Because no other weapons can work,' she snapped her fingers excitedly, words rushing out. 'Bombs, sniper shooting, the Feds, NYPD, Secret Service, they'll have Javits locked down. Fire is easy to start. A matchstick isn't seen as a weapon. Not these days.'

'Won't he have to be present to start a fire?' Beth asked dubiously.

'He could set one off with a time-delay switch.'

'Which could be detected by the security staff,' Chloe objected.

'You notice where he set this fire?' Zeb asked them, slowly.

'A curtain store,' Beth answered promptly. 'Javits will have lots of them. Curtains. Ceiling to floor ones. Wall hangings. There'll be a heck of a lot of fabric in there.'

'I think he is figuring this out, too,' Zeb answered slowly. 'The first two kills were to see if whatever he's using for fire, works. The third was to check how fast the flames would spread.'

Meghan lunged towards her cell and dialed a number rapidly.

'Chang,' she said. 'Get your ass over here. And your sidekick's, too. Nope, I won't tell you over the phone.'

'We're up to our necks in work,' the cop said, his whine audible to all. 'Investigations. That's what the NYPD does, in case you've forgotten.'

'There's coffee waiting.'

'We'll be there in half an hour,' Chang said as his resistance folded. 'We're not far from your place.'

'Burke?' Zeb asked Broker.

'She's in DC.'

'We'll get her on a call when our friends arrive.'

Chang and Pizaka arrived promptly in half an hour. The rumpled-looking detective's eyes flew over the office and settled on the jugs and cups. He poured a large shot for himself and his partner, drank his beverage greedily and smacked his lips.

'Now, I feel human. Talk,' he commanded the twins.

Beth made to sneer, caught Meghan's warning glare and held back. Now wasn't the time for barbs.

'We're getting Sarah Burke on the line,' she said as she dialed the FBI agent's number.

Chang's eyebrows almost touched his hairline. 'Something's happened?'

She held a finger up to silence him as the phone rang twice.

'Burke.'

'Sarah, Beth. Can you talk?'

'Shoot.'

'I've got Chang and Pizaka with all of us. I'm putting you on speaker.'

'What's up?'

'I've emailed you a few video clips. Play them. Start with the first. I'm putting it up on the screen here for the cops' benefit.'

She brought up the first video: the killer in Eaton's store.

'That's the man in Colbert's apartment. The one who killed his accomplice.'

She ran through the details. Vinnie Godinez's killing. McCree. Eaton and the video.

'I won't ask how you got McCree to confess,' Burke said when she had digested the revelations.

'Don't,' Chang said feelingly. 'This lot …' he trailed off when Bwana stared hard at him.

'Play the second one,' Beth commanded and brought up the jerky Times Square video.

'Yeah, I heard about this. Chinese tourists, right? Both died. This is an NYPD matter. What's the connection?'

'Play the third video,' Beth answered in reply. She looked quickly at the cops and bit back a smile. They were watching in fascination as the curtain store video played.

'That's from yesterday,' Chang's jaw dropped. 'It's not our investigation, but we heard of it. Heck, the whole city knows of the fire. How did you get that video?'

'You see the arsonist?'

'How could I miss him?'

'Burke, play the last video.'

Something clattered at the FBI agent's end when the final clip played out. They heard a muttered curse. Chang sucked breath noisily. He rose, tried to straighten his jacket, gave up. 'That's—'

'The arsonist is the man who was at the Colberts,' Burke finished for him. 'He's the one on your radar. Possible terrorist.' Her voice sharpened. 'What's he doing setting fires? 'We think that's how he's going to attack Javits.' Chloe filled her cup with coffee and inhaled the aroma. She explained quickly how they had arrived at that conclusion. 'Burke, get your people to compare the videos. See if they'll arrive at the same match we made. Chang, Pizaka, you too.'

'Where is he?' the FBI agent snapped, her voice reflecting the buzz in the room.

'Somewhere in New York, going by these fires.'

'We can flood the city. The FBI and NYPD, find him—'

'How?' Meghan demanded. 'What description do you have? A man wearing a hoodie?'

Burke paused. Gathered herself. 'What do you suggest?'

'Chang, Pizaka, find out how he started those fires.'

'It'll be with the arson squad,' Pizaka muttered under his breath as he drew out his cell. 'Maybe FDNY's BFI is leading it.'

New York's fire department, FDNY, had a Bureau of Fire

Investigation that looked into arson cases. It worked closely with the NYPD in such cases, and jurisdiction was sometimes shared.

'Burke?' Zeb stirred.

'Yeah.'

'We want to visit Javits. Can you arrange it?'

Chapter 28

Pagac was driving to Tucker's gas station even as the warriors, the NYPD and Burke were meeting in New York.

He had flown down to Newark and rented a car at the airport.

He drove slowly, window down, enjoying the drive, feeling the wind in his face. He hadn't told Tucker he would be coming. No council member ever did. They liked to catch their chapter presidents unaware. Of course, there were times when such unexpected arrivals turned into no- shows. Like when a chapter head didn't turn up for work.

Tucker runs a gas station, for chrissakes. Where else would he be? Pagac silenced his doubts.

The council member was burly, short and in his fifties. His wrists were beefy, his knuckles raw from boxing without gloves. He had been an enforcer at one time. He had enjoyed *disciplining* White Freedom members. A couple of times, he had been involved in the disappearance of snitches in the organization.

He thought about how much he loved those days. *Wayne, me, Spinka, the other council guys, beating the heck out of someone. Killing a rat.* He still went along to witness such acts when he could. He wasn't beyond landing a punch or a kick. Or worse. He preferred the *worse.*

One part of him wished Tucker was bad. *I can then join the enforcers and wreck him.* Not that he had anything against the young man. He rubbed his knuckles. It was just that he hadn't roughed up anyone in a long time. Or killed anyone.

He drove up to the gas station pump, got out, stretched and yawned. 'Howdy, ma'am,' he greeted the woman filling at the other outlet. She smiled back at him and turned to her children.

The service station doubled as a convenience store, with big windows from which the manager could keep an eye on the pump area. He saw Tucker's startled glance and nodded imperceptibly. He fed the hose into his rental and stretched some more.

It was the routine he had with Tucker. He would come in unannounced. Fill up and head to Tabernacle, a small township where the chapter president's home was.

The young man would get away from his duties and meet him in the only bar in the vicinity. Pagac was a stranger, but no one took any notice of him. It was that kind of town. People minded their own business but were always ready to help those in trouble.

He longed for those days. *They'll come. We're winning on social media. This upcoming attack will get us more supporters.* White Freedom hadn't affiliated itself to any political party, but he, Wayne and the other councilors were already making plans. *Elections are two years away. Morgan will get a rude surprise, come voting day.*

Morgan. He made a face and spat. Apologized promptly

when he saw the woman's shocked expression. 'I've come down with something, ma'am,' he explained hurriedly. 'Throat feels jammed up.'

She shepherded her children into her car, jumped in and drove away.

Only then he recollected how she looked. Mexican. These immigrants, they had no manners. They didn't know how to live in the U.S. It was Morgan's fault. He had encouraged foreigners to arrive.

That will change, Pagac vowed to himself and went inside to pay. He met Tucker's eyes and conveyed a silent message.

'What's up?' the chapter manager asked him an hour later, in the Tabernacle bar. They were by a corner window, two bottles of beer on their table.

'How's it going?' Pagac asked casually.

'Good, good. My members are clear. I think you know that.'

'Yeah, you've got nothing to worry about.'

'Did you find any snitch?'

'Your men are good.'

'So, we're all clean? Whi—' He caught himself. 'The movement?'

'Investigation's still ongoing,' Pagac said, noncommittally. *And you're on the radar, bud.*

Tucker nodded in understanding, waiting, knowing the council member hadn't come that far for just his company.

'You got to make yourself available a few days before the summit.' Pagac took a long pull and wiped his lips with the back of his hand. His eyes were narrowed as he watched the man opposite.

Tucker showed curiosity. 'The summit? The G-'

'Yeah. Don't say its name.'

The young man's eyes widened. 'We're …' he looked around. 'We're planning to—'

'Something like that, yeah. Pick four of your members. The best ones. Reliable, trustworthy. Get yourself alibis. You know the drill.'

'Yeah. Can I tell them—'

'No.' Pagac's voice hardened. 'You know the rules. Don't act like it's your first gig.'

'Yeah, sorry. I just thought—'

'Leave the thinking to us. Get your men ready. Make yourself available. That's all you're getting from me.'

'How long do we have to be away for?'

'Three days at the most. Might not come to that, even.'

'Three days,' Tucker repeated, fingering his bottle.

'That a problem?'

'Not for me. Josh, Kev—' He broke off when Pagac looked blank. The council member didn't know his chapter members. 'I know some of my folks can't be away for long. I'll have to check.'

'Be ready. Have your men,' Pagac warned. He didn't care about the details. He reached for his wallet and placed a few bills on the table, a generous tip included. 'Oh, yeah. I nearly forgot. You'll be joined by four more from Texas.'

He chuckled when the young man gaped at him. 'What we're planning is big. It'll send the right message to the right people. You need a bigger team.'

Tucker nodded, his mind whirling, thinking of logistics. Eight men to manage, half of them he hadn't met before.

'They'll come here?'

'Yeah. They're good. When they get here, I'll call and let you know the mission details.'

The manager leaned forward. 'This involves any fatalities?'

Pagac sat back in his seat and smirked just a little, letting Tucker dangle for a while. 'You'll see when you get the details. You getting squeamish? Every member knows what joining the movement means. You getting cold feet, boy?'

'No,' Tucker replied firmly. 'It's just that we'll need real tight alibis.'

'Do that. There should be no blowback. If you get caught—'

'Yeah, I know. It's every man for himself.'

The council member stood up and patted the younger man on the shoulder. 'Relax. We know you can do this. There's a reason we chose you. You've got the skills. There's a future for you.'

When he was back in his car, he dialed a number. 'Where are you?'

'Following him. From a safe distance,' a gravelly voice replied. One of the Houston PIs who was looking into Tucker.

'Just you?'

'I have a partner, sir. We work in two-man teams. There's another team to relieve us when our shift ends. We'll have eyes on Tucker round the clock.'

Pagac smiled in satisfaction. *If he turns out to be a snitch ... I'll punch his ticket myself.*

Chapter 29

Zeb and his entire crew drove to Javits in two vehicles. Meghan in the front with him, Beth and Broker at the back. Standard seating arrangement, their vehicle in the lead. Bear was at the wheel of the second, Bwana, Roger and Chloe filling it up.

Their revelations to the cops and FBI the previous day had triggered a flurry of activity.

'Titanium powder, finely ground,' Chang had reported in the evening. 'That's what the arson investigators have figured out. Sprayed from an aerosol can, lit by a lighter. Cannot be extinguished by water. Which is why the Chinese tourists and the homeless man died. The people who rushed to help them threw water. It didn't help. By the time EMS arrived, it was too late. Same situation with the curtain store.'

Sarah Burke had confirmed that the arsonist was the same person who bought the guns in Eaton's store. 'We brought in the dealer for questioning. He's singing. He's ratting on his customers, gangs. His info should help us close down some of those outfits.'

The two vehicles rolled up at a Javits security entrance after clearing several checkpoints. Zeb climbed out, crossed his arms and leaned against the vehicle.

Bear joined him. 'We waiting for someone?'

'The foreman.'

Rusty wasn't a happy man. He had a load of work to do. The piping under the dais had developed a crack. It needed to be fixed. The refrigeration system had died. Scaffolding inside the auditorium had to be taken down. That fricking Pete, he had managed to fall from his perch where he was fixing the ventilation system.

'He had harnesses and all. And still, the dumbass fell,' the foreman grumbled to himself. And now he had to fill out countless forms and answer questions from a safety committee.

On top of that, these new arrivals.

He lumbered out of the gate and glared at the two vehicles. He had a bunch of papers gripped tight in his left hand.

He shuffled through them and read a name.

'Carter?' He made no attempt to hide his hostility.

A brown-haired man straightened. Came towards him. The way he walked reminded Rusty of a panther. Not that he had seen many of those animals, but back when he'd been young, he'd visited a zoo.

'You're Carter?'

'Yeah.'

'Eight of you?'

'Correct.' The man gave some kind of a signal. Doors opened, men and women stepped out. Rusty gawked at the three females. Their looks, their air of competence. He snapped his jaws shut when an ebony-skinned man cleared his throat.

'The Feds, the cops, the Secret Service, any other agency can take you around. Why me?'

'The FBI said you know the hall best. You're here day in and out.'

'Just who are you people?' He peered at Carter suspiciously.

'What does it say on those papers?'

'These?' Rusty waved them, 'Nothing. Your names, faces, is all they've got. You must have some juice to get a visit organized. No one's allowed to come to this entrance. Heck, most folks don't even know of its existence.'

He didn't get a reply. He swore under his breath and glared when a tall man chuckled, one who looked like a model. Roger. That's what his name was. He squared his shoulders and stomped off towards a room. 'You got to go through that,' he said, pointing to a fingerprint-controlled barrier.

Two women went first. Sisters, judging by their looks and names. The barriers opened. Rusty's eyes bulged. *Juice. These folks have juice. Not only did the Feds get them these invites, they uploaded their prints in the system overnight.*

'Give us the tour,' the one called Meghan told him when all eight were on the other side of the gate.

Rusty did her bidding.

Three hours later, he wiped sweat from his forehead. They were back at the fingerprint-controlled barrier. Beyond them, a few workers looked at them curiously as they went about their job.

'Remind us again, how many work in there?' Carter jerked his head towards the conference hall.

'Thirty.' Rusty took a long pull from his water bottle, capped it and slipped it into a pocket. 'More in the entire building. Javits is huge. But only those thirty, and that includes me, are allowed to go beyond those gates.'

'And you'll be working right till the day of the summit?'

'No, sir,' the foreman laughed. 'A week before the event, we're off. Then, Federal government folks take over.'

'Why the security?' That model dude pushed his shades further up his nose and patted down his hair.

Rusty looked at him suspiciously and wondered if it was a trick question. Surely it was obvious?

'To stop strangers from getting inside. Bad people, like terrorists, you know. Folks who just might want to plant bombs,' he explained patiently. Sometimes you had to take it slow with visitors. Tell them the basics.

'Fingerprints alone will deter those people?' the dude persisted.

'Friend, me and my people, we've all been vetted by the FBI. By the Secret Service. Lord knows which other agency. Our lives have been examined. Our financial records, our families, friends, everything has been turned over. We started working here only after getting those clearances.' *Got it, dumbass?*

'Just asking,' model dude held his hands up.

'And even then, the FBI runs random checks on us. A bunch of them appear unannounced, interview us, make us go through all the work we've done. Get us to walk through our week,' Rusty carried on, hammering his point home.

'Yeah, yeah,' the dude shrugged and turned away.

'I don't see an iris scanner,' the older sister frowned.

'Don't need one. My team has been together for several years. It's the longest serving construction team in Manhattan,' the foreman boasted. 'We know one another very well. That fingerprint device,' he snorted, 'that wasn't needed, either. But hey, who asks me?'

At those words, the visitors looked at him. The large man,

the one with the beard, seemed to be amused but didn’t say anything.

‘Hey, look.’ Rusty shuffled his feet. ‘I gotta go. Things to do, you know.’

‘Thanks,’ Carter said, gripping his hand, ‘you’ve been a real help.’

The foreman didn’t believe him. All he had done was give the man a tour. He nodded at the other visitors and, when those sisters flashed him a blinding smile, his cars turned red. He honest-to-God blushed.

Zeb drove in silence after they left. The Javits conference center looked secure enough. *Law enforcement would have crawled over it, vetted everyone who worked in it.* There was no way a killer could get through.

So, how’s he planning his fires? If that’s what his MO is?

He had no answers. He looked to his right. Meghan was staring straight ahead. Her lips curved into a smile when she felt his gaze.

‘Don’t ask me,’ she drawled, reading his mind. ‘I’ve been trying to figure out the same problem.’

She craned her neck to look back and made a disgusted sound. ‘Beth, she’s not thinking at all. She’s texting Mark. She –’

Zeb’s phone rang and connected to the SUV’s audio system.

‘Zeb?’ Bwana.

‘Tucker called. He wants to meet right away. He sounded nervous.’

‘Go.’

Chapter 30

‘Pagac came,’ Tucker blurted that evening when Bwana and Roger met him in the Plumsted Township bar.

‘Pagac? Who’s he?’ The dark-skinned man swiveled in his chair to signal the server. Used the move to check out the other patrons.

There were fewer than twenty, none of whom were paying them any attention.

‘Markus Pagac,’ Tucker hissed. ‘He’s on the council.’

Roger frowned at Bwana. *Be serious,* he messaged with his eyes. *Tucker looks scared.*

‘What did he want?’ he asked softly, planting his elbows on the table.

‘Asked us to plan for a three-day away trip. To New York. Just before the summit.’

Bwana’s face turned granite. A muscle twitched on his cheek. *‘Us?’*

‘Four men from my chapter. Four more coming from Texas.’

‘You know who your four are?’

Tucker nodded. ‘Yeah. Pagac asked me to pick my best people. I know who those are.’

'What about the Texans?'

'Don't know them. He said they'll come in time for departure.'

'What's the plan?'

'He said he'll tell us when those others turn up.'

He looked around casually. Smiled when the server caught his eye. Shook his head when she mouthed, *Do you want anything else?*

'He asked us to arrange for watertight alibis. I asked him whether any killings were planned.'

'What did he say?'

'He laughed. Asked if I was being squeamish. He didn't confirm. Or deny.'

Roger rotated his beer glass with his fingers and watched the liquid swirl. Three days. That was enough to execute just about anything if plans were in place.

'There's something else.'

He raised his head when he heard the strain in Tucker's voice.

'I asked him if they had found any informer,' the snitch said. 'Pagac said my men were clear.'

'So?'

'His words. Your men are clear. He didn't say you are all clear. He didn't include me.'

Roger sat back and surveyed the snitch. Tucker looked composed, and to any watcher, it would appear as if the three men were good friends. Talking about a hunting trip or fishing or cars, the way men did.

Roger knew the man's appearance was deceptive, however. *We've been undercover. We know how it is. He must be close to cracking.*

'You're reading too much into his words. That's just the way he speaks, probably.'

The informer shook his head stubbornly. 'You don't know them like I do. Bernier, Pagac, the rest of the council members, they're careful with words. Very careful. They know exactly what to say, how to say it, and when to say it.'

'Okay,' Bwana made a hand gesture. 'Let's assume you're right. That what he meant is you aren't cleared. That you're under the scanner. Why would he do that? It doesn't make sense. One moment he's entrusting you with a danged big mission. The next he's saying you can't be trusted?'

Tucker wet his lips. Grabbed his beer glass and emptied it. He wiped his lips with the back of his hand. 'There are rumors. Talk that Pagac likes to see people suffer. Some say he goes with the enforcers.'

'They're the group's—' he started to clarify at Roger's expression.

'Enforcers,' Bwana cut in heavily. 'I can imagine what they do. Name doesn't need an explanation.'

'Yeah,' Tucker agreed. 'Word is that Pagac likes to do his share of roughhousing. Even killing.'

'So, you're saying the dude wants to see you squirm. That's why he said what he said.'

'That's what I figure.'

'Come away with us,' Roger said abruptly. 'We'll pass this over to the FBI. They'll act on it—'

'I told you. We've got sympathizers there.'

'Tucker,' Bwana rumbled, 'we'll arrange protection for you. *We*. Not the Feds or the cops.'

'No. I've got to see this through. Next time I'll wear a wire. Get you the recording. *Then*, you can hide me.'

'This isn't a game,' Roger said angrily. 'White Freedom doesn't play nice. Bernier will have you and your family killed. He'll make it look like you disappeared. Come away with us, right now.'

The informer shook his head. 'No. The only way to bring down Bernier and Pagac and the rest of the council is to record my every conversation with them henceforth. I am staying put. Even if it means I die.'

'You've seen those two before?' Rowan Windler asked Russell Harber.

His partner shook his head and kept snapping pictures of Tucker and the men he was with. Windler and Harber, the investigators from the Houston firm, were in a rental car they had hired under an alias. They had arrived in New Jersey the previous day, along with Howie Stroman and Bill Pouros, who took the day shift.

Shadowing Tucker had proved to be uneventful thus far. The gas station manager had a routine of home, service station, and back home. He didn't deviate from it in the short time they had been following him.

Until that evening, when the man had spoken briefly to co-workers and left early. Windler and Harber had followed him from a safe distance and driven around in the parking lot until they had a view of Tucker through a window.

Neither was a lip reader, and even if they had been, it wouldn't have helped. The manager had his side to them and, for the better part of the evening, his face was turned away.

'Do we follow him or those men?' Harber wondered, drumming the wheel, a nervous habit that drove his partner up the wall. The two men had been state cops in Texas. They had taken early retirement to join Red Earth Security and had found life in the private sector was far more profitable and comfortable.

'Follow the men,' Windler responded as he placed his hand over his friend's. 'And stop that. You know it drives me nuts.'

'That's why I do it.'

Tucker came out of the bar with his companions. He seemed to be arguing with them. The large man was clearly angry, gesticulating forcefully, but the manager seemed to hold his own. The visitors shook their heads in defeat, gripped the manager's hand, spoke a few final words and stalked away to their ride.

'Nice wheels,' Harber admired as he noted the vehicle's plates. 'Who do you think they are?'

It was a game they often played. Trying to guess the occupations of the people they came across.

'Not bankers, for sure,' his partner replied. Neither of them shrank in their seat or made any sudden movements when the handsome man looked their way. They were confident they couldn't be seen in the darkness. 'Not lawyers, either. No briefcases or files. I haven't seen any doctors or accountants look like them. They're too smartly dressed to be cops.'

He fired up his engine when the SUV's lights came on. Waited until the vehicle left the parking lot and then followed.

Harber craned his neck to look back. 'Looks like Tucker's headed back to the gas station.'

'Uh-huh.' The road was deserted that time of the night, and he held back a good distance from the dark vehicle in the front.

They followed the visitors in the night to the I-195 West until they got to the New Jersey Turnpike. Windler looked at

Harber, who shrugged. That direction of travel … there was only one destination city, New York.

The Turnpike was busier and enabled them to maintain a three-vehicle distance from the SUV. The night rolled on, as did the highway, and when they reached Woodbridge Township, the investigators gave up.

They pulled into a service station. Fueled their vehicle and put coffee and burgers inside themselves.

Harber made a call. 'Boss, we're sending several photographs your way. Tucker met a couple of strangers. Might be worth checking out who they are.' He recited the SUV's plate numbers. He grunted in acknowledgement as Thurman Bayer, the founder of the security company, rapped out orders. 'Gotcha,' he said and hung up.

He made a second call as Windler looked on. 'Sir,' he told Pagac when the council member came online. 'We have emailed you several photographs. Tucker met two men today in Plumsted Township.'

He broke off, listened for a moment. 'No, sir. We haven't seen them before. But we've been here for just a day. Yeah, Thurman will be looking them up. He should get back to you.'

'Let's go,' he told his partner when he had ended the call.

It was when they were heading back that it came to him.

'Notice their hair?'

'Yeah,' Windler replied. 'Closely cropped.'

'FBI?'

'Nah. They would be in suits.'

'But some kind of operatives?'

'Seems likely.'

'If they are law enforcement, why would Tucker be meeting them?'

Chapter 31

Zeb couldn't sleep. He tossed and turned in his bed in his apartment in the Columbus Avenue highrise. When the warriors had bought the building, they had deliberately repurposed it, turned the higher floors into apartments for themselves, with the office on a lower level.

That still left some spare office space that they rented out to other companies. The basement was theirs to use exclusively, however. It was where they had their garage, where they tooled their vehicles. It was also where they had their armory.

Zeb had another apartment in Jackson Heights. That was home, but he often spent nights at Columbus Avenue when on a mission.

He rose for the umpteenth time and went to the kitchen to drink water. Something was bothering him. Something that hovered at the edge of his consciousness, frustrating him.

He looked out at the darkened city through the window, swore and went back to the bedroom. He slipped into jeans and a t-shirt. Grabbed his shoulder holster and went to the elevator.

Four am. The time registered on him automatically when he entered the office.

And stopped in his tracks when he saw a head at a desk, back to him, headphones on the ears. Bobbing to some beat.

Meghan.

She had a sheet in front of her, Eaton's video playing on her screen, music leaking faintly from her headset.

She sensed his presence, looked up, ripped off her headgear, flashed a smile and filled the room with light.

'You figured it out?'

'Figured what out?' he dropped into a chair next to her.

She waved the sheet at him. He took it, recognized it immediately. Rusty's staff list. Thirty names. Three of them circled with a red pen. Meghan's doing.

He ran his eyes over the names. Mike Pollenbergh. Miguel Fonseca, Michael Gerlach.

He cursed when that elusive memory came to him suddenly.

Of course.

'Now, you get it?' she smirked, reading his face. 'You're getting old, Zeb. There was a time you'd work it out first.'

He gave the sheet back, crossed his arms behind his head and leaned back. Access to the conference hall had stumped them. How would the killer get in?

The red-outlined names were his answer.

The killer already had access.

That's the only way he can get close enough and plant his fire devices.

'Mike, Michael, Miguel,' he repeated.

'Yeah. All of them could sound like the *Mi* in Eaton's video. I've got their details.' She was almost vibrating with excitement. 'Pollenberg's an air-con expert. Fonseca is a civil engineer. Gerlach's a safety engineer.'

'All three would know how to trigger an attack. They would know the hall's vulnerabilities. They would know about fire.'

'Correct. Their physical builds are just about right.' She zoomed in on their photographs. 'Nothing about them is especially memorable.'

'They would be thoroughly checked out.' He played devil's advocate.

'Our killer would have *assumed* their place after the security clearances.'

'Impersonating another person who's in close contact with co-workers, a team who have been together for a long while. That's almost impossible.'

'Come on, Zeb,' she scoffed. 'You've done it. You impersonated an officer in Iran's IRGC.'

The Islamic Revolutionary Guard Corps was a branch of the country's armed forces. It was an extraordinarily powerful group whose role was to protect the country's system and stamp out dissidents, democracy supporters and any kind of movement that it saw as *deviant*.

It was brutal, feared, and favored by the country's Supreme Leader, its highest ranked political and religious authority.

'You studied that soldier for a year. Absorbed everything about him, his walk, his mannerisms, his speech, everything. You became him. It is difficult but not impossible.'

'Gait analysis? Any kind of comparison?'

'Those three against the clips we have?' her hair flew when she shook her head. 'We have nothing on those men. Just their photographs.'

'If you were a betting person—'

'The two Mikes. Gerlach is a divorcee. Lives alone in the Bronx. Pollenberg's single. Never married. Doesn't date. Either candidate is a good fit for our killer to take over.'

'Bwana and Roger are back?'

'Yeah. I haven't spoken to them, though.' She cocked her head at him. 'Tomorrow?'

'Today,' he corrected her. 'It's already daylight. We start shadowing these men once our team's up.'

Chapter 32

Wayne Bernier fingered the photographs that his assistant had printed for him. 'I haven't seen them either,' he told his visitor, Markus Pagac. 'I don't like his look.' He tapped the black man's picture.

Pagac wasn't sure if the White Freedom founder was objecting to the man's skin color or something else. He sat quiet, waiting for Bernier to articulate his thoughts.

'They aren't cops?'

'No,' the council member assured him. 'I checked with our friends in law enforcement. They aren't in the FBI, nor with Texas, New Jersey or New York police forces.'

'We could ask Tucker,' he ventured, when his boss—that's who he was, effectively—made no comment.

'And give it away that we're having him and other chapter heads watched?' Bernier snorted. 'Nope. Leave it with me. I'll make some calls to DC.'

The warriors divided into two-person teams. Zeb and Broker. Bwana and Roger. The sisters. Bear and Chloe.

Each unit drove a yellow cab, the most ubiquitous vehicle

in the city. Three teams to shadow the two Mikes and Miguel, the fourth team to take over whenever a team needed a break.

'No cops, no FBI,' Zeb had decided when they met in the morning and Meghan had gone through her deduction of the previous night. 'We don't know who this man is. Who his information sources are.'

'Sarah won't like it,' Broker said darkly. 'Neither will Chang or Pizaka.'

'We'll live.' And with that they set out, Zeb and Broker tailing Pollenberg, Bwana and Roger behind Gerlach, and the twins shadowing Fonseca. Bear and Chloe parked their cab at Javits and snoozed.

Zeb punched his cell the moment he settled behind the wheel.

'Rog, talk!'

Roger broke down their meeting with Tucker. 'He's stubborn,' he concluded. 'He's pretty danged committed about bringing Bernier down.'

'Bernier keeps his hands clean,' Zeb said bitterly. 'See how he sent Pagac. He can always say the council member was acting on his own, if there's blowback.'

He swung out from his parking spot when Pollenberg stepped out of his building. The air-con man had his hard hat dangling from his belt, a bag in his left hand.

'Lunchbox,' Broker murmured as he steadied his camera and began shooting.

They followed the air-con expert to the subway, where Broker got out and followed him inside. Zeb continued driving towards Javits. Similar scenes played out with the other two units.

'Seems to be an upright citizen,' Beth said in the evening

in disgust, over their headsets. 'Fonseca's done nothing that would make us suspicious.'

'Gerlach, too,' Roger added. 'Zeb, what about you folks?'

'Pollenberg's returned from work. Gone home. No beer stop, no hanging out with friends. We're outside his building.'

'He's still in there?'

'Yeah. We can see the lights. There's no rear exit. We checked.'

At 11 pm they returned to the office. Handed their surveillance videos to Beth, who got Werner to run comparisons with the ones they had.

'No match,' she said in disappointment.

She turned to Zeb, who offered an encouraging smile. 'If the killer has assumed one of their identities, he would have got everything right. Speech pattern, walking style, the works. Gait analysis isn't an exact science. It can be spoofed—'

'Yeah, I get it. What now?'

'Now, we break into their apartments.'

Chapter 33

Wayne Bernier could have made the call, but some matters were better handled in person. He flew to DC in a Gulfstream—it helped to have billionaire friends—and rented a cab at Reagan Airport. The person he was meeting worked in the Pentagon, a three-star general who supported White Freedom. Not that he could express it openly.

The two met in a bar on McPherson Square and whiled the time away talking of world matters while their server brought their orders.

'Word is that the president wants to strike a defense treaty with China,' Sidor, the LTG, lieutenant-general, said in a lowered voice.

Bernier made a face and looked at his drink sourly. It was no secret that President Morgan wanted to de-escalate the rising tensions with the second largest economy in the world.

'He should be going hard on them,' he said bitterly. 'Increasing trade tariffs. Disallowing Chinese investment. Beefing up our military.'

'On that.' The Pentagon man cut a healthy portion of his

steak and chomped on it. 'I hear he wants to scale back our budget.'

Bernier glared at noisy eaters at the next table, swallowed and controlled himself. 'He didn't change his colors. I'll give him that. That was his manifesto when he was campaigning. He's stuck to that.'

'You came to DC to discuss him?'

'No.' He reached inside his jacket and brought out Harber and Windler's photographs. 'I need to know who these two are. Whether they served.'

The general glanced at them briefly and discreetly covered them with a table napkin. 'Anything I should know?'

'It's better you don't.'

They finished their meal quickly. He had detected a Texas drawl in the server's voice. If he didn't support the Lone Star state's citizens, who would?

They shook hands outside the bar and were turning to go their separate ways when a thought struck him.

'General,' he called out.

The military man turned.

'The week of the summit. It would be healthy to stay away from New York.'

The official stared at him for long moments, nodded and walked away.

Bernier hung around in the square. He scanned stationary vehicles and people who loitered. A woman was reading a newspaper on a bench. Another was jogging past, talking to someone in her headset. Two men in suits waited at a light to cross.

Nope. No one seemed to be paying him any attention. Checking his six had become habit to him, ever since White

Freedom became a prominent movement. He was confident the general would have measures to throw off any tails.

He'll find out who those men are. And then we'll deal with Tucker.

Beth and Meghan were dressed casually. That meant a tat painted on the elder twin's neck. A piercing in the younger woman's left eyebrow. Scruffy jeans and trainers on both of them. Fonseca's apartment was in a building that had several young occupants. 'Hipster look. That's what Broker calls it,' Beth chuckled as they approached the entrance.

'It's mainstream now.' Meghan rolled her eyes. 'Not that Broker would know.'

It was the second day of their surveillance. They had followed the Javits man to the conference hall. They had then returned and waited for his wife to do the school run. She worked in a pharmacy and wouldn't be back until the evening.

The sisters didn't take the elevator. They climbed to the seventh floor. Went down the hallway, which was crowded. A raucous bunch of younger people outside an apartment door.

'You want to join us?' a dude with slicked back hair shouted at them. 'We've got beer. And weed.'

'Carry on,' Beth said, smiling politcly.

'You don't know what you're missing out on.'

'We do,' she said sweetly.

The bunch disappeared inside the apartment. Noise levels dropped off immediately.

'Fonseca lives next to that?' Meghan shook her head.

Beth didn't answer. She was checking out a blue door, the Javits workers' entrance. 'No camera.' She kneeled and eyed the lock. 'Standard make.' She reached into her backpack, drew out a toolkit and got to work while her sister kept watch.

Ten minutes later they were inside the apartment, gloves on their hands, their hair rolled underneath their ball caps. It wouldn't do to leave traces of their presence.

A living room. Dining table at the far end. Leading to the kitchen. Three bedrooms, a bath. They split and commenced searching. Looking for anything that wouldn't fit in a family apartment. Like aerosol cans that contained metal sprays.

Two hours later, they exited the apartment, having found nothing incriminating.

'Got enough photographs.' Meghan held her cell phone up. 'Werner can go through it and let us know.'

'I've got prints, too.' Beth replied. She had lifted several of them from glass tumblers.

They went down to the street level, back to their cab, and headed back to Javits.

'What do you think?' the younger twin asked her sister.

'He's clean. That apartment didn't give me any vibes.'

'It wouldn't. Not if he was a professional, stone-cold killer.'

'Yeah. But I still think he's not our man.'

Bear and Chloe were in Gerlach's apartment in Harlem. They'd had enough of hanging around in their cab and had taken over the break-in from Bwana and Roger.

Chloe had her hair rolled tight, cap visor low over her forehead, shades on her eyes. Bear was himself. His build and beard couldn't be hidden.

He knocked politely on the safety engineer's door. No response. Which was good, since the man was in Javits.

Getting around the lock wasn't difficult. The search took less than an hour because the apartment was bare.

Some furniture in the living room. A bed. Cutlery in the kitchen. No pictures. No mementoes. No decoration.

Bear raised his eyebrows at Chloe, who shook her head sadly. 'This is how you end up after a messy divorce. Looks like he's cleaned out. Emotionally as well.'

Werner's file on Gerlach was extensive. His extramarital affairs had led to the separation. He and his wife had sold their bigger home and had divided the proceeds. The engineer had bought the smaller Harlem apartment with his share of the sale.

'You got prints?'

'Yeah.' Chloe held up a plastic baggie. 'You got photographs?'

'Enough to start a gallery.'

'Let's go. This place depresses me. Let this be a warning to you. You mess with me, you'll end up like this.' She indicated the state of the apartment. 'I won't stop there. I'll cut off your testicles as well.'

'Yes, ma'am.' Bear, one of the most lethal men in the world, followed her meekly to street level.

Zeb gained entry to Pollenberg's apartment the same way his friends had. Illegally. Which meant any evidence obtained wouldn't stand up in a court. Which didn't bother him. That was for Chang, Pizaka and Burke to worry about.

He stood still in the apartment's silence, Broker next to him. They didn't move for a long while, absorbing the *atmosphere*, watching motes of dust swirl in the air.

Zeb moved. He ran a gloved finger on a chair and inspected it. No dust. The air-con expert might live alone, but it looked like he cleaned his apartment regularly.

The two men didn't speak. Broker brought out a device and checked for listening devices and cameras. *Clear*, he mouthed before disappearing into a bedroom.

Zeb looked around the living room. Books next to a couch. Popular thriller authors. Texts on industrial air-conditioning on a chest of drawers. A squeeze ball. A pair of weights.

He searched thoroughly and came up with nothing to prove that Pollenberg wasn't who he claimed.

He joined Broker, who had put his gear away and was searching as well. 'No bugs, no cameras,' his friend said.

'Nothing at Gerlach and Fonseca's apartments, either,' Zeb grunted as he raised a mattress and looked underneath it.

Two hours of painstaking effort, followed by an hour to replace everything back in its previous position, and all they had to show for it was sweat trickling down their backs.

'If we draw a blank?'

'We look into the rest of Rusty's team.'

'If that's a dud as well?'

'Then we get NYPD and FBI to plaster his face on TV,' Zeb replied as they drove back.

Which would be a failure, because it would get the killer to go deep underground. And still carry out his attacks.

They gathered in their office in the late evening, Zeb playing with one of the paper airplanes Beth had made.

'I'll transfer the prints to Werner,' she said, trying hard to sound cheerful. 'Maybe something will turn up.'

'Go for it.' Bear stifled a yawn, waved at them and followed Chloe out.

At about the same time, the general logged into a file and ran a search for Bwana and Roger, using a facial recognition algorithm.

The results came back quickly.

Two files.

He clicked on one.

And blinked when it was empty.

He clicked on the other one.

Nothing in it, either.

He thought for a moment and then reached for a phone.

It didn't take that long for Werner to look at the fingerprints. He messaged the twins, knowing they would be happy with what he had found, and got back to his reading.

That Nietzsche dude was an awesome writer.

Chapter 34

Beth and Meghan were at their desks when Zeb arrived. He had returned to his Jackson Heights apartment the previous night and as a result was the last person to come to the office.

Chloe got his attention the moment he stepped in. She waggled her eyebrows in the twins' direction.

He looked over to them. They had their backs to him, working on their screens, busy. But their postures. The way Meghan flicked her hair back.

They're bursting! They've found something?

He went to the kitchen, filled his cup with coffee, wandered out. Glanced at his watch.

'Why're you all here?' he asked casually, playing along with whatever the sisters had up their sleeves. 'Gerlach, Fonseca, Pollenberg, they still need to be watched.'

'I stopped them,' Beth replied in a bored voice.

'Why?'

'Werner found something strange.'

'AprintinPollenberg'sapartmentthatwasn'this' Meghan couldn't contain herself, words rushing out of her.

'Sis!' Beth glowered at her, then broke into a wide grin.

'We found a print that doesn't match him! In Pollenberg's apartment. A male.'

'It's him,' Meghan nodded so fast her hair bounced on her head. 'Pollenberg's our killer.'

'Those two men.' The general was in his car, using a burner phone to call Bernier.

'What about them?'

'They were service personnel. But their files, there was nothing in them.'

'Nothing? How's that possible? You folks keep extensive records, don't you?'

'There's only one explanation.' The general took a breath.

'What?'

'They worked in some black-ops unit.'

'You're sure?' National Security Advisor Daniel Klouse rocked back in his chair. The call had been made by one of his contacts in the Pentagon.

'Yes, sir. The general accessed those files. He then made a call—'

'Don't say names.' It was DC. Walls had ears.

'Yes, sir. But the person he made the call to doesn't have access, either.'

'Thanks, buddy. I owe you one.'

'I owe you my life, sir. It's nothing.'

Klouse replaced his phone and frowned. He didn't like what he had been told. There was no reason for a general to go digging into Bwana and Roger's files. Any of Zeb's team's files, for that matter. He glanced at his watch. He had a meeting with President Morgan in fifteen.

He grabbed his jacket and strode out of his West Wing office. 'Emily,' he told his EA, 'I won't be back before lunch.'

He brought out an encrypted phone when he was out of hearing range from anyone.

'Clare,' he said without preliminaries when the director of the Agency came on line. 'An LTG's been sniffing around Bwana and Roger's files. Zach Sidor.'

'I know of him. You know why?'

'Nope.'

'I'll deal with it. You're heading to President Morgan's briefing?'

'Yeah.'

'I'll see you there.'

The NSC advisor shook his head. *That Clare. A nuclear missile could be heading her way, her cool wouldn't crack.*

Zeb broke away from the excited chatter in his office and walked to a window.

'I've heard of Sidor. He was lined up to lead JSOC at one time,' he told his boss.

'Correct. He didn't cut it. Behavioral issues. He's on his way out. He doesn't know it yet. Why would he be interested in those files?'

'I'll find out.'

'Zeb,' Meghan called him before he could give the matter further thought.

'Yeah.'

'We bring him in? Pollenberg?'

'No.'

'What? Why?'

'It's a strange print. Nothing more.'

'It was on a bottle of water. That was half-empty. Recently used, from the looks of it.'

'He's a loner, Zeb,' Beth chimed in, exasperatedly. 'He doesn't have friends. No one visits him.'

'I know, but we still need something more to link Pollenberg to the killer. Right now, we have a theory and a print. That's it.'

'So we watch him?' Chloe asked.

'Yeah. Most of us. We shouldn't lose sight of him.'

'That will be vehicle surveillance, on-foot—' Bwana began, when Zeb cut him off.

'Not you or Rog. A Pentagon general has been looking at your files.'

A moment's silence.

'Lieutenant General Zach Sidor,' he told his team. 'We need to know why.'

Werner gave them the answer half an hour later, as they were making plans for Pollenberg's surveillance.

'White Freedom.' Meghan projected a photograph on to the wall. 'He knows Bernier.'

They stared at it in silence. It was a DC neighborhood that they recognized easily. McPherson Square. Two men in front of a building, a bar, from the looks of it. One man walking to the left, the other heading in the opposite direction. Their profiles were clear. The White Freedom leader and the general.

'When was this?' Bear popped a knuckle, the sound loud in the office.

'Yesterday,' she exhaled loudly, blowing hair out of her face.

'How did you get this image?'

'Werner's been tracking Bernier's movements ever since

Tucker turned informant. There's a lot of data on him residing in the cloud. This photograph is from a drone in the square. A kid who uploaded his pictures to his social media account.'

'It could be coincidence,' Beth said, half-heartedly.

'It isn't,' Broker replied grimly. 'The two men know each other.'

'Someone spotted you,' Zeb looked at Bwana and Roger. 'No other explanation.'

'Only one place to do that.' Roger's eyes were narrow slits. Gone was the Texas mirth. In its place was cold anger. 'The bar where we met Tucker.'

'Which means they had eyes on him. Bernier isn't stupid. He'll suspect we're with a covert unit. He'll figure out why Tucker met us.'

'They'll send the enforcers.'

Chapter 35

Khalili had ground more titanium powder in his workshop three days before. Alone in the night, with a single light bulb for illumination. He also had plans to visit a chemicals dealer and check out sodium purchases.

He was still undecided. Titanium or sodium? And how? He felt nervous. Jumpy. Irritable. He had never felt like that before and wondered if he was coming down with some illness.

No. It's just the difficulty in this mission. I underestimated the security setup, he thought darkly as he worked in Javits.

He had spoken briefly to the Man, who had flared at the lack of progress and threatened him again. The killer had shot back angrily, and the two men had hung up.

Khalili wiped his brow and rested on his haunches for a while. He gazed vacantly at Rusty, who was stomping about in the distance, muttering under his breath.

I might fail.

Failure was always a possibility in any mission. *On this one, I might fail without even trying.*

And that was what burned away in him. That he might not

even be able to place the flammable material on the site.

Rusty came closer, his grumbling now audible.

'Metal sheets. How hard can that be? I told him to order ten by four aluminum sheets. And what does he do? He buys steel. First, Carter and his people. Wasting my day. Now these sheets.'

Khalili looked away and bent to his work. He wanted no part of the foreman when he was in such a mood.

His head jerked up suddenly.

Wait. What did he say? Carter?

'Rusty,' he rose and wiped his hands on his coveralls. 'What's up, buddy? You seem stressed.'

The foreman needed no further invitation. He let loose a stream of curses and ran through his litany of woes. Incompetent suppliers. Late shipments. Pressure by the Javits executive board to finish the work faster. And then those visitors.

'Who were they?' Khalili asked.

'Didn't you see them? Of course, you didn't. I plumb forgot. You were off that day.' Rusty slapped his palm to his forehead theatrically. 'They never said who they were. I get a call from the FBI. You know how that bunch is.' That prompted another string of swearing.

Khalili restrained the urge to shake his foreman. He put on a sympathetic expression and nodded his head in understanding.

'What did the FBI want?'

'They cleared the visit of eight people. Sent me a list of names and descriptions.' Rusty hawked and spat in anger. 'These folks turn up. Don't smile. All of them quiet. They want to see the conference hall, they say. I checked them against the letter. They matched it. I hoped they wouldn't pass through the barrier, but the gate lifted. They must be tight with the Feds.' The foreman brooded for a moment on the injustices of the world.

'They weren't Feds?'

'Nope. Well, they didn't say who they were. But they certainly weren't wearing suits.'

'All they wanted to see was the hall?'

'Every inch of it. The area that's closed to the public, that requires security clearances. They asked a lot of questions. About how many people work here. What exactly we're working on. How our crew is vetted. Waste of time, if you ask me. I betcha they were nothing but a bunch of tourists who happened to know people in high places. It's the FBI's fault. They're responsible for the delays. I can't kick my supplier's ass without their permission.'

'They gave their names?' Khalili brought the foreman back on track.

'Carter was the main dude. Zeb Carter. The others …' The foreman patted his pockets. 'I've got the letter somewhere. Three women in them. Lookers, too. Two of the largest men I've seen in that bunch. One of them gave me the stink-eye when I looked at the babes. I was just looking! Anything wrong with that? What's this world coming to when a man can't appreciate beauty? Hey Mike, don't you have work to do instead of jawing with me?' And with that Rusty stomped off.

Darkness swamped Khalili. *Carter!* He felt faint, short of breath. Sweat beaded on his forehead and he swayed on his feet.

He went to the recesses of the conference hall, to the air-con section, and leaned against a large tank. It was cooler there, which helped.

Why did Carter come here? Does he know? Do the cops know?

Questions raced through the killer's mind. His palms sweated. His chest pounded.

Control. Got to control myself.

He breathed deeply as he paced. Sucking on oxygen, letting it fill him until the fog enveloping him started to recede and his mind started to work again.

No. They don't know who I am. Otherwise I would be arrested.

That left an uncomfortable possibility, though. Did Carter suspect him? And if so, how?

Khalili knew he had been careful. He hadn't survived this long just by getting lucky. He knew he hadn't shown his real face to any camera. He kept up with the Pollenberg disguise—walk, talk, mannerisms and all—as long as he was impersonating the air-con man. Nope. No one could have guessed who he really was.

Then why did Carter come there? It was too much of a coincidence.

Khalili was suddenly glad that he had spent the last few nights in Pollenberg's apartment. He hadn't detected anyone following him, but if they were, at least his Queens apartment and warehouse wouldn't be discovered.

'Mike!' Rusty roared from somewhere outside.

'Coming.' He wiped his hands, picked up a tool to show he was working, and headed out.

The killer tried to work as normally as he could for the rest of the day, but it was hard. He was glad when evening arrived and his shift ended. He removed his hard hat, wiped his face with a sleeve and joined the bunch of workers filing to the exit.

'Hey, Chip.' He tapped a co-worker's shoulder. 'Can you give me a ride? I need to get to the Bronx. You live over there, right?'

'Yeah,' Chip nodded. 'You got another girl there?' he asked slyly.

'Nah, nothing like that.' Khalili put on an embarrassed act.

'How's it going with your babe? You fox, you never tell us anything about her.'

'It's going well. I don't want to jinx it.'

'Yeah, yeah. But come to Uncle Chip if you need any advice, you hear?' His co-worker slapped his thigh and laughed loudly.

The killer climbed into his friend's truck without looking back. If Carter was having him followed, it wouldn't be obvious. The man was a pro. There would be at least two vehicles. And if he knew Khalili's routine, there would be someone on foot as well, to tail him through the subway.

The assassin kept talking, laughing at the right moments as Chip regaled him with stories. They reached Columbus Circle, waited at a light. Khalili readied himself.

His co-worker accelerated when the light turned and started another story. The assassin looked ahead, assessed their speed and the weight of traffic. A light turned yellow, up ahead. Chip slowed.

'Oh, there he is. Jake!' he lowered his window and yelled out. 'Sorry, Chip. Gotta skip. I need to talk to that dude. He owes me money.' He wrenched the door open and jumped out before the truck had stopped moving.

He threaded through the traffic, ignoring the angry honks

and shouted curses. Went to the sidewalk and entered a café. Headed through the crush at the counter and went to the bathrooms at the far end. One was empty. He removed his Pollenberg disguise, dumped it into his backpack, cracked the door open and peered out.

No Carter, no cops.

He shouldered his way through, head bent, and walked out. He picked up a newspaper someone had left on a table and made a show of reading it, watching his surroundings from the corners of his eyes.

No tails that he could detect.

He headed to the subway, changed trains randomly a few times before finally catching one to Queens.

He walked swiftly to Pollenberg's apartment, using the cover of other people.

And when he neared the building, his saw them.

A bunch of cruisers parked outside the dead man's building, lights flashing, several cops outside the entrance.

They know about me.

Chapter 36

'You spooked him!' Meghan tore into her visitors, Chang, Pizaka and Sarah Burke. 'You screwed it up. All you had to do was shadow him. But no, New York's finest and the FBI decided to go to Pollenberg's apartment and wait for him there. And you did it so obviously that the dumbest killer could have spotted your presence from a mile away. And this man isn't dumb!'

They were gathered in the Columbus Avenue office. An early morning meeting. Eight of them and the three visitors. It wasn't a friendly gathering.

They'd had two vehicles outside Javits the previous day. Zeb and Broker in one cab, Bwana and Roger in another. They would follow Pollenberg if the man used a vehicle to get home.

The sisters, Bear and Chloe were on foot. They would shadow him if he used the subway.

The plan was to tail the suspect, find out what his routine was and whether he had another hide-out.

They hadn't anticipated the move the man had made. Running out of his co-worker's vehicle. They had lost him at that point.

'Do you think he made us?' Bwana asked in their headsets.

'No idea,' Zeb confessed. 'It's possible Rusty told him about our visit. Pollenberg, if that's who the killer is, saw Meghan, Beth and me at the Colberts' apartment.'

They had circled back to the man's apartment, only to find the not very subtle presence of law enforcement.

It turned out that the FBI had arrived at the same theory as they had.

They, too, had worked out that the killer could be a Javits worker and had narrowed down on Pollenberg, based on his loner lifestyle and the *Mi* the killer had said in Eaton's store.

Burke had reached out to Chang and Pizaka immediately, and the NYPD and FBI had then mounted a joint operation.

One that didn't yield any result.

'What were you thinking?' Beth asked Burke savagely. 'You couldn't have consulted us beforehand? And you!' she rounded on the cops. 'You didn't think of telling us—'

'Enough,' Burke rapped out. Her face was pale, her lips thin. 'Our priority is to stop an attack in Javits. We don't have the luxury of shadowing a suspect. We acted on credible assumption. And what about you? You were shadowing him. You didn't tell us about that. You didn't even tell us about the fingerprint!'

In the heated discussions, Beth had let slip about the mysterious print.

'This is why we didn't tell you,' Meghan burst out, her face red with anger. 'We knew you and the cops would screw it up. The print. You know it isn't admissible. We got it illegally. We were—'

'Protecting me,' Burke sneered.

'Yes, we were!' The elder sister slammed her palm on the table.

Burke went to a window, her body tight with anger. She shrugged away Broker's hand and stood in silence, her back to them.

Chang found something of interest in the ceiling and didn't meet anyone's eyes. Pizaka spent a long time polishing his shades.

Meghan looked at them hotly and then at Zeb. She made to speak, but clamped her jaws shut when he shook his head.

'There's one upside,' he said. 'Pollenberg, this killer, won't be returning to Javits. He knows he's been found out. Burke, you should secure the place. Check it out thoroughly—'

'Don't tell me how to do my job.' She left their office without a word.

'Should I—' Broker started after her.

'Let her be,' Chloe grabbed his arm. 'Let her calm down. Relax. This isn't the first time we've argued with her. It won't be the last. You both are good. Still. Though I don't know what she sees in you.'

Zeb tuned out and joined Meghan at the window.

'He's out there, somewhere. And now, he could be planning anything.'

Pagac was with Bernier at the Texas billionaire's ranch. A separate building, away from the main residence, served as an office, and that was where White Freedom was headquartered.

'There's no doubt about these two?' the council member fingered the two photographs on the table.

'My contact is sure they are from some special-ops outfit.'

'In that case, we know what to do.'

'Yes,' Bernier confirmed. 'Take as many enforcers you want. Grab Tucker. Sweat him.'

'And if he turns out to be a snitch?'

'Make sure he's not seen again.'

Pagac's face lit with unholy joy.

'Bwana, Rog? Any news from Tucker?' Zeb asked.

'No,' the Texan stirred, 'we messaged him. he hasn't responded.'

Zeb rose abruptly. 'You need to get to him, right away. Pollenberg, he occupied all our attention. We forgot about him. You can bet Pagac and Bernier haven't. You, Bear, Chloe, get to New Jersey. Make him come with you. We'll figure out witness protection for him.'

'What if we are too late?' Bwana asked, concern etching deep lines in his face.

'No,' Zeb shook his head. 'Bernier will take some time to evaluate his options. The enforcers,' he looked at Meghan, 'they're scattered all over Texas, right?'

'Yeah,' she nodded. 'Those that we know of.'

'It'll take some time, a day or two, to form a team. Plan the logistics. But you need to go, now!'

'What about us?' Broker asked when their friends had left.

'No luck?' Zeb looked at the twins.

'No,' Beth knew what he was referring to. 'Werner's got no positives on anyone looking like the killer in the city. He's gone to ground.'

Chapter 37

Khalili had spent the previous evening walking the city in a daze. There was no police presence at his Queens apartment. No cruisers at his workshop, either.

He had changed into a hoodie and stepped out of his residence. Wandered aimlessly, head bent, one thought swirling in his head.

I failed.

He had prided himself on being one of the best assassins in the world. Not that there was a world ranking, a leaderboard somewhere, but he knew how good he was. The Man, too, considered him as possibly the greatest.

I failed.

The thought filled him with bitterness. Helplessness. All his careful planning had come to nothing. He hadn't even come close to planting a bomb or his fire-making metal.

I did nothing.

His cell phone buzzed. Khalili let it ring several times. He was tempted to ignore it, but he finally took the call.

'What's happening? You haven't updated me in a while,' the Man grated.

Some subconscious instinct made the killer press the record button on his device.

'They made me,' he replied, dully.

'Explain,' the spymaster rapped out.

Khalili explained.

The Man didn't shout. He didn't rage. He was surprisingly gentle.

'You know what this means, don't you?'

'Yes,' the assassin replied. He didn't, but neither did he care.

'I'll call you back in some time.'

The killer pocketed his phone and kept going. A light rain started. He didn't feel it. His shoulder bumped into someone, who cursed. He didn't respond.

An hour later, his phone rang.

'Click on that link,' the Man said softly. 'I'll call you back in fifteen minutes.'

Khalili had leaned against a lamppost. He didn't care that passersby could see his screen. He tapped the link and it opened to a video.

He felt nothing as he watched the Man's goons awaken his parents, made them kneel in their cell, and shot them in the head.

He felt nothing when he watched the clip again and recorded it.

'You are responsible,' the Man said kindly when he called, as if explaining to a child. 'I warned you what would happen if you failed. You are a dead man walking now. You can't return to our country. You can hide in America, but my killers will find you one day.'

The assassin didn't respond.

'There's a way you can redeem yourself,' the Man continued. 'Kill Carter.'

Khalili had kept walking as the rain beat down on him. He didn't see anything other than the few feet of sidewalk in front of him. Everything else was a blur. People. Cars. Buildings.

Something green and leafy and large to his left. Ozone Park. It registered on him automatically.

'Got a light?'

He raised his head slowly as if it was an effort.

Two hoodie-wearing men. One with a cigarette dangling off his lips, patting his pockets.

The killer didn't reply. He side-stepped, to walk past, when the second man produced a knife.

'Everything you've got. Now!'

Khalili reacted without thought. His right hand shot out before the mugger had finished speaking. He grabbed the man's wrist and yanked him toward himself.

The assailant wasn't expecting that move. He stumbled forward and then went down when Khalili's elbow smashed between his eyes.

The killer continued moving balletically. He swooped down and picked up the fallen knife. Swung it up and across, and the second man screamed as the blade ripped him open.

The assassin tossed the weapon on the fallen men and continued walking without a backward glance.

Light and sound and emotion had returned to him later, much later, when the rain had turned into a downpour.

He lifted his head up and felt drops smash into him, as if trying to force him to the ground.

Hate had come to him.

But he wasn't sure whether it was directed at Carter or the Man.

He returned to his apartment, removed his sodden clothing, dried himself and went to bed.

He knew what he would do next.

Khalili was in his warehouse at the same time that Meghan was raging at Burke and the cops.

The killer filled his aerosol one last time and put it in his backpack. A Glock, spare mags, a knife, gloves, and various tools joined it.

He looked around one last time, brought the shutter down, and then, when he was one block away, the timer-controlled explosives blew up and reduced the warehouse to rubble.

He took the subway to Manhattan, changing trains randomly, even though he was sure he wasn't being followed.

And then took one last, rattling, steel-encased train ride to his final destination.

Amsterdam Avenue. Maggie Colbert's apartment.

Pagac and eight enforcers landed at Newark Airport at 11 am. They rented three vehicles and set off towards Tucker's gas station.

The plan was simple.

They would go to the man's house in Tabernacle, where the enforcers would alight. Pagac would drive on towards the service station and signal for the manager to meet him at his home.

Where the enforcers would be waiting, and Tucker would meet justice.

The council member couldn't help grinning. His heart beat savagely, his blood thrummed. It was a good day to be alive.

At 11 am, Bwana, Roger, Bear and Chloe were on the New Jersey Turnpike, in slow-moving traffic.

The Texan tried calling Tucker. No reply. He sent a message. *Get away. Now!*

The manager didn't respond.

Tucker didn't, because he was having one of those days when everything went wrong. A conservation group had organized a litter-picking drive in Wharton State Forest that day. Over a hundred people had turned up, driving all manner of vehicles. Pickup trucks, cars, SUVs, a few tractors. Since his gas station was the only one in the vicinity and had ample parking space, all the pickers converged on it.

It was great for business, but it meant that he was woefully short-staffed and had to be out and about himself. On top of that, one of the pumps had broken down. In the chaos, he forgot about his cell phone, which lay in a drawer beneath the counter, buzzing away silently.

At 11 am, Beth raised her eyebrows at Meghan, who shrugged. The two looked at Zeb, who lay on his couch, eyes closed, apparently asleep. They knew looks were deceptive. Their friend could spring to action in an instant.

Beth turned to her cell.

Still stuck in traffic. A message from Roger. *How's Zeb?*

Sphinx mode, she replied.

You two?

Waiting for something to happen.

At 11 am, Khalili emerged from the 72nd Street Broadway subway station and started walking up Amsterdam Avenue.

Maggie Colbert's apartment was two blocks away.

Chapter 38

Pagac and his crew reached Tucker's home at 1 pm. The enforcers hung around while the council member climbed the porch and rang the bell.

No answer, which was expected.

'Open it, Randy,' he ordered the largest man.

Randy, a hulking figure, approached and inspected the door. Wood, but not sturdy. Tabernacle was a township with less than ten thousand residents. Crime was virtually unheard of. There wasn't a need for elaborate home security.

The enforcer raised his leg and kicked at the door, which splintered and rocked back on its hinges.

'Won't he suspect game's over when he sees that?' another enforcer asked.

'Let him,' Pagac said callously. 'It'll be too late for him. Y'all make yourself comfortable. Stay away from windows. We don't want nosy neighbors.'

Randy looked around. Tucker's house was set back from a solitary road, from which a badly maintained driveway led to the residence. A thicket of trees obscured the house from the street. There were no immediate neighbors. A small, white house stood in the distance, about half a mile away. Tabernacle was that kind of township.

'Not much danger of that,' he said.

'Do it,' Pagac said roughly. 'I'll be back shortly, with him.' He shouldered past the enforcers and climbed inside one of the vehicles.

Bwana made up for lost time when they left the Turnpike and got on US 206. Long stretches of highway when he floored it. He glanced sideways momentarily and grinned. Roger, his eyes narrowed, fingering his cell phone. Behind them were Bear and Chloe. All of them armed with their Glocks, knives, armor beneath their jackets. Shotguns at their feet. They were ready.

They blew past towns: Mansfield, Springfield, another long stretch, and then, Southampton Township.

'Try him.'

'What do you think I've been doing for the last few hours?' Roger glowered at him. Nonetheless, he tried. 'Nothing,' he said, giving up when Tucker's phone continued to ring.

'No reports of any assault,' Beth piped in through their headsets. She was monitoring New Jersey State Police chatter. 'There's something in the local news. A litter-picking drive today. Big turnout. That might be why he's not answering. He could be busy.'

Bwana squeezed more juice out of his vehicle and sent it barreling towards the gas station.

Khalili approached the Colberts' building. No drunk outside its entrance this time. He looked up at the twelfth floor, but his target apartment didn't face the avenue.

The window-washers were still at work on the building, ant-like men stuck to its mirrored surface, working hard. He shook his head in bemusement. Two weeks since his last visit and they hadn't finished.

He adjusted his backpack and followed a couple who were heading inside the building. He joined them in the elevator and jabbed the button for the twelfth floor.

Pagac rolled into the gas station and looked towards the glassed office. No Tucker behind the counter. There was a long line of vehicles at one pump and several more parked in the lot. Foot traffic. Middle-aged men and women, coffee cups and doughnuts in hand, along with several children.

What the heck's going on?

He spotted the manager, who was talking to an elderly bunch, and stared hard.

Tucker felt his gaze and turned. He looked startled. He approached Pagac.

'What's up?' he asked, his lips barely moving.

'We need to meet,' the council member replied.

'Now? You see this? I can't get away in this rush.'

'NOW!' Pagac said coldly. 'This can't wait.'

'I'll try.' The manager paled under his intense look. 'I'll need to talk to Jim—'

'Get moving. And Tucker—'

The manager turned back toward him.

'Let's meet at your house. I doubt we'll have privacy at the bar. Not with this lot around.' Pagac nodded at the volunteers.

He drove away, but didn't go far. He circled back, parked behind an RV and watched.

Tucker spoke to a man forcefully, drew a long face. The

manager handed over something that looked like keys. He greeted some volunteers, went to his car and drove out.

Pagac called Randy.

'He's coming.'

Chapter 39

Tucker was halfway to his home when he realized he had forgotten his cell phone in his office. He swore, eased off the gas and was tempted to turn around. But Pagac was waiting. It wouldn't do any good to annoy him. Not at this stage of the operation.

That triggered another thought. What did the council member want? Perhaps he wanted to brief him on the operation.

He can't suspect who I am, can he? The manager thought about it as he drove fast. *No,* he decided. *I know how the enforcers work. I would already be dead if they knew about me.*

He turned in his driveway, gravel flying out from beneath his tires. He frowned as he stopped the vehicle. Three vehicles? Pagac always came alone. Who had he come with, this time? Was that … yeah, his door was smashed open.

His gut clenched. A sense of foreboding gripped him. He thought of turning back, fleeing to safety.

He was preparing to dive back into his car when a hand slapped his back.

'Got you, boy.'

Khalili checked out the hallway. Empty. This time of the day there would be only stay-at-home moms or dads. Or the elderly. No sounds came from the other apartments.

He knew the Colberts were at home. *I know their schedule inside out.*

He rang the buzzer and crouched beneath the peephole. He heard footsteps approaching, pausing, then retreating.

He pressed it again.

The person returned, faster. A deadbolt rattled, a lock turned … and the killer rammed his shoulder against the opening door.

It flew back. Slammed into the person behind it, who went sprawling. The daughter, Grace Colbert. Someone screamed. The mother, who stood in the living room, eyes wide in fright, a hand cupped to her mouth.

The son came running from somewhere inside the house. He took a quick look. Lunged towards a phone.

Khalili was faster. He smacked him on the side of his head, a hard blow that felled him to the ground. The killer removed his Glock from his backpack and pointed it at the mother.

'Tell your daughter to shut the door. If she escapes, you die.'

'Please … please,' the woman sniffled, her face terror-stricken.

'I won't ask again,' Khalili said softly. He felt nothing. The Colberts were tools. He could kill them and walk away, but that wasn't his intention.

'Grace,' the mother's voice cracked. 'Do as he says, honey.'

The daughter rose from the floor, wiped blood from her

forehead and glared at him. Her face was pale, her hands trembled, but she was angry. Khalili liked that. The kid had spirit.

She slammed the door shut and went to her mother, who grabbed her and hugged her tight.

'You want to kill us?' the daughter asked the assassin, contemptuously. 'Go ahead. Or maybe, you want to rape us first.'

The mother cupped a palm over Grace's mouth. Her eyes widened. Tears rolled down her cheek. 'Shush, honey. Please, mister. Take our money. Take—'

Khalili backhanded her. Her lips split. She fell against a chair and then on the floor. Her children looked on in shock. And then Travis leaped at him with a sound of rage.

The killer pirouetted out of the way and shoved him away with one hand. The son crashed into a wall cabinet. Cutlery smashed onto the floor.

'I have a gun,' the assassin said mildly. 'It's not for show. Get her up,' he ordered the daughter, pointing his Glock at the mother. 'The three of you, sit quiet.'

They did his bidding.

He looked at them when they were settled, the mother trying hard to control her fear, the kids, scared and angry, glaring at him.

'Call Carter,' he told Travis.

The son blinked. 'Who?'

'Carter. The man who was here last time. Who came through the door with those women.'

'We don't have his number,' Travis blustered.

Khalili raised his Glock and, at that, the mother screamed and thrust her body in front of her son.

'No, don't, please!'

'Call Carter. I won't ask again.'

Grace shot out of her chair and went to the phone. She scrabbled around, searching for something. Found a card and held it up. 'That's his number.'

'Call him. Put it on speaker.'

Bwana slowed down as he approached the gas station. It was crowded. A line of vehicles at one pump, bunches of people gathered in the forecourt.

'It's that litter-picking crew. Volunteers,' Beth said. 'They must be using this place as their meeting point.'

'See Tucker anywhere?'

Four heads craned and swiveled.

'Nope,' Roger said.

Bwana parked at the second pump, which seemed to be out of order. He stepped out, his tall figure drawing some attention.

He went inside the store. No manager in sight.

'Where's Tucker?' he asked the pimply-faced young man behind the counter.

'He's not here.'

'Where did he go?' Bwana asked patiently.

'He said something about going home.'

'Is that normal?'

'Uh, no. Who are you?'

'Did he get any calls?'

'Dude, who are you?'

'Answer me,' Bwana warned.

The man sized him up and gulped. 'No calls. He was outside all day. All of us were. I saw him speaking to someone.'

'Who?'

'I wasn't paying attention. A middle-aged man. White. Hey, who are—'

Bwana raced out of the store, climbed into the vehicle and gunned it before he had belted himself in.

Tires squealed. Rubber burned.

'Pagac's here,' he said grimly.

Chapter 40

Zeb was playing with one of Beth's airplanes when the call came.

He paid no attention when the phone rang. They had a system. Whoever was closest to the instrument would pick it up. Beth was. She lifted the handset.

It was her utter stillness that made him look up. She was staring at him. 'Yes,' she replied. 'He's here. Who are you?'

She jabbed a button and a voice came on.

'Carter?'

'Yeah?' He squinted, bent to read what Beth was hastily scribbling, sensing Meghan come from behind and lean over his shoulder.

Maggie Colbert's home. It's—

She stopped writing when the voice spoke.

'You're looking for me.'

He sucked his breath sharply. Looked at Beth, who nodded her head. *It's him. The killer.*

'I am looking for many people. Who are you?'

'Don't play games with me, Carter. I am waiting at the Colberts' apartment—'

'Are they dead?'

'No.'

'Put Maggie Colbert on the line.'

'Hello,' her voice shook when she spoke.

'Ma'am, are you and the children hurt?'

'He … slapped us. Hit Travis.' She broke off in a choked sob.

Zeb tightened. The familiar rage started stirring in him. The beast waking up. Meghan put a hand on his shoulder. The beast subsided.

'How badly are you injured?' Beth asked briskly.

'Not bad,' Maggie Colbert steadied her voice. 'I don't know what he—'

'Enough,' the killer returned. 'You've got your proof. They are alive.'

'What do you want?'

'You're the woman who came with him? I want Carter. And both of you.'

'Why?' Zeb cut in.

'You'll know when you get here. Get here fast. Otherwise I just might start killing.'

He ended the call just as someone moaned in the apartment.

Zeb stripped to his waist even as the twins raced out of the office. He was fastening his armor when they returned.

'We have ours,' Beth patted her jacket.

The three grabbed their go-bags and went to the elevator. Silent. Controlled anger. Adrenaline pumping through their bodies.

'No cops?' Beth asked when they reached their SUV.

'No cops,' Zeb confirmed.

They would deal with Pollenberg, or whoever he was, by themselves.

Bwana swore and jammed the horn when the line in front of him, the volunteers' vehicles, moved at a snail's pace. He swerved suddenly, got on the green swathe beside the road, and passed the line. The ground was uneven and he had to navigate around trees and ditches.

'How many do you think they'll have?' Roger gripped an armrest tightly. He trusted Bwana with his life in combat situations. But not when his friend was driving.

'Four or five,' Chloe ventured. 'Tucker lives alone. They'll figure he doesn't suspect anything. Pagac and some heavies should be sufficient.'

They glimpsed the manager's home in the distance, obscured by trees.

'Perhaps you should—'

Bwana brought the vehicle to a skidding stop before Bear finished. The four of them climbed out, collected their weapons, spread out and ran towards the residence.

'Meg?' Bwana called out on his comms unit. 'We're nearing his house.'

'We aren't in the office anymore. The killer called us. He's got the Colberts.'

Bwana looked to his right. Roger, fifty feet away, raised a fist. He had heard. Chloe, to his left, nodded. Bear, further away, didn't respond. They ran faster.

Zeb parked the SUV a block away from the Colberts' building. They walked briskly, two women and one man, taking in everything around them.

Passersby seemed to read something in their faces and bodies. Foot traffic scattered.

Zeb paused when the highrise appeared. The window-washers caught his eye. 'We'll go to the roof.'

Beth nodded and glanced at her sister. They caught on.

Inside the lobby and up the stairs. No elevators, because the killer just might be watching the security cameras.

Climb five flights. Catch breath for a minute. Resume. On the seventh-floor landing, they encountered an amorous couple who broke apart on sighting them. The woman turned red and adjusted her neckline furiously. The man found something of interest on the wall. The sisters made no comment. Neither did Zeb. It wasn't their business. They carried on and several minutes later, were on the roof.

Air-con blowers, water tanks, signs of a helipad. New York sprawled around them. Highrises catching the sunlight and glinting. A chopper buzzing in the sky. The faint sounds of traffic reaching them.

Beth hurried to the parapet and placed her go-bag down carefully. She unzipped it and removed a bulky item. Unfolded it, straightened its wings and rotors and turned it into a drone.

It was coated with stealth paint that made it near-invisible to radar and detection technology. It had camouflaging technology. The device adopted the color of its surroundings and made it harder to be spotted. The drone wasn't available commercially; Broker and the twins had custom-built it, and its capabilities included thermal imaging, infrared capability, LIDAR, a mobile tower, and more.

She handed the bird over to her sister while she dug out a remote control.

The younger twin turned on the machine and made it hover a few inches. Their screens lit up as the drone's HD cameras synced.

'Zeb?' she looked around and called out.

'Yeah?'

'You got an infil?'

''Yeah. The same way he escaped that time.' He tugged at several cables fastened to securing hooks on the roof. The window-washers' lines.

Meghan joined him and peered over the roof. Four lines snaked down the sides of the building, all of them spread apart. She helped Zeb move them closer, to approximately where the Colberts' window would be.

'Go,' she told her sister when they had finished.

The drone rose in the air and floated down, controlled expertly by Beth. Images flashed on their screens as the bird's cameras captured the building as it flew lower.

A woman hanging her washing in a living room. A TV turned on to a baseball game in another apartment. Several units empty.

'It's sunny. Curtains are open,' Beth said to herself. 'Let's hope … yeah!' she exclaimed in satisfaction when the drone arrived at Maggie Colbert's floor. Their screens showed the drapes were pulled back. That was important.

She zoomed in the camera and looked up at Zeb when the images streamed in.

There was the mom. Grace to her left. Travis on the right, seated close together to the left of the room. Dining table between them and the window. More chairs to the right.

And there was the killer, opposite them, watching them.

'What's that in his hand?' Meghan asked.

Beth trained the cameras and gasped.

It was an aerosol.

'He means to burn them!'

Chapter 41

Bwana and Roger circled to the back of Tucker's house, while Bear and Chloe continued approaching it.

'Four vehicles,' Chloe murmured. 'Tucker's and three SUVs. Front door looks broken. Two men at the front.'

'One man, smoking, in the backyard,' Bwana grunted.

Chloe crouched low and ran to the thicket. Bear joined her, and they studied the house for a moment.

'You've got the looks,' Bear said after a while. Chloe punched him on the shoulder and walked towards Tucker's home. Casually. A neighbor out for a stroll.

'Hi,' she waved at the men as she got closer.

The returned greetings were less enthusiastic.

'Something happening?' she queried, 'I'm Tucker's neighbor, over there,' she waved vaguely behind her. 'I saw the vehicles and got curious. Tucker rarely gets visitors. You're all carrying guns?' Her voice sharpened as she reached the front steps of the porch.

'We're friends of his, from Texas,' one man replied. The other glanced at him sharply. 'We're planning a hunting trip with him. Have a good day, ma'am.'

She climbed, peering behind their shoulders. 'Is he at home?'

'He's busy.' The two men moved, blocking her view. 'We'll tell him you called, Ms—'

The Glock appeared in Chloe's hand as if by magic. She swung it in a wicked blow, catching the first heavy on his temple. The second man started, moved forward. And collapsed when Bear came from behind him and knocked him out with a single blow.

Chloe caught the first man before he fell to the wooden porch. They dragged the unconscious men away and dumped them by the side of Tucker's garage.

'One man down,' Roger whispered.

'Two here,' Chloe replied and entered the house.

Zeb caught hold of the line with gloved hands, braced his knees against the edge of the parapet and looked at the sisters.

They were similarly poised.

'We want him alive. If possible.'

Meghan nodded and went first, sliding down the safety rope, gloves whispering against it, rappelling down swiftly, Beth and Zeb half a second behind.

Mirrored windows flashed in front of them. A startled face in one of them. No visible occupants in most of them.

'Five,' Beth started counting out as they neared the Colberts' floor.

'Four.' Another apartment flashed past, a man sprawled on a couch in its living room.

'Three.'

Zeb gripped the line harder, slowing his descent.

'Two.'

He inched his right hand closer to his shoulder holster.

'One.'

They were just above the upper edge of the Colberts' window.

'NOW!'

They kicked against the building's side, swung out in empty space, sliding down several inches as they did so.

Three Glocks flashed out as they swung back like pendulums toward the Colberts' window. They fired at its two upper corners. Glass shattered. The window gave away when they crashed into it, and then they were inside the apartment.

Chloe, Glock pointing straight ahead, crouching to offer the smallest target, moved slowly through the hallway. Living room to the left. She ducked inside, barrel first.

Clear, she indicated.

Bear followed impassively.

No update from Bwana or Roger, which was standard operating protocol. When in close quarters, keep radio silence unless there was an emergency.

Sounds reached them as they went deeper, past a bedroom, which too was empty.

Indistinct words. A sound, repeated frequently, that made the skin at the back of her neck prickle. Flesh striking flesh.

Past a dining room. No occupants. She slowed when the sounds and words grew louder.

Pagac and his men seemed to be in the kitchen. She inched forward, toward the open door. Stopped when she saw the scene.

Three men, their backs to her, standing, guns dangling by their sides. Heavies One, Two, and Three, she named them.

Three others facing her, their eyes focused on the action in the center of the kitchen.

Tucker, bound to a chair, his head nodding, his chest bare, face limp, eyes closed. Lips split, nose apparently broken, eyebrows cut, welts across his chest, blood streaming down his body.

Pagac pacing in front of him. Gloves on his hands, his shirt red from spatter.

'You're a snitch, aren't you? You turned on us. Who are you ratting to?'

The council member slammed a fist in the manager's gut. Tucker groaned, heaved, retched and spat blood.

'No … one.'

'You lie. You're a good liar.' Pagac hit him again, this time on his throat. The prisoner jerked and gasped hoarsely, sucking in air desperately, his eyes bulging.

Chloe sensed movement behind her. She didn't look back. She knew what Bear was doing. Recording.

She watched for a few more moments, allowing her partner to capture the brutal interrogation, and when she felt him put away his cell phone, she straightened.

'Pagac,' she called out. 'This's your idea of fun?'

Heads jerked toward her. Hands reached for AR 15s.

She was diving before the first round whistled past her. Landed on her left shoulder and took out Heavy One, who had his back to her and was spinning around to shoot.

The kitchen exploded in sound as weapons went off. She snapped a look. Bear and Roger had entered from the rear and joined the fray. A man yelled. It was Pagac, who was cowering behind the refrigerator.

Someone screamed, got her attention. Heavy Two, who was cursing in anger. He got off a round that over her head, before Bear's shot blew a hole in his chest.

A bullet buzzed angrily an inch from her face. That was from Heavy Three, who had leaped back to make more room for himself. His AR15 was chattering, scything through the air. She crabbed sideways as quickly as she could, knowing that Bear couldn't cover her; he was still in the hallway leading to the kitchen.

Heavy Three smirked, took his time to aim—and that was his mistake.

His head exploded like a melon. Bwana shooting as he dived across the kitchen, smashed into Tucker's chair, sent him to the floor and covered him.

Chloe, Bear and Roger covered him, aiming at the three remaining enforcers, who made the wiser choice.

They dropped their weapons, their hands reaching for the sky.

'Go on, take a shot,' Bwana urged them.

They didn't.

'What's the world coming to?' he swore. 'Bad dudes ain't what they used to be.'

'Pagac,' Chloe called out. 'Come out. Slowly. Hands high.'

The council member didn't move from his hiding place. They could hear him breathing loudly. Almost sobbing.

She fired in the air, in his direction.

'Don't shoot,' he pleaded.

'Show yourself.'

Pagac peered around the refrigerator. Looked at the scene. Came out from behind his cover. Rage and fear twisted his face.

'I should have—' his lips clamped shut when he saw Bear was recording him.

'You might as well sing,' Chloe suggested. 'You won't be tasting freedom for a long time.'

She went behind him, cuffed him with plastic ties, helped Roger secure the other prisoners. Four of them. Two dead.

'How's Tucker?' she asked Bwana, who had cut Tucker free and was leaning over him.

The manager forced one of his swollen eyes open. 'Your timing,' he managed a weak smile. 'It needs improvement.'

Chloe made calls. To the state cops. To Sarah Burke. Then she checked her screen.

No messages from the twins or Zeb.

Chapter 42

Beth and Meghan landed on the dining table as someone screamed. They slid across its surface and slammed into the mom and her children, taking them down to the floor, covering them.

Zeb's entry was ungainly. He smashed into a chair and stumbled and lost his gun.

The stumble saved his life.

The killer reacted instantly when they broke into the apartment. He lunged away from the wall. His right hand reached behind him. A gun appeared. The round blew through air where Zeb's head had been a few moments before.

Zeb dived to the floor. He grabbed the chair and flung it against the assassin. Heaved himself off the carpet and charged at the killer, who was ducking to avoid the incoming missile.

He bodyslammed into the man, grabbed his gun hand and smashed it to the floor. The weapon caromed away.

The assassin was strong, wiry and fast. He kept twisting his body, preventing Zeb from locking him down. He slashed at the warrior's face with the aerosol can, a jarring blow that rocked Zeb's head back.

He caught sight of the killer's face, lips drawn back, eyes darting to the object in his hand.

He's going to spray!

He brought his right hand up to cover his face as the can hissed, weakening Zeb's hold on the assassin, who swung the canister and jabbed it into the warrior's throat.

Zeb fell back, gasping, struggling to breathe. His vision darkened. He felt the killer slip away and reached out to grab him by his leg. The assassin anticipated his move, kicked out savagely and broke away.

A blur of movement. Beth pounced on the assassin with a yell. The assassin dealt with her by grabbing her outstretched arm, twisting it and shoving her away.

'Stay down!' one of the sisters shouted at the Colberts.

The killer froze for a millisecond at the warning, not knowing who it was intended for. That pause was enough for Meghan. He went flying back when she pounced and grabbed him by the waist. The two crashed into the wall. A blur of motion as they exchanged blows. Something fell to the floor and rolled. The spray can.

The assassin roared and used a judo hold to send Meghan staggering away.

Zeb attacked him then. A hard chop to the killer's neck, followed by a blow to the gut. Parry and duck as the killer retaliated.

Krav maga moves, Zeb thought dimly, *an expert.* He crowded the gunman against the wall, cutting off his movement, twisted in time to take the upraised knee on his thigh. He reeled back when the assassin headbutted him. His lips split. A knuckled drive to his chest sent him a step back.

The killer needed just that opening. He dived toward the can.

'No!'

Zeb lunged to his fallen Glock, grabbed it, twisted on his shoulder and trained it on the killer, who now had the aerosol in one hand, a lighter in the other.

The assassin took a step back, to the window.

'Drop it,' Zeb warned.

'You can't escape,' Beth added. She and Meghan cut off the killer's approach to the Colberts.

'I didn't want to do this,' the assassin surprised them by speaking.

'Do what?' Zeb asked, getting to his feet carefully. '*DON'T MOVE!'*

The killer took a contemptuous step back.

'I had given up killing. But he found me.'

Zeb shook his head imperceptibly in warning when Beth raised her Glock.

Let him talk. We have three guns on him. We can shoot to wound if he tries anything.

She settled into a shooting stance but didn't fire.

'Who are you talking about?'

The assassin ignored Meghan's question. He was looking into the distance, his body slack, the can and the lighter drooping.

'He told me to attack the G20 Summit. I told him it was impossible. He said I am the best assassin in the world. That's right, isn't it? You never knew of me.'

'You could be a street thug,' Zeb said dismissively.

'You know the killing in Italy some years back? The British ambassador to the U.S.'

'You could have looked that up,' Zeb scoffed.

'The Israeli ambassador in Cairo,' the killer said,

knowingly. 'You know how he died?'

'Enlighten us.'

'In a fire. It wasn't an accident, even though that was what the media reported.'

A cool breath blew through Zeb's mind. He was aware of the sisters looking at him. *They wouldn't know of these killings. The Cairo one ... it was hushed up. The Egyptians and Israelis never revealed that it was an assassination.*

A jigsaw piece fell into place in his mind.

Can it be—

'That was me. Both times,' the assassin said, simply. No boasting. No gloating. 'You never had a clue about me. That's why he chose me.'

'Who?' Meghan asked impatiently. 'Get to it.'

'He gave me an incentive,' the killer ignored her. His dark eyes were fixed on Zeb, his face giving nothing away.

'Money?' Beth guessed. 'Must be lots of it, to pull off such an attack. You failed, though.'

'He took my parents. They are old. In their seventies. Every day, his men tortured them. He sent me their videos. Made me watch. Sometimes he worked on them himself.'

Maggie Colbert moaned softly. She drew Grace close to her.

'He sent me one final video when I told him I failed. His men made my parents kneel. They shot them from behind.'

He lowered his right hand. 'I'm not reaching for a gun,' he said when the twins' fingers tightened on their Glocks. He brought out a cell phone and tossed it on the floor. 'I recorded his last calls. The video of my parents' execution. It's all there.'

Beth's face was ashen. She wet her lips, wiped a palm on her jeans and settled back in her shooting stance.

'And then he told me I could redeem myself,' the killer continued, no inflection in his voice.

'How?' Meghan asked.

'By killing Carter.'

His lips thinned as he looked at the warrior. 'He hates you. There's no one he wants to see dead more than you. I could have killed you. All of you. I knew where your office was. I followed you. You didn't even know I was there. I could have taken you out anytime.'

'Why didn't you?' Zeb heard his own voice as if from a distance. He knew who the killer was referring to. Everything now made sense.

'I told you. I had given up killing. When he asked me to go after you, he gave me an idea. He was right. I could redeem myself. But not in the way he wanted. You have figured it out, haven't you? You know who he is.'

Zeb nodded, feeling slow, sluggish. *How could I have overlooked that man? He had the capability, the resources. He had the motive. Hate.*

'You will go after him.' The killer moved with blurring speed. The can hissed. Deadly spray flew and settled over his body.

Beth lunged forward. Zeb grabbed her by the waist and held her back.

His lighter sparked.

His clothing caught fire.

Grace and Maggie screamed.

'You will avenge my parents.'

The can dropped to the floor. As did the lighter. The killer took another step back, towards the window, his entire body alight.

'What's your name?' Zeb asked, struggling to hold Beth, who was straining, shouting.

'My plans … the G20 Summit, they couldn't have worked.'

'I know,' Zeb said, almost gently.

'Reza Khalili. That's who I am.' The killer climbed onto the windowsill. 'Only my parents and he know that name. Now you.'

And with that, he stepped away.

Zeb let go of Beth, who ran to the window and leaned out. Meghan joined her. They watched for a moment and turned to Zeb.

'We could have stopped him,' the younger sister rounded on him. 'We could have shot him in the shoulders.'

'He was a dead man walking.' Zeb felt empty. 'He wanted to die.'

'He had information. We could have—' Meghan stopped her with a hand to her shoulder.

'Zeb,' the elder twin asked. 'Who is he? This man he was talking about.'

She turned pale when he uttered the name.

'Major General Zarab Tousi. Head of the IRGC, Iran's Islamic Revolutionary Guard Corps.'

Part II

Chapter 43

Four Months Later

'You didn't clear the road?' Major General Zarab Tousi snarled at his driver.

He was in the back of his black, armored Mercedes, in a foul mood. The ride usually calmed him. He liked it when citizens recognized his vehicle and bowed, when traffic emptied as his vehicle was escorted by motorcycle outriders and security vehicles.

'It is clear, agha,' Hassan Rezghi, his chauffeur and bodyguard, responded.

Tousi leaned forward and looked through the windshield. It was clear. Far ahead was one security vehicle filled with five soldiers. Two Sepah men on bikes ahead of them. Behind him was another vehicle with five more armed men. In the distance, the Beit Rahbari loomed, the official residence of the Supreme Leader.

'We should have made quicker time,' he grumped.

Rezghi looked at his boss in the mirror and shrugged mentally. He had been driving Tousi for years. He was used to the man's rages.

Many said his boss was the most powerful man in Iran, after the Supreme Leader.

Sepah, as the IRGC was known locally, protected the country's religious, political and social system. It was a branch of the armed forces with over a hundred thousand personnel. It also controlled the Basij, a volunteer force of close to four hundred thousand personnel.

The organization was responsible for protecting the Persian Gulf and the country's nuclear facilities.

Its real power reached beyond its military capabilities, however. Sepah stamped out political protests in Iran. Brutally. It arrested Western reporters. It protected the Supreme Leader and the government from internal threats. It had wide-ranging economic interests. It owned or invested in oil companies, construction firms, weapons manufacturers. Sepah was everywhere. It was feared by many, hated by many more—and that was precisely the effect Tousi wanted. He reported only to the Supreme Leader and, over the years, had consolidated his and his organization's power to the extent that it outstripped that of the clerics.

Tousi had started his career as an undercover spy, infiltrating Western agencies, converting their agents. He had risen to be a spymaster, one so successful that he had been dubbed the Handler for the way he ran agents in different countries. The Supreme Leader had personally appointed him to his current role. He was well suited to it. He had the smarts, the guile; was ruthless and brutal. He didn't mind getting his hands dirty, a much-needed quality to stamp one's authority on Sepah.

Rezghi looked at his boss again as he maneuvered the vehicle through Beit Rahbari's gates. A vein pulsed on Tousi's temple. *He's nervous,* the driver thought, as he rolled down the window and waited for guards to peer inside.

'Wait for me,' his boss snapped, as he strode out of the vehicle. A needless command, since the driver always waited.

'You promised to destroy the G20 Summit,' the Supreme Leader hissed, his dark eyes fathomless. He was seated on a platform, Tousi on a chair, at a lower level. Power play at work.

'You said everything was in place,' the leader said, sipping on his chai, watching his subordinate the way a hawk watched its prey. 'If everything was ready, why did the summit go ahead without any incident?'

Tousi bowed his head as if in supplication. He gritted his teeth and put on a sorrowful expression. The Supreme Leader brought this up every time they met. He wanted to make the Sepah head squirm before he got to the matter of the day.

'My assassin failed, agha. He was the best and I thought he could pull it off, but he didn't.'

He hadn't told the leader of the details of what had transpired. Khalili had failed and then had disappeared. He had failed to kill Carter, too, and that riled Tousi even more than the summit no-show.

'Failure. That's all I hear these days from you,' the leader spat. 'You said you would destroy Israel. Look what happened.'

Tousi didn't have to look. He knew what had gone down. The whole world knew. Israel had recognized Palestine as an independent nation, a move that had President Morgan's backing, widely welcomed by the world. It had resulted in a dramatic reduction in worldwide terrorist activity.

He kept his head bowed as the leader carried on in the

same line. His rant turned to the protection of Islamic culture, how it was threatened by Western influences, how little Tousi was doing to eradicate those evils.

'You know about the speech I am making?' The leader switched track suddenly.

Tousi looked up and brought his mind to the present. 'Yes, agha. At Tehran University.'

It was to be a rare outing for the Supreme Leader. He usually addressed the public in Imam Khomeini Hussainiya, which was in the office building.

Tousi and he had discussed the university event in depth, and both had agreed that the leader needed to be seen outside the confines of his residence.

The address, to university students, would cover the usual topics: Iran's willingness to defend itself against internal and external threats. Denouncing Israel, President Morgan, and the evil influences of Western culture.

The speech would be more of the same but was necessary. The USA's sanctions were hurting, the economy was in a tail-spin, citizens were angry and frustrated. Tousi and the leader hoped that his speech would go some way toward soothing heightened tensions.

'I won't be making it,' the Supreme Leader stunned him. 'You go in my place.'

'Agha, but—'

'You have let me down several times, now. Is that going to happen again?'

Tousi closed his mouth and bowed in acceptance. He went back to his car, seething in anger. He didn't see anything of the city as his driver took him back to his office.

The speech wasn't what rankled him. He could and would

address the students. It wasn't a big deal. Khalili's failure with the summit didn't rankle him, either. Sure, it would have been a mighty blow for Iran if the killer had succeeded. But Tousi hadn't invested much in the mission. He had made an advance payment to the assassin, and that had been it. And then he had gotten the man's parents killed.

No, what made the Sepah head bitter was Zeb Carter. It looked like Khalili had failed there, too.

The American agent had foiled him in Israel. He was the one man Zarab Tousi feared.

Tousi could taste the hate in his mouth.

Carter. Where was he? How could he be killed?

Chapter 44

Zeb had acted swiftly after Khalili's death. He and the sisters had checked out the assassin's phone. The stored calls and videos on it confirmed what the killer had said.

The voice on those calls was a match for Zarab Tousi.

The Pentagon, when Clare disclosed the findings in a tense meeting at the White House, wanted to conduct a military strike against Iran. The CIA wanted to go in and abduct the Supreme Leader.

The Agency's Director had persuaded President Morgan to not act hastily.

'Sir, we can't just capture him without a proper plan for what happens next. We know what happened in Iraq when we captured Saddam. That country's still unstable. Besides, the Middle East will explode in war if we engage with Iran overtly.'

'Clare, we can't let that country get away with this.'

'It won't, sir.'

'You mean…?'

'Yes, sir. We'll get Tousi. Let my people handle it.'

The Pentagon didn't like it. Other three-letter agencies suggested they could take on the mission. The President ignored their demands and greenlighted the Agency.

'Grab him, how?' Beth demanded when Zeb relayed the developments to his team.

'We'll go to Iran and get him.'

The *we* ended up being Zeb and the sisters. None of the other male warriors could blend in. Chloe could, but she had a family commitment that meant she wasn't part of the infiltration team.

Zeb handed over Khalili's cell phone to the NYPD, who shared it with the FBI. Those two agencies took over. They traced the assassin back to his Queens apartment and warehouse. FBI agents and cops took apart the residence and the remains of his workshop and pieced together the assassin's plan.

'He was thinking of sodium,' Sarah Burke called one night, a week before the summit. 'It wouldn't have worked, however. He still would have needed a triggering mechanism of some kind and we would have spotted it.'

Zeb grunted in acknowledgement. He remembered the killer's final words. *Did he want to fail? He said he didn't want to kill anymore.*

'You don't seem interested,' Burke brought him back from his thoughts.

'It's your investigation, now.' Neither the FBI Assistant Director nor the cops knew what he was planning. 'You've checked out Javits?'

'Yeah. Thoroughly. It's clean. We've checked out the foreman's crew, the rest of it, and every other worker. We've put them under the scanner. They've all come through. No threat there.'

She paused. He made no comment, his mind in Tehran, his attention focused on his old foe.

'You've heard about Pagac and Bernier?'

'Yeah.'

The council member had cut a deal with the FBI. Reduced sentencing in return for dirt on Bernier. That resulted in the White Freedom leader's arrest, who had immediately lawyered up.

We took down Khalili. We brought down Bernier. Tucker's in witness protection.

As far as Zeb was concerned, the Agency's job was done on those two operations. It was time to focus on Iran.

He and Avichai Levin, Mossad's Director, had planned to go after the Iranian spymaster, but that hadn't materialized. Agency missions had cropped up.

'You've got an idea, haven't you? About how we'll pull it off,' Meghan asked, as they began planning for the mission on the day of the summit.

Zeb turned up the volume on their office TV. Thunderous applause blasted from its speakers as the G20's two special guests walked on stage.

Israel's Prime Minister Yago Cantor and Palestine's President Ziyan Baruti.

He listened to their speech for a moment and then muted the sound.

'We'll take a page from Khalili's playbook,' he told the sisters. 'We'll get close to him as IRGC soldiers.'

They got Werner to run through the Sepah database for likely candidates for them to impersonate.

And there they hit jackpot.

Hassan Rezghi, Tousi's driver, matched Zeb in height and build. Levin sent over an entire dossier on the driver that had photographs from several angles, videos, a detailed background.

'He's married. He's got kids,' Meghan exclaimed when she skimmed through it. 'How'll you work around that?'

'I won't be taking over his life, the way Khalili did with Pollenberg. We need one brief opportunity where I can substitute for him and grab Tousi,' Zeb replied. A vague plan was forming in his mind, but there were too many intangibles that needed to be resolved. 'Let's work on the face mask.'

'Hey, what about us? Who will we be impersonating?'

The Mossad director came to the rescue again during a video call.

'Tousi's creating a secret cadre of women soldiers. Secret because Iran allows only men to join their armed forces. He's been studying us, Mossad in particular. He has seen our success with our operatives of both genders. He wants to copy that. He wants to have women as spies and soldiers. He's got fifteen women stationed on Greater Farur Island. They have been training for three years and we have credible intel that they have been involved in some operations in Iraq, against ISIL. Alongside Yazidi women.'

'Farur Island is in the Persian Gulf, isn't it?' Zeb's brow furrowed as he tried to recall what he knew of it. 'It's where the IRGC's naval unit trains. It's remote. No inhabitation.'

'That's why it's perfect for a secretive women's battalion,' Levin responded drily. 'Meghan, I've sent you another file. This has everything we know of those women.'

Zeb leaned over the sisters as they opened Levin's folder.

It contained dossiers on the fifteen women, their photographs, close-up as well as long distance, training videos, images of them in traditional dresses, going shopping.

'You've got someone in-country,' Meghan said suspiciously.

Zeb nodded. The kind of detail in Levin's files required an implant, an agent who was stationed semi permanently in Iran.

'Two of them,' the Mossad director boasted. 'You know them well. Carmen and Dalia.'

'They're there?' Beth asked in excitement. The sisters had met the Israeli kidon in a previous mission and had bonded quickly.

'Yeah. Khalili didn't invent impersonation.' Zeb had kept nothing back about the Iranian assassin from his friend. It was how the two worked. 'Mossad agents have been doing that for years.'

'Yeah. Mossad's operatives can walk on water, too,' Beth mocked.

'I can't reveal all our capabilities,' Levin winked and hung up.

The three of them studied the women soldiers and finally decided on Pouri Vakili and Akhtar Nassour. Those two resembled the twins the closest.

Meghan got their faces manufactured at a laboratory they trusted. Special purpose latex. Hand sewn in parts. Face painted by graphic artists who were world-renowned for their skills.

In parallel, the three of them started getting into their roles. Walk, talk, mannerisms, habits. Their challenge was that while the Mossad files were extensive, they weren't sufficient enough. Impersonating another person required in-depth knowledge of that person. They didn't have enough of that.

'We can't do this here,' Zeb decided, a week after the summit. 'We'll need to be in-country.'

They went to Tehran.

The capital, with its eight million people, was the largest city in the country. It was situated at the foot of the snow-capped Alborz Mountain Range and was a mix of the old and the new, the West and the East. The city had seen Arab, Turkic and Mongol invaders and its architecture reflected that heritage.

Palaces and castles juxtaposed with urban highrises. The past co-existing with the modern. Grand towers, the most prominent of them, the Azadi Tower and Milad Tower.

The former was commissioned by the last Shah of Iran to commemorate the two thousand five hundredth year of the formation of Imperial Iran. Milad Tower, seen from most parts of the city, was the sixth tallest in the world and was part of a convention center.

The city had a modern and traditional divide. The northern districts were cosmopolitan, and expensive, while the southern neighborhoods were more orthodox, relatively cheaper. The middle was where most of the government offices and shopping centers were located.

Zeb and the twins flew separately, commercial, using one of the many aliases they had as Agency operatives. Zeb was Chad Amin, Beth was Amy Arsalan and Meghan was Kate Arsalan. All three were Iranian-Americans, visiting the country of their forefathers. The sisters covered their heads with scarves and wore manteaus over their clothing. Iranian law. It required women to keep their heads covered and wear modest clothing.

They stayed in different hotels in Hasan Abad which was a central neighborhood, one of the oldest in the city. The locality and its surroundings had a significant number of ministerial offices.

It was convenient given that Azarbayjan, where the Supreme Leader's office was located, was a brisk walk away. That would give ample opportunity for Zeb to observe Rezghi as he drove his boss to and fro from the leader's residence. However, that wouldn't be enough observation to impersonate the driver without any risk. *We'll figure something out.*

The twins had a bigger challenge. There was no way they could go to Farur Island and watch the two soldiers whose identities they would assume.

I am not planning a Khalili style impersonation, however. All we need to do is replace them for a brief moment of time.

Which brought up another hurdle they had to overcome.

Who would they replace Tousi with?

Chapter 45

If Iraq, Afghanistan, the Arab Spring and several other operations across the world had taught Western intelligence agencies anything, it was that it wasn't enough to remove a despotic government or politician or agency head. The replacement had to be someone better, otherwise all the effort, investment and loss of human life was wasted.

Grabbing Tousi was fine. But what if his replacement turned out to be equally bad or worse?

Zeb and Levin had mulled over that problem for months, even before this sortie to Iran. It was one reason a joint Mossad-Agency mission hadn't materialized.

They had one possible candidate: Brigadier General Rostam Golzar, the deputy head of the IRGC. Tousi's number two man. Golzar would be the one promoted if anything happened to the Sepah boss.

There was one problem with Golzar.

They knew next to nothing about him. Even Mossad, with its formidable resources and sayanim—Jews who helped the Israeli state in various countries—hadn't found anything on Golzar. Anything that they could exploit.

Zeb set about rectifying that when they arrived in Iran. He and the twins, Carmel and Dalia, alternated between discreetly following Rezghi and video-ing him, and shadowing the Sepah's deputy head.

Simultaneously, Meghan and Beth practiced their Persian. They went out with the Israelis, who spoke the languages fluently with the right accent, assimilated the culture, and played the roles of Iranian women. They could safely assume the identities of the soldiers, since Vakili and Nassour were on Farur Island and their homes were in remote parts of Iran.

They didn't get any dirt on Golzar. They found that he behaved the same way as his boss. He aggressively criticized Western culture and made sure he was seen when Sepah soldiers arrested protestors.

'I'll have to go in,' Zeb told the women, one night over dinner.

Carmel sucked her breath in sharply. 'Even Mossad hasn't broken into his home. Or Tousi's.'

'Your boss won't like that admission,' Beth grinned cheekily. 'There is nothing Mossad hasn't done, according to him.'

'Yeah, the ramsad is a character.' Ramsad was the Israeli name for Mossad's director. 'It's risky.'

Zeb shrugged. What they were planning was risky.

One moonlit night, when the clock struck 2 am, he scaled the high walls that surrounded Golzar's government residence in Pamenar.

He and the twins had prepared for this by running drone surveys and had learned the routine for the foot patrols inside the walls. They hadn't detected any sensors on the walls.

Zeb stood stationary when he landed. He was wearing a dark skinsuit, armor and jacket, carrying his Glock, a blade sheathed to his thigh, and a backpack. He carried no identification. He knew if he was caught, it was unlikely he would be seen again. He wore a headband, in which was mounted a wireless HD camera.

He withdrew a monitor and ran it around him. No motion sensors. There were CCTV cameras, but his drone, hovering high up, made sure, with some highly sophisticated tech no layperson had heard of, that the cameras looped the feed endlessly.

The bird in the sky was controlled by Beth, who sat in a dark van a street away that looked as if it had broken down. With Meghan in the vehicle were the Israeli kidon, following Zeb's headcam feed.

'No dogs,' the younger sister whispered over the encrypted channel.

Zeb crouched low and ran toward a glass door, which seemed to open to a reception area, curtained from the inside. He peered at the lock. Yeah, he could pick it. He looked for wires and spotted something that looked like a junction box in the upper corner inside.

A door alarm?

'Our drone has jammed the alarm system,' Beth confirmed. 'Go.'

He broke inside the house carefully and peered through a gap in the curtains. It was dark. A dim light coming from a hallway to his left.

There were security personnel inside the residence complex, but they were in an annex. No guards in the house itself. Just Golzar, his wife, Leila, and their two young daughters, Roya and Sara.

Zeb padded across the reception room. Checked out the

other rooms on the ground floor. A guest bedroom, which was empty. Kitchen. Dining room. Another reception room. A playroom. A study stacked with files. Zeb was tempted to grab the briefcase lying on the desk. Nope, that wasn't why he was there.

He climbed the marble steps and entered another hallway. Dim lighting. Snoring from a room to his right. He bent low and tried the door. It gave. He pushed it open an inch. A large bed. Moonlight filtering through drapes. Two shapes underneath the spread.

He searched the rest of the floor. He found the daughters in a bedroom, sleeping on twin beds. Another room seemed to be their study. A dressing room that seemed to be the wife's. Two large bathrooms.

He stood still for a moment. He didn't know what he was looking for. It wasn't as if Golzar would leave anything incriminating in the open. This was Iran. The man worked in Sepah. He would be scrutinized. He would have eyes on him always.

Best to go to the study and check his files out.

He was turning to leave when something glinted on the floor, near a bathroom door jamb.

Golzar's snoring stopped.

Zeb froze.

A bed creaked.

The snoring began again.

He went to the bathroom's entrance and got to his knees. Picked up the tiny piece of jewelry and stared at it.

Why would there be a cross in Golzar's house?

Chapter 46

‘They are devout Muslims,’ Dalia asserted when he showed them a picture of the cross. ‘Both he and his wife grew up in Tehran. We have their family histories. No Christians in their lineage. Besides, someone of another faith wouldn’t be allowed to join Sepah, much less be so highly ranked.’

‘It must be something the daughters brought home,’ Beth surmised. ‘From one of their friends.’

Both Roya and Sara went to a private school in Abshar, a nearby locality, where the children of other government officials studied.

It’s possible, Zeb thought. But Golzar has cleaners, cooks, an entire staff of servants. *They would have discovered the cross and either reported it or thrown it away.*

‘I’ll go in again.’

He ignored the cries of protest that followed. The cross, if it meant anything, could be the lever they needed.

He broke inside the house an evening later, when the Golzars were at a diplomatic reception organized by the Syrian embassy.

Nine pm. The house was well-lit, but security was decidedly

lax. Two guards were smoking in a corner of the manicured lawn, their backs to the infiltrator who ran across its breadth and paused at the glass door. Six more personnel were in the annex, drinking coffee, their eyes on a soccer match playing on a small TV. None of them paid attention to the camera feeds. Even if they had, they wouldn't have spotted the intruder. The drone was at work again.

Zeb headed to the adults' bedroom and searched the wardrobes. Nothing. He looked beneath the mattress and pillows. Opened the side tables, looked beneath the carpet, went to the attached bathroom and searched.

He returned to the wardrobe and commenced a second search. This time, he probed its construction, searching for hidden compartments. He found one in a lower drawer and brought out a thick roll of U.S. dollars. He peered inside the opening. Nothing else there. He counted the bills, took pictures and returned the roll.

He tapped the bottom of Leila's side of the wardrobe and … there!

A hinged panel collapsed. He shone a light and surveyed the jewelry. Necklaces. Pearl and gold ornaments. He was looking beyond them, however, his eyes riveted on a simple chain, on which was a small cross. A second hook on the chain was empty. He brought out his phone and compared his picture to the ornament in his hand. Yes. A very good match.

He riffled through the other jewelry carefully and felt something thick inside. Brought it out slowly and whistled softly when it turned out to be a small, well-thumbed Bible.

He took more pictures, put back the contents of the compartment and sealed it shut. He searched the male side of the dresser and found a similar compartment. Only two items in it. Praying beads on top of a religious picture. That of a Christian saint.

Zeb leaned against the wall when he had finished his search. His head was buzzing with multiple thoughts, but the foremost one was, *Rostam and Leila Golzar are Christians!*

Chapter 47

Rostam Gulzar went to his favorite chai-khaneh in Narmak the following afternoon. The Syrian reception had been exhausting. He had eaten too much and now his belly was complaining.

A dark, strong tea would help. It wouldn't, of course. It would add to the acid in his body, but the Sepah deputy boss was firmly convinced of the therapeutic qualities of the beverage.

He nodded to the man behind the counter, who flew out from his perch and escorted his guest to a corner table. Golzar's security personnel were outside the café, standing guard, weapons visible. Inside, men, for it was a male-only establishment, looked at the new arrival with interest. Those who knew of the Sepah man looked away quickly. It didn't do to stare at an IRGC boss openly.

Golzar sipped his beverage slowly, idly perusing a newspaper. He flipped a page. Froze when he saw a photograph nestled inside the pages. Praying beads on top of a Christian saint.

He looked up sharply. No one was watching him.

Looked around. No one was paying him any attention. The proprietor looked his way, sensed his agitation and hurried across.

'Any problem, agha?'

Golzar closed the page, hiding the photograph. 'That tea was too hot,' he snarled. He grabbed the newspaper and strode out of the room, ignoring the owner's apologies.

He climbed into his vehicle. 'Wait,' he ordered his driver, who was preparing to wheel away. He brought out his cell phone and, under the pretext of checking his messages, looked out of the window.

There didn't seem to be anyone looking his way. He craned to look out of the rear window. The usual traffic.

He opened the newspaper again and took out the photograph. His fingers trembled. The picture fell to his lap.

He picked it up again, and then he saw what had been written on its back.

A cell phone number.

He shoved the picture into his pocket with a shaking hand. 'Let's go,' he told his driver.

He couldn't focus on his work for the rest of the day. Each time someone knocked on his office, he dreaded the worst. Tousi, with armed officers to escort him to prison.

Prison? They'll execute me and my family.

He couldn't take it anymore and went to his superior's office. 'Agha, I am not feeling well.'

The Sepah head looked him up and down. 'Yes, you're pale and sweating. Go home. Don't infect others.'

Empathy wasn't Tousi's strong point.

'Did we have any visitors?' Golzar picked Roya up and kissed her, did the same for Sara.

'No,' Leila replied. She took his briefcase and put it in his study. She brought him a cup of steaming tea and wiped his forehead with a towel. 'Are you feeling okay? You are flushed.'

'I don't know,' he lied. 'I might be coming down with something. That's why I came home early. So, no visitors?'

'No, why do you ask?'

He debated telling her. *No*, he decided. *No point in scaring her.*

He walked over to the annex. Guards sprang up and stood to attention, surprise on their faces. It was highly unusual for the deputy head to visit them.

'Everything okay with our security? Any intruders? Any alarms?'

'No agha. We are vigilant,' the eldest officer replied.

If you were so alert, how did someone break into my house?

There was no point bringing that up with the security detail. It could end up exposing him and Leila.

He returned to his residence, and while his wife directed their servants to lay out dinner, he searched the secret compartments.

Yes, everything was in place. Nothing had been stolen. He went to his study and returned with another bag. Removed a bug detector and deployed it in the bedroom. No surveillance devices.

He went downstairs. Played with his daughters. Had dinner. Watched TV until his wife went to bed and then inspected the doors and windows. No signs of forced entry that he could detect. The alarm's control panel said it was working fine.

He went to his study and brought out a burner phone. He had several of those. They came with his job.

He dialed the number.

A male voice picked up immediately. 'No names,' in Persian. 'Meet me tomorrow. At the gym you go to. Your usual time.'

'Who are you—'

But the man had hung up.

Sweat beaded on the deputy head's forehead. Whoever the man was, he had not only broken into his residence and discovered his secret, but also knew his routine.

Golzar went to a gym in Narmak, not far from his favorite chai-khaneh, every alternate day. He went at lunchtime, had a light workout and a massage, and spent time in the sauna.

Given his standing, the gym's managers emptied the establishment of all other members when he arrived. Only the trainers, the masseuse and the reception crew remained.

I should go to the fitness center with officers. Arrest him.

Fool, his mind argued back. *He'll reveal who you are. He has proof.*

What if I destroy the cross, the beads and the Bible?

He sprang up. And then sat down heavily when a chill raced through him.

He might have videos of Leila and me praying.

No, his best bet was to go to the gym, hear the man out. And then deal with him.

I am the second most powerful man in Sepah. I can make him disappear.

Chapter 48

At 12 pm the next day, Golzar stepped out of his office. His driver straightened and held the door open for him.

'Gym, agha?'

'Yes.'

The Sepah deputy boss strode to the fitness center when they arrived, his driver a step behind him, carrying his workout bag.

A trainer took the bag from his driver and escorted him inside.

'It's empty?' Golzar asked sharply.

'Yes, agha.'

Security personnel checked the establishment before his visit. Routine protocol. He relaxed. That man won't be able to get through.

He punished himself with weights, on the bike and the treadmill. Made the masseuse dig deep into his back and neck, and then headed to the sauna.

It had wooden benches and could hold ten men at a time. Thick steam swirled in it, reducing visibility. He entered and peered through the gloom.

No one here.

Relieved, he occupied the highest bench, sat, rested his aching back against the wall and closed his eyes with a sigh.

'How long have you been Christians?'

He yelped and jumped. Looked to his left and made out a shadow in the corner. His mouth felt dry. He hesitated. Should he call out? There was a trainer not far away. His security guards were in the fitness center. They would come rushing.

'I can kill you before you make a sound.'

He subsided like a punctured balloon.

'Who are you?' he rasped.

'How long have you been Christians?' the man repeated.

Golzar wet his lips. 'Do you know who I am?' he blustered. 'I can have you arrested. You'll not be seen anymore. Just like that,' he snapped his fingers.

'Go ahead. Call your men.'

The Sepah man was tempted. He opened his mouth.

'Think what will happen to Leila.'

His courage fled him.

'Who are you? What do you want?' he whispered.

'You didn't answer my question.'

'Why is that important? Is this about money? How much do you want?'

'Tell me.'

Golzar stayed quiet, his mind racing. What were his options? *I don't have any,* he thought. *Not until I know how much he knows and what he wants.*

'After I became a commander in Sepah.'

'That was when?'

'Ten years ago.'

'Both of you converted at the same time?'

'She was already a Christian. Since she was a student. Her friend was from that faith. She learned about it from her and then converted. She didn't even tell her parents.'

'And your children?'

'You want to expose me?' Golzar snarled, 'Go ahead. But leave my children out of it.'

'What are they?'

'What do you think?' he spat. 'They are brought up as Muslim children. We don't have a choice. They are too young to live a double life like us. What do you want from me?'

'How many people have you tortured?'

Golzar blinked at the sudden turn in the questioning.

'What?'

'How many people have you tortured and killed in Sepah?'

'Why does that matter? You want to blackmail me? State what you want. You want a favor? To buy some government land? Tell me.'

The man's voice hardened. 'I ask questions. You answer. Or you and Leila have your lives destroyed and Roya and Sara will be orphans.'

His words hit the deputy head like bullets. 'I haven't tortured anyone,' he admitted softly. 'Tousi. He likes it. He made me watch several times. Now, in my position, I have others to do it.'

'Do you understand where I work?' he burst out when his interrogator stayed silent. 'This is Iran. Sepah has to be feared. I don't have a choice.'

'Did you know Reza Khalili?'

'How …' Golzar was stunned. 'How do you know him? Who are you?' he inched closer.

'*STAY BACK*!'

He retreated.

'Answer me!'

'I never met him,' he said, swallowing. 'Tousi handled him.'

'Did you order his parents killed?'

'That was Tousi. Are you Khalili's brother? Are you related?' He dreaded the answer, because if the man was, then he, Golzar, was dead.

'How's your relationship with the Supreme Leader?'

'It's good.'

He wants to expose me? He wants to kill me? He wants money? What does he want? The Sepah man stopped trying to work out what his blackmailer's intentions were.

'How often do you meet him?'

'Once a month, along with Tousi. But my boss meets him more often.'

'If anything happens to your boss, you'll be promoted?'

Golzar stared through the steam, trying to see the man. 'Yes. That's how it works in Iran.'

'You asked me what I wanted? I want Zarab Tousi.'

The Sepah licked his lips. He wasn't sure he had heard correctly.

'I don't know … what you mean.'

'It's simple. I want your boss. I want you to take his place. You'll help me do that.'

The Iranian rose, reaching out blindly to the wall for support.

'Sit down.' The stranger's voice was like a whiplash. He sat down automatically.

'What … How …' he stammered, lost for words, his mind a blank fog. 'What you're asking is impossible,' he said finally, when he had gathered his thoughts.

'As impossible as getting inside your house and finding out who you really are? As impossible as finding Khalili and stopping him?'

Golzar's heart nearly stopped. Tousi had told him everything about the assassin.

'Who are you?' he whispered.

'I am Zeb Carter,' the shadow moved. Steam parted and Golzar saw for the first time the man whom his boss hated with all his life.

Chapter 49

Golzar gaped. He recognized the American immediately. Sepah had a slim dossier on him, with a few photographs. They matched the man in front of him.

He knew how Carter had foiled his boss in Israel and in other missions. If Tousi were in his place, his boss would have launched himself at the man.

'How did you get here? You speak Persian? What do you mean by *replacing my boss*? What do you want from me?'

Words spilled out of his mouth. One part of his brain wondered if the American was going to kill him. Another part toyed with shouting, to draw the attention of his guards.

'I want to take out Tousi. I want to know his movements. His schedule. Everything about him—'

'I can't.'

'You know his schedule, don't you?'

'Yes.'

'What's the problem, then?'

Golzar's thoughts were scrambled. This wasn't what he had envisaged when he had arrived at the gym. To take Tousi's place? Yes, that had always been his ambition. But he knew it wouldn't happen as long as his boss was around.

But taking Tousi's place would mean …

'Yes, you'll be our man in Sepah. Just the way your boss infiltrated several Western agencies. And Mossad.'

Golzar paled. He knew the mission Carter was referring to.

'I can't pull that off.'

'You can, and will.' There was steel in the American's voice. 'I have read your file. You were a highly capable operative before you became management.'

'I will be betraying my country.'

'You betrayed your position by becoming a Christian. I want Tousi. Your state secrets … they'll be of interest only if you threaten my country or our allies. You can shape Sepah. Make it less brutal. Focus it on internal security and not external aggression. Isn't that what you want?'

Yes, that was what Golzar wanted. He didn't want IRGC to be the brutal, feared organization it currently was. He wanted to make it like America's FBI.

'How will this work?' he whispered.

'You don't need to know. Keep giving me intel on your boss's schedule—'

'I can't be implicated.' Fear gripped him suddenly.

'You won't be. Are you on board?'

Rostam Golzar had read about people's lives flashing in front of their eyes. He had scoffed at those accounts. But he experienced it now.

'I need time,' he whispered.

'I can't give you time.'

'I can't make a decision like this so quickly.'

'You can. You can change your life in a second. You can decide to continue to live your life, which is a lie, which goes against all your values, or you can do something about it.'

'If it fails …'

'I will protect you and your family.'

Golzar looked at the American. He stood steady, tall, as steam swirled around him. Zeb's exploits were legend. His boss hated him, but Tousi also had grudging respect for Carter.

Rostam Golzar made a decision in the gym. One that would change his life.

He nodded.

'Go,' Carter told him. No change of expression on his face. No delight, no joy, no shaking of hands. 'Call me on that number. I or my associates will answer. Bible verses will be passwords. You start off, we'll finish them. Use new ones every time you call.'

'You aren't alone?'

'No.'

The Sepah man nodded. He looked out at the gym. 'How did you get in here?'

'It's not important. You need to leave now. You have overstayed. Your guards might wonder.'

'And Golzar?'

He stopped.

'Don't think of double-crossing me.' Carter's voice was silky. 'You've seen what I have on you. If that's not enough, I have recorded this conversation.'

Rostam Golzar turned and looked at him. He looked in the American's eyes. 'You have read my file?'

'Yes.'

'Then you know I don't do betrayal. That's what Tousi does. Not me.'

The second time Zeb met him was a week later. It was evening. The Sepah man was at a government function in a fancy hotel in downtown Tehran.

Golzar was in the restroom, washing his hands at the sink when Zeb entered. Just the two of them.

The deputy boss wiped his face with a paper towel and threw it in a bin. He caught sight of the arrival and his eyes widened in surprise.

'Rezghi? You're here? Didn't you drive the boss away?'

'When one member suffers …'

'All the members suffer' the Iranian completed automatically. And then his jaw dropped. Shock flooded him.

'Carter?' he whispered. 'Is that you?'

'Anything on his schedule?' Zeb replied.

Golzar swallowed.

'This is how you'll pull it off?'

'Will it work?'

The Sepah man stepped back. He surveyed Zeb. 'You look just like him. You speak like him as well, with his southern accent. The way you hunch your shoulders …' he shook his head in admiration. 'Yes, you are his driver. No one will think otherwise. His schedule—'

The door opened. Two men in Sepah uniform entered, joking with each other. Zeb recognized them immediately. They were from Tousi's security detail. They shadowed him wherever he went. Elite soldiers.

He must have given them the evening off.

They stopped laughing when they saw Golzar. Saluted smartly at him. Nodded at Rezghi and proceeded to the urinals.

One man spun back on his heel, suddenly. 'Hassan? You got back so soon? I saw you ten minutes ago driving the boss.

Majid, didn't you see him?'

Zeb was facing the mirror, drying his hands with a towel. He met the soldier's eyes. Didn't say a word.

Majid turned around as well.

'Hassan! He asked you a question.'

Zeb straightened and tossed the towel in the bin. Golzar was to his right. The men were behind him, four feet away.

He made an almost imperceptible gesture with his hand at the Sepah deputy head, *stay where you are*, and hoped the man would understand.

'Abbas, call the boss!' the second soldier commanded. 'Something's wrong. Why is Hassan here? *YOU!*' he roared at the driver. '*ANSWER US*.'

His hand darted to his holstered gun. Abbas reached for his cell phone.

Zeb acted. A knife hand strike that slammed into the first soldier's throat, crushing his trachea. A choked scream escaped him. The second soldier leaped back. His gun rose.

'Hassan!' he yelled, 'What are you doing?'

Zeb grabbed Abbas by the waist and collar, twisted his body and sent him hurling toward Majid. The two men fell. A gun clattered to the floor. A shout burst from one of them.

'Get the door,' Zeb snapped at Golzar, and pounced on the fallen man.

An elbow to Abbas's throat. Finger jab to the eyes of Majid, who was pinned beneath his friend. Followed up with a brutal blow to his neck, destroying his windpipe.

The fight didn't last long, even though the Iranians were highly trained soldiers. Zeb had been prepared. He had controlled the attack, and two minutes later, two Sepah soldiers were dead on the restroom floor.

'You … killed them,' Golzar whispered, his face pale.

'I had no choice.'

Zeb went to the sink and washed his hands carefully. He watched the deputy head in the mirror, alert for any move.

No threatening move came. Golzar bent over the soldiers and felt for their pulses.

He looked up. Two windows high up.

He climbed onto the restroom's counter and peered out of one.

'Lawn,' he said to himself. 'No buildings. No roads nearby.'

'Wait here,' he told Zeb. 'Seal the door from inside.'

He went out and returned shortly with an *Out of Order* sign. He placed it on the outside of the restroom's door.

'You'll have to spend a few hours in the restroom. I'll return late in the night. We'll get their bodies and dispose them.'

Zeb nodded. *This is what I wanted to see. His reaction.*

He turned off the bathroom's lights and waited. It came easily to him. Waiting patiently was one of the first skills an operative learned.

Golzar returned at 3 am.

'My vehicle's just outside, on the road. This part of the hotel is empty. I have placed several *Do Not Enter* signs in the hallways. We won't encounter anyone.'

They grabbed one body and heaved it out of the window. The second body followed the first. They carried the bodies across the lawn and placed them in the back of the Iranian's vehicle.

Golzar slammed the door shut and wiped his palms on his jeans. He was dressed casually. A sweater on top, scarf around his neck, trainers on his feet.

'I'll take care of them—'

'How will you explain their disappearance?'

'They just disappeared. Deserters. It has been known to happen. Tousi will ask me to investigate. I will do so, thoroughly, and find nothing about them. Their names will go up on a list: *Arrest on sight*. That's how we treat deserters. Of course, we'll never find them.'

'Won't Tousi find it suspicious? These are his hand-picked men, aren't they?'

Golzar shrugged. 'He'll have to find the bodies to suspect anything. In Sepah we have ways of disposing them. Nothing of them will be found.'

'I'll come.'

'No. You don't need to know all our secrets.'

Zeb glanced at the hotel. 'You could be seen. There are cameras.'

'Their security system has had a sudden outage. Quite coincidental, don't you think?' Golzar's teeth flashed in the night. 'There are ways to enter the hotel. VIP entrances that the lay person does not know of. We do. Sepah knows everything about these fancy hotels and auditoriums.'

He looked at his watch. 'I'll get going.' He headed to the front of the vehicle. Stopped when a thought struck him.

'Carter?'

'Yeah?'

'This was a test, wasn't it? You wanted to see if I was committed.'

'What do you think?'

'Did you have to kill them?'

Zeb's grin faded.

'I have read Abbas's and Majid's files.'

'How do you have them?'

'That's not important. One man was a serial child molester. The other was a murderer. They got away with their crimes because they were Sepah soldiers and Tousi's bodyguards. You should know all this.'

'I do. They should have died a long time ago.'

Chapter 50

Four months in-country. Zeb's Rezghi disguise was as good as it would get. He impersonated the man carefully. It wouldn't do to repeat what had gone down in that hotel bathroom a few months ago. He couldn't risk anyone doing a double-take and asking, 'Weren't you driving the boss just now?'

He went to the driver's haunts just after Rezghi had left the establishments, so that the proprietors wouldn't think much of the driver returning.

No opportunity so far, he thought, as he sipped his tea. *Golzar's giving us Tousi's schedule, but there's no window in that*.

Laughter reached him. Four women at another table, their heads covered, bent over a phone. The chai khanch in Enghelab was one of the few in the city that allowed the other gender.

Zeb didn't look at the women. He knew who they were. Meghan and Beth, in their Vakili and Nassour disguises, and Carmen and Dalia, impersonating two other Iranian women soldiers. None was in uniform.

They met in restaurants, cafes or parks. Never in their

rooms. It wouldn't do for a man to go to their rooms. Not in Iran.

'He said he would come, didn't he?' Beth spoke in his headpiece.

'Yeah … there he is.'

A stir in the tearoom as Golzar arrived with his security detail. The proprietor scampered and escorted him to his usual table.

The Sepah man sat back and looked around arrogantly. He didn't blink when his eyes passed over Hassan Rezghi, sitting alone. Nor did he pause when he spotted the four women.

Over the course of the past months, as trust built, Zeb had introduced the four women to him. The Iranian had another jaw-dropping moment when the twins met him the second time in their soldier disguises.

'How did you know about them?' he asked Zeb in astonishment, referring to the women soldiers on the remote island.

Zeb hadn't replied. He hadn't mentioned that Carmen and Dalia were Mossad kidon, either. Rostam Golzar didn't need to know everything.

Golzar's tea service began. The other patrons drank theirs.

Forty-five minutes later, the Sepah deputy head rose. He didn't pay. No one from Sepah had to, in any establishment in the country.

He strode out without giving a second glance to those around him. In his position, everyone else was beneath him and had to be treated accordingly.

His hip bumped the women's table. Crockery crashed to the floor. He bent half-heartedly but Vakili, Beth, was faster. She apologized profusely, even though it wasn't her fault, and picked up the pieces. The proprietor rushed over, helped, and after bowing and scraping escorted Golzar out.

Calm returned to the tea house.

Beth wasn't calm when she spoke. Her voice shook with excitement.

'He slipped a note. Tousi's speaking at Tehran University in a week's time.'

'Yes,' Golzar spoke guardedly when Zeb called him over his burner phone. 'The main guest declined. Asked him to take over.'

They didn't use names, even though Zeb was using an encrypted line.

'Audience?'

'Students. About a thousand of them …' He hesitated. 'This could be it.'

'We'll need to see the place.'

'That …' the Iranian bit back his protest. By now he had realized how Zeb worked. 'Hassan Rezghi, the women soldiers, can't be seen there,' he said softly.

'We won't be going in those identities. I'm sure you can think of something.'

'Rostam, come to my office,' Tousi ordered his deputy over the phone.

'Sit.' He rocked back in his chair and held up a sheaf of papers.

Golzar sat.

'Listen to this.' And he launched into his speech.

Sepah's number two put on a suitably awed expression as his boss covered a multitude of topics. The might of Iran, harsh criticism of Western influences, insults aimed at President

Morgan and the USA—Tousi covered all bases.

'Agha, present your profile when you're attacking Morgan. It will go down very well with the media.'

The IRGC's head thought about it for a moment. He thrust his jaw out and presented his side-face to Golzar. 'Like that?'

'Exactly like that, agha. You look strong. Determined.'

Tousi didn't preen, but came close to it. 'How's my speech?'

'Fantastic, agha.' He looked around nervously as if the walls had ears and lowered his voice. 'Better than anything the Supreme Leader could have given,' he whispered.

'Rostam, you don't need to flatter me.'

'I am not, agha,' Golzar insisted. 'I have heard you address Sepah soldiers, and we both have heard many of our leader's speeches. I know the difference. I am sure this speech is just the start of many great things for you.'

'You think so?'

'Yes, agha. I have a feeling the Supreme Leader has been keeping an eye on you for some time. For bigger roles. I think he has grand plans for you. Why else would he ask you to take his place?'

'He's not happy with the Israel and G20 missions.'

'Pfft,' Golzar said scornfully. 'You have served our country for so long. You have destroyed many of our enemies' intelligence agencies. You have turned so many CIA operatives that the Americans fear you. What's a couple of losses? No, agha. I am confident the Supreme Leader wants you for bigger things.'

'I will serve him in whatever capacity he thinks fit,' Tousi said, trying to sound humble. 'Rostam, you will take over when I leave this agency. No one can do a better job than you.'

'I can't fill your shoes, agha.'

'You will be a great boss yourself, Rostam. Don't underestimate what you have achieved in Sepah.' The IRGC boss picked up his papers and started reading his speech. Cue for Golzar to leave.

'Rostam,' his boss stopped him.

'Yes, agha?'

'You're taking care of the university's security?'

'I am on it, agha. I'll be personally handling it.'

Zeb met with the twins and the Israeli kidon that evening. In Laleh Park, not far from the university. He buried his head in a Persian-language newspaper while the women gossiped. Or made a pretense of it.

'We have Tousi's schedule,' Beth told him over their encrypted comms channel. 'He will be arriving at 6:45 pm. He will be greeted by the chancellor, who will take him around the main building and introduce him to his key staff. Tousi will enter the auditorium at 7:15 pm. His address will commence at 7:20 pm. It will last for an hour—'

'An hour?'

'Yeah. Golzar has heard his speech. It looks like Tousi has a lot to say. He will leave for his office at 8:40 pm after the event.'

'He won't stay for dinner?'

'No. He is the Sepah boss. He has to be aloof.'

'Route?'

'He has a meeting with the Supreme Leader before the speech. He'll be taking Daneshgah Street, then Qods and Taleqani Street to get to the university. Armed guards, patrol vehicles on all those roads.'

'Rezghi will be with him?'

'Yes. He doesn't go anywhere without his bodyguard.'

Zeb thought. He looked across the green toward the university buildings. At the families playing in the park.

'There's only one place to grab him,' he said. 'At the university. After his speech.'

Chapter 51

It happened as they were leaving the park late in the evening. The sun set around 8 pm in the summer, and rainfall was rare.

However, that evening, rain clouds had gathered, darkening the city, and as they started crossing Keshavarz Boulevard, the first raindrops fell.

People burst into a run, heading to storefronts and awnings for shelter. The twins raced with the Israelis. Crossed the road and huddled together under a drooping canvas that was propped up by poles. Jewelry in a shop window behind them.

'Hurry up, slowpoke,' Beth chided Zeb in his headset, as the rain intensified.

He didn't. He was looking to his side, at two Sepah men. They were in uniform, a hundred feet away, at the junction with Qods Street. They were talking to a woman who was adjusting her head scarf. No one else near them, as tended to happen with IRGC soldiers. Most people gave them a wide berth.

He watched them for a moment, feeling the beat of the shower on his face.

He shrugged and moved on. He wasn't in his Rezghi

disguise. He didn't know how many soldiers knew of Zeb Carter and didn't want to find out.

He had taken two steps when he heard the distinctive sound of flesh on flesh. A wet sound. A slap.

He looked back.

One soldier had his hand raised, and even as he watched, struck the woman, who had fallen to her knees.

His inner beast exploded. No warning, no trigger. One moment he was heading to shelter. The next, cold, dark, killing rage had filled him.

He turned towards the soldiers.

'Zeb,' Beth warned. 'Leave them be. Come over.'

He ignored her. The street was in sharp focus. A car raced past on the boulevard, its lights on, spraying him with water. Shadows under shelter. People. A few watching the scene, most not.

He was close enough to hear the woman arguing. Crying in protest as blows rained on her. Words came to him in snatches.

Her headscarf had fallen away as she had run when the rain started. The soldiers had stopped her for that and had commenced slapping her when she had argued back.

She screamed when a blow struck her face. Lashed out with a leg, heaved to her feet and ran down Qods Street. A car swerved to avoid striking her. Tires squealed. A horn blared. The driver cursed.

The soldiers laughed. Broke into a jog, following her.

Zeb followed, hands loose at his sides, seeing nothing other than the Sepah men. Hearing nothing.

The street was darker, overshadowed by buildings on either side. The woman had slipped and fallen near a parked vehicle. The soldiers reached her.

One bent down and hauled her up by the arm. She shouted and beat at them with her hands. The other IRGC man slapped her. Yelled at her that she had broken the law.

'What law, you fools?' she shrieked. 'My scarf slipped in the rain.'

Slap!

The beast roared.

Zeb was fifteen feet away. He recognized them now. They were Tousi's men, part of his protection detail. They sat in the second vehicle that followed the Sepah boss around.

The woman's wide eyes fell on him. Didn't register his presence. They were full of fear and anger. Blood trickled from her burst lips.

Small details. The beard of one soldier who was holding the woman, thick hair matted with rain. The lips of the other twisted back in a sneer. Yellowing teeth. Rain dripping off the eaves of a roof, streams of water glinting in the light.

'Leave her.' His voice came out cold, flat.

Both men jerked and looked at him, astonished.

'Go away,' Sneer said contemptuously. 'This is a Sepah matter.'

'Leave her.'

'Do you know who we are, fool?' Beard shoved the woman towards Sneer and faced Zeb. 'We are Sepah. We'll—'

'I won't tell you again.'

The soldiers looked at each other and then at Zeb. Beard swore and lunged at him, his hand darting to the baton at his side.

Zeb went inside the blow. His left hand grabbed the incoming weapon, used its momentum to yank the soldier forward, knuckle-punched him in the throat, brought a knee up to groin-crush him, slammed his forehead to break his nose and shoved away the man, who was blacking out as he fell.

One man down in less than five seconds.

The second soldier watched in shock. And then reacted with a yell of rage. He thrust the woman away. Shouted in anger. Reached for his holstered weapon.

Zeb's Glock appeared in his hand as if it had a life of its own. His first shot blew a hole through the man's head. His second round punched him in the chest and sent him staggering backwards. He fell in an ungainly heap. His gun clattered to the ground. He stood motionless as the beast raged and roared inside. Growled and grunted and dissolved in his bloodstream.

He became conscious of the rain. Of drops running down his face. The woman on her hands and knees, her mouth wide open, aghast, fearful.

He holstered his gun, conscious of her eyes. He checked the first soldier. He wasn't unconscious. He was dead. Zeb's blow to his throat had finished him. Sneer was beyond living, too.

'Do you need help?' He looked at her finally, not moving towards her, not wishing to scare her anymore.

She scrambled to her feet, wiped her lips with her sleeve and choked back a sob. She didn't look at the fallen men.

'I don't know why they picked on me. My scarf fell off. I told them. I didn't remove it. They didn't listen …' she buried her face in her hands and burst into tears.

'Zeb!'

He cupped a hand to his ear. No, not in his headset. Voices behind him.

Beth, sprinting toward him. Meghan, Carmen and Dalia,

behind her. They slowed to a stop. Took in the scene at once.

'We have to get away.' The younger twin grabbed his sleeve. 'Are you okay?' she asked the woman who had raised her head on their arrival.

'I … yes,' the Iranian nodded, replying unconsciously.

Beth tugged at Zeb again, urgently.

'Let's go,' Meghan hissed.

Zeb didn't move.

'If the police ask you, tell them what happened. That a strange man killed these men,' he told the woman.

'I didn't see anything, agha.' She straightened, her dark eyes taking him and his companions in, blood a dark smudge at the side of her mouth. Her hands moved and set her scarf on her head. 'I don't know how they died. I wasn't here.'

'I should have acted sooner. The moment they hit you.'

'Agha … go, please. They are right. You shouldn't be here.'

'I should have—'

'Agha, I don't know who you are. Who these women with you are. Those men could have raped me if you hadn't been here. It has happened. No one questions what Sepah does. But you have to leave, now.'

'What about you?'

'I'll go back to my life. And every day, I'll say prayers for the man who came to my rescue.'

Zeb didn't resist this time, when Beth dragged him away. He followed the twins, and when they were almost at the end of the alley, the woman shouted.

'Mam'nooman.'

Thank you.

Beth took them through twists and turns, away from the

scene of the fight. She looked once at him, saw the set expression on his face, and kept quiet. She waited until he was back in his hotel and then joined her sister in Meghan's room. Carmen and Dalia were there, silent, as the elder twin made a call.

'Rostam, there are two Sepah soldiers on Qods Street. Dead. You'll need to recover their bodies and make them disappear. There's no time. You'll have to go right now.' She explained quickly what had gone down, hung up and breathed deeply.

'How is he?'

'In his shell,' Beth replied.

No one spoke. No one moved.

Dalia flopped on Meghan's bed finally and brushed her wet hair back. 'What happened back there? He put the mission in danger.'

Beth wiped her face. Didn't answer.

'Beth? Meghan?' Carmen's face was hard. 'Dalia asked a question.'

'It was a trigger reaction, I think,' Meghan said, tiredly.

'Reaction to what?'

'Zeb and his family were captured and tortured not far from that street. His wife and child were killed. In front of him.'

Chapter 52

Zeb stood outside the women's hotel the next day.

He had made a call the previous night and had found that Golzar had disposed of the bodies.

'At this rate, you'll wipe out Tousi's security detail,' the Iranian had joked.

'I put you, everyone, at risk.'

'Yes. But we were lucky. No one found out what happened. I got there, alone, and recovered the bodies.'

'Thank you.'

'Zeb …' there was something in the Iranian's voice. 'Those two, Sohail and Nozar. They, too, were violent, brutal men.'

'Yeah,' Zeb said noncommittally. *I screwed up. Doesn't matter how bad they were.*

You saved her from them.

Yeah, but what if other soldiers had entered that street? What if the bodies had been discovered by cops? I let blind rage get the better of me. I let my control slip. Let the past take hold of me.

He drew a deep breath. Closed his eyes momentarily and went to the white space in his mind. A wall of filing cabinets, each indistinguishable from the other, all of them storing individual memories.

That night, all those years back ... it's there somewhere.

He rarely recalled those events. The past was behind. What lay ahead was the future.

I died when they did. Remembering does not make any difference.

He opened his eyes and he was back in Tehran, awaiting the women.

Who didn't turn up. Men drifted out of their hotel. Soldiers in uniform. Families. Teenagers. Other women. But no Beth or Meghan or Carmen or Dalia.

Someone tapped him on his shoulder.

He spun around.

A soldier in Sepah uniform, three others with him. Stern-faced. Glaring at him.

Until a smile cracked his face and he spoke in Beth's voice. 'Told you he wouldn't recognize us.'

Beth? That's Meghan and the Mossad agents?

Of course! Golzar must have provided them with the identities, to check out the university. Those are great disguises.

'I am sorry,' he said immediately.

Beth's grin faded. She looked searchingly at him.

'How are you?'

That's why she and Meg are in the Agency. Lesser people would have criticized him. But not them. *I haven't told them what happened to my family, though they know from the others. They haven't ever asked. They won't, even now. I nearly jeopardized our operation yesterday, and all she asks is how I am.*

'I am sorry,' he repeated, ignoring her question, and got

a sun-blinding smile in return, along with a dismissive wave of her hand.

The matter wasn't to be discussed any further. She was like that. Meghan, too.

He turned to Carmen. He could now detect the Israeli's features under the disguise, and got a wink from her.

Yesterday was a closed chapter for them, too.

Meghan handed him a bag. 'Your uniform and credentials are in it. Change in the hotel's restroom. We'll be waiting here.'

Colonel Farrokh Mozafari, Zeb, showed up at a side entrance of the university. Beth, his driver, sprang out of the vehicle and held the door open for him.

"This is the last time I do this for you," she whispered, her lips barely moving.

Zeb didn't acknowledge her. He climbed the short flight of stairs and shook hands with the officer waiting there. Lieutenant Colonel Javad Kianian, the man responsible for getting the university ready for the event.

'I haven't seen you before, agha. Or heard of you.'

'Good,' Zeb barked. 'I and my team,' he jerked a shoulder in the direction of his four soldiers, 'work in an elite group. We report directly to Brigadier General Rostam Golzar. You know why we are here?'

'To check progress?'

'Yes. Do you know who we are?'

Kianian swallowed. His eyes fell away from the name plate on Zeb's chest. 'I understand, agha. You and your men never visited. A secret, surprise inspection. If I may say—'

'Yes.'

'It might be better if you remove your nameplates. That way no one will remember who you are.'

Zeb looked at him gravely and then nodded. 'Good idea. The Brigadier General did say you are one of the smarter officers. I can see why he said that.'

Kianian squared his shoulders and puffed out his chest as the visitors pocketed their credentials and followed him.

'Agha,' he took them down a hallway where activity bustled. Workers put up Tousi's posters, carpets were laid. Flower vases were placed on pedestals. Armed soldiers stood at regular intervals, saluting as they passed. 'This area,' he waved a hand at their surroundings, 'is cut off from the university. No one is allowed to enter as we work. Everyone here is vetted.'

'Here—' he pushed open double doors and pointed to a concrete drive. 'This is where the Brigadier General will arrive. Only three vehicles will be allowed here. His vehicle and that of his two security teams. It is at the back of the university and usually used by the chancellor and senior staff.'

Zeb inspected the drive. It was a dead-end, with spaces for vehicles to park.

'It is ideal, agha, which is why we chose it. The university's senior staff park there.' Kianian pointed at bays fifty feet away.

He pointed to the ceiling on their way back. 'Cameras. And the control room—' As he pushed against the wall in the corridor, a concealed door opened. '—is here.' He waved grandly at the array of consoles and uniformed men in front of them.

Zeb took in the scene. Security camera images flickered on screens, covering the drive, the hallway, the theater, the front of the university.

'We'll have snipers on rooftops, strike teams in the university … it will be the safest place in Tehran on that day,' Kianian said proudly as he led them away.

'Golzar said he'll delete our presence from the feeds,' Meghan piped in his flesh-colored earpiece.

Zeb nodded imperceptibly. He followed the Sepah officer, to the left and across a barricaded hall.

The Iranian pointed to a set of glass doors. 'The students will enter through those. They will be security-checked. Body scanners. No bags allowed. Only those who have registered will be let through. They won't be allowed to go to any other part of the venue, except the auditorium.'

He pushed through another pair of doors just opposite the entrance, and they were in the theater. A side entrance.

Rows of cushioned seats. The stage to their right, a hundred feet away. More soldiers and workers. Photographs of Tousi going up on the walls.

The elevated dais had curtains at the back and the sides.

'We'll check for explosives; we'll have sniffer dogs,' the Iranian continued his commentary as he narrated the security arrangements. He led them down the central passage between the rows and approached the dais. A passage stretched in front of it, going to each end of the venue.

'There are doors there, and normally they would be open for entry. For this event, they will be sealed shut.'

'How many will be attending the speech?'

'One thousand, agha. All of them undergrad and post-grad students. They have already registered and we have profiled them. No security threat there. We are not taking any more registrations. The chancellor and the vice chancellor will be on stage with the Brigadier General.'

Zeb's eyes lingered on the curtains. 'Who else will be on stage?'

'Hassan Rezghi, three or four soldiers from his security team. The chancellor and vice-chancellor. No one else.'

They climbed the stage and faced the empty chairs.

'Here.' the Iranian parted a side curtain, walked them down a passage, and opened another concealed door. 'This is an emergency exit,' he said proudly.

Zeb looked around. They were in the hallway they had inspected moments earlier. The exit to the drive was less than fifteen feet away, to their right.

'This will save us a lot of time in case we need to leave quickly. It is how the boss will enter the auditorium.'

'Good planning,' Zeb said approvingly. He tapped the wall. Behind it was the control room.

'Yes, agha. That secret passage runs along its side.'

'Did the university already have these hidden doors and passages?' Beth asked gruffly, the hard-boiled sweet in her mouth helping to disguise her voice.

'No. We partitioned a lecture room to make room for that emergency exit and built those doors. We—'

His cell phone buzzed. He answered it. Straightened unconsciously and nodded. 'Yes, agha. I'm coming.'

'I have to go,' he pocketed his phone. 'The boss is here. Major General Tousi.'

Chapter 53

'Rostam,' Tousi snarled as he entered the university. 'Where are Sohail and Nozar? I usually have ten men with me all the time, and now I have only six. You haven't found what happened to Abbas and Majid, and now two more soldiers have disappeared. What's happening?'

Golzar, a step behind his boss, looked around discreetly.

The Sepah head had surprised him half an hour earlier. He had barged into his deputy's office and said they needed to inspect the university. The number two said he had it under control. Tousi didn't listen and got Golzar to join him.

'Abbas and Majid are nowhere to be found, agha,' he replied. Where was Carter? If Tousi saw the American in his Mozafari disguise … he suppressed a shiver. 'We investigated thoroughly. They aren't in their villages. They definitely aren't in the city. It's as if they have disappeared from the face of the earth. It's a similar story with Sohail and Nozar.'

'I know all that.' Tousi looked back and glared at him. 'My question is, where are they? I feel naked with just six soldiers around me.'

Golzar breathed a sigh of relief when they entered the auditorium. No Carter. No women. No Kianian, either. Soldiers saluted them smartly and answered questions.

'Those six are the best we have, agha,' the deputy answered his boss's question when they exited the theater. He raised his voice. *Hopefully Carter will hear and get out of our way.* 'And don't forget, you have Rezghi as well. He's always at your side. In the meanwhile, I am interviewing other men. We need the right soldiers to protect you, agha. I don't want them to disappear the way those fools did.'

'I want them thrown in prison, when they are found. All four will die. After I have interrogated them.'

'Yes, agha.'

Golzar went inside the control room, checked it out swiftly and then made way for his superior. 'Everything's ready for your speech, agha. Not even a fly can enter the university. Not without our permission.'

Tousi grunted, questioned several soldiers who were seated in front of their monitors, nodded in satisfaction at their answers, and swept out as arrogantly as he had entered.

Golzar took him down the hallway and was opening the doors to the driveway when he sensed movement down the corridor. He stiffened when he saw five figures cross the width of the passage and go in the direction of the theater.

Kianian, Carter and his companions.

His boss sensed his gaze. Was turning to look when inspiration struck Golzar.

'Agha, you know there will be many female students at your speech. I have an idea.'

'What's it?' Tousi looked at him.

'You know our reputation. That we are brutal. Violent.'

'We have to be to control this country, Rostam. You know that.'

'I do, agha. But these students, they want to change the world. You know how they are. They watch American and British TV. They think our culture needs to change.'

'They are young. What do they know?'

'I agree, agha. But perhaps there's a way we can get them on our side.'

'How?'

'Get four of our women soldiers to the speech. Let them take the place of those missing men. Let them be on stage with you. The impact that will make …' he trailed off when Tousi held up his hand.

'No one knows about them, Rostam,' he said thoughtfully.

Golzar breathed out a sigh of relief. *He hasn't rejected the idea.*

'Armed women protecting you, hardened soldiers—think of the optics, agha. The students will love you. That sight, along with your great speech, it will bring the house down.'

Tousi stood taller. 'Do it, Rostam.' He clapped his deputy on the shoulder. 'It's a brilliant idea.'

'Thank you, agha,' Golzar bobbed his head modestly. 'I know just the right women to accompany you.'

Chapter 54

‘This way,’ Zeb commanded Kianian, the moment he heard Golzar’s voice in the distance. He went inside the emergency passage, the women and the Iranian behind him. ‘I want to check this out again.’

‘But … our boss,’ the lieutenant colonel stammered. ‘Don’t you want to meet him?’

Zeb turned sharply on his heel and drilled the Sepah man with a cold stare. ‘The purpose of this surprise *inspection* is to see the readiness of the site and your people. Rushing to meet the boss is *not* preparedness.’

The Iranian flushed and nodded jerkily. ‘I apologize, agha. I wasn’t thinking. Let’s carry on.’

‘The boss also doesn’t need to know we were here. He doesn’t like it when a surprise inspection no longer is a surprise.’

‘I get it, agha,’ Kianian swallowed. All thoughts of a rapid promotion seemed to be disappearing in front of his eyes.

Zeb turned his back contemptuously on the IRGC man. Caught a fleeting look at Beth, who was staring stonily ahead. Her lips … she was biting down a smile.

He listened carefully as they moved ahead. *Smart of Golzar to warn us with his voice.*

They reached the dais. He went through the motions of checking the curtains, fingered them. Looked up at the walls, patted a sniffer dog and then nodded approvingly.

'Everything seems to be in order.'

Kianian's shoulders slumped in relief momentarily before he straightened again.

'Your men. Where do they stay?'

'Here, agha. On site. No one will leave until the event is over. We sleep in these seats. We use the university bathrooms to freshen up.'

'Show me those.'

There were two large restrooms to the left of the theater's side entrance, just off the glass doors in the front. A bank of urinals and stalls in the men's and a longer line of stalls for women.

'They will be checked, too. We will have security men standing outside.'

'What if the boss needs to go to the bathroom?'

The Iranian took them back to the theater, onto the stage, and parted the curtains. A small hallway that dead-ended to a small bathroom. Two stalls and a sink. 'This is for VIPs only. Only the boss will use this.'

'You have thought of everything,' Zeb praised him. 'I will submit my report to Brigadier General Golzar. I am sure he'll be happy with you.'

'Thank you, agha.'

He took them back to where their vehicles were parked. There was a moment when they crossed the hallway, at the far end of which were Golzar and Tousi. The men were facing each other, loud voices reaching them.

Zeb felt the sisters tense behind him, and then they were through.

They shook hands with the Sepah man, climbed into their vehicles and made a swift getaway.

'That was close,' Carmel sighed. 'For a moment, I thought we would have to shoot it out.'

'You got any ideas?' Beth glanced at Zeb as she weaved in and out of traffic.

'Some.' He turned to the Israelis. 'We need to talk to your boss.'

They met in Azadi Square in the western part of the city, where throngs of tourists surrounded the soaring Azadi Tower at its center.

Neither Zeb nor the women were interested in climbing the monument. He sprawled on the grass and closed his eyes, the picture of a man enjoying the evening sun, while the women sat a distance away and brought out a pack of playing cards.

Beth did her thing with electronics and patched Avichai Levin and Broker in on a conference call. Encrypted channel with voice distortion. Despite that, they spoke carefully and didn't use names.

'You've got friends here?' Zeb asked the Mossad director.

Friends was code for sayanim.

'A few,' Levin replied cautiously. 'What are you thinking of?'

Zeb ignored him. 'You've got birds?'

Broker answered, knowing the question was directed at him. 'Several,' he drawled. 'Tell me when and I'll be ready.'

The agency could commandeer any government satellite,

but those weren't the ones Zeb was interested in.

Several billionaires owed them as a result of either Agency missions or their security consulting operations. Many of those enormously wealthy friends had their own telecoms infrastructure. They readily gave access to their birds. They didn't ask questions. They didn't balk. What Zeb and his team had done for them was beyond repayment.

'A vehicle that our friends travel in?' This was aimed at Levin.

He thought for a moment. *Friends? Which ones was Zeb referring to?* 'Your bestie?'

'Yeah, and his friends.'

Sepah!

'Yes, that's no problem. What's on your mind?'

'You know what our American friend was trying?'

Meghan looked up sharply.

Khalili? she mouthed.

Zeb nodded.

Burn the place? she mouthed.

Zeb nodded.

They would use Reza Khalili's idea.

Chapter 55

Zeb and his team spent the remaining five days ironing out kinks in their plan.

First, they tackled how they would start the fire.

Levin helped with that. He directed them to a reputed firm in Amir Abad, a Tehran district, that provided interior furnishings to the wealthy, many of whom were in government.

Morsad Arik, its owner, was bald, had a paunch and peered through thick-lensed glasses when the twins and the Israeli agents entered.

'We have a mutual friend in Israel,' Carmen told him in Hebrew. 'Call him, verify who we are.' She rang the Mossad director on her cell and gave it to the proprietor. He took it and spoke for several minutes, his eyes never leaving their faces, then hung up.

'What do you want?'

'A curtain. Floor to ceiling, this shade, this feel,' she produced a snip of fabric that Golzar had provided. She gave him the size.

Arik fingered it. 'What's so special about it? You can get this anywhere.'

'It has to be made of flammable material. Highly flammable.'

The owner looked up once, but no expression crossed his face. 'When?'

'Tomorrow?'

'Three days, not before then.'

Carmen calculated mentally. No, that wouldn't work. That would be too close to the event. It wouldn't give them enough time to install it.

'You'll get a bonus if you do it quicker.'

'It can't be done before then.'

'You know there's a reason if the ramsad is involved.'

'There always is. But that size of curtain, in the kind of fabric you want, cannot be made faster. There's no way.'

Carmen sighed. She looked at Dalia, who shrugged.

'Can you install it?' Meghan asked him in the same language.

'Where?'

'The university.'

Arik stared at her for several moments, then at the other women. He glanced once at Carmen's phone, which was on the glass counter between them.

'How will my people get in?'

'We'll arrange that.'

'I don't want them to be suspected.'

'They won't be.'

'You can guarantee that?'

'No.'

The proprietor fingered the snip of cloth, bowed his head and thought.

'It will be ready in two days,' he said. 'How can I reach you?'

Carmen gave him her burner phone's number.

'We need to test it. If you make a separate sample, we want to see it burn.'

Arik didn't blink. It was as if this were a routine request from his customers.

'Come tomorrow. I'll have something ready for you.'

'Why are you doing this?' Beth asked him as they were leaving.

'If I don't, who will?'

'He must have made the connection to Tousi's speech,' she told the Israeli agents when they left the curtain store. 'He must have suspected something when we asked him about flammable. But he didn't say anything.'

'The sayanim don't,' Dalia explained. 'It's why Mossad is so successful. If they can help, they will. No questions asked.'

'Don't they fear for themselves?'

'That's our responsibility. We take all precautions to minimize risk for them.'

They took a chai break while they ran down their shopping list. Zeb wasn't with them. He was going over the route Tousi would take to the university, looking for blind spots where pieces of their plan would be executed.

'You've got it easy, hotshot,' Beth jibed.

'You got the curtain?'

'We've placed the order. What are you doing?'

'Lying on my belly, beneath a broken-down truck, watching Qods Street. Oil's dripping on my back, a dog's sniffing my legs.'

'I feel for you,' she replied unsympathetically and hung up.

'A dog thinks he's a lamppost,' she told the others when Meghan raised an eyebrow. 'What's next?'

'The Sepah vehicle.' Dalia munched on a biscuit and drank her beverage. 'The ramsad's arranged for us to meet Yehuda Malbim. He runs a garage in Nazi Abad. It's in the south of the city—' She broke off when Carmen and the twins rose.

'I haven't finished,' she protested.

'There will be enough time for chai, later,' Carmen growled and strode out of the establishment.

Malbim's garage was in an alley that was crowded with vehicles in various states of repair. It was a dead-end street, and his was the only establishment on it.

Inside, there were several cars on raised lifts, men in blue coveralls working on them. More workers outside, sounds of clanking and hammering and yelling and whistling around them.

No one paid any attention when they arrived.

'Because we're women? We should be ignored?' Meghan's lips curled contemptuously.

She marched inside, brushed past a worker, who looked up in astonishment, and knocked on the window of an office.

A man was on the phone, speaking loudly. He turned around. Cocked an eyebrow, spoke hastily and hung up. He opened the door and looked at her and her companions.

'Come in,' he said brusquely, and held the door open.

'Call our friend,' Carmen began.

'I am Malbim. There's no need for that. He described you well.' The proprietor wiped his hands on a dirty towel, drank water from a bottle and capped it.

'You want a particular vehicle?'

'Yes. It should be—'

'I know what you want. He was specific. Come with me.'

He took them outside his office, along the wall, to the far end, where the garage branched out to a quieter, darker area. He turned on lights and revealed several vehicles that were covered by tarps.

He uncovered the nearest one and waited for the women to stop coughing when dust flew. 'Mercedes GL Class SUV,' he said proudly, as he walked around the black-painted vehicle. 'Bulletproof windows, run-flat tires, souped-up engine,' he ran through its features. 'You can't distinguish it from a real Sepah vehicle.'

Meghan surveyed it, hands on her hips. With the grille covering the windshield and side windows, the light bar on top, it did look like one of the rides Tousi's men went around in.

'What do you do with this?'

'I rent it out for movies. I have more.' He pointed to the other covered vehicles. 'Army trucks, Jeeps, I can provide them all. Sometimes, even the police rent from me,' he snorted in amusement, 'when they need vehicles for VIPs.'

Dalia held out her palm. He tossed her a bunch of keys. She grabbed it, slid into the driver's seat and started the vehicle.

It growled satisfyingly. *Fuel gauge is full*, she noted. *Tire pressure's good. Looks like he prepared it for us.*

'What do you think?' She huddled with her partner and the sisters.

'It'll do,' Carmen replied. 'It only needs to pass visual inspection, which it does. Golzar will provide us with license plates.'

'We'll take it,' Meghan told Malbim. 'In two days. Make sure it's here.'

'It will be.'

'You don't want to know why we need it?'

The garage owner smirked. 'No. This isn't the first time I have helped our mutual friend.'

'Your men … they'll have seen us come. Four women in a garage. They'll talk.'

'They won't. You noticed not one man looked up? They all know what we sometimes do. They were ignoring you deliberately. For your safety and theirs.'

'You trust our friend that much? That even your workers help?'

'With my life.'

'There's something else.'

'What?'

'You or your men, whoever it is we don't care, need to set off fireworks.'

'Fireworks?' Malbim was dumbfounded.

'Yes,' she explained, prepared for questions.

None came.

'We'll do it,' the owner replied simply.

'Wait for our call. Set them off only then.'

'Yes.'

Meghan was silent on their way back to central Tehran. She was thinking about Malbim and Arik. Of their helping without any expectation of reward. Just because they were sayanim. She thought of Avichai Levin and his friendship with Zeb. *Without him and Golzar, our mission would be a non-starter*.

'What's next?' she asked when they reached Laleh Park.

Dalia threw herself to the grass and glanced at her watch. 'At 7 pm we have an appointment with Senen Kalish.'

'Who's he, and, where is he?'

'He runs a vehicle dealership in Niavaran.'
That's in the north. 'What do we need from him?'
'Two bikes and a fuel tanker.'

Chapter 56

Kalish was in his fifties, dressed in a suit. He shook hands with them when they arrived and spoke in monosyllables and grunts.

'Two motorbikes as ordered. In police colors.' He pointed to the vehicles.

BMWs, Meghan thought, as she knelt beside one and felt it. *K 1200, one of the fastest bikes available.* They weren't standard issue for NAJA, Iran's police. *They are getaway rides, which is what we need. Golzar will provide number plates for them, too.*

'Who will be riding them?' the dealer asked.

Meghan looked at Beth and suppressed a grin when she saw the longing on her sister's face. *Who wouldn't want to ride these beauties?*

'Those two,' she said, pointing at the kidon who were inspecting the vehicles.

'You want a test drive?' he asked Carmen.

'Yes.'

'You can't go dressed like that,' he frowned.

'We'll come back tomorrow evening.'

'The fuel truck?'

'At the back.'

The truck was painted white and carried the logo of a local chemical company. Hazard signs were painted on its back and sides. Beth tapped it with her knuckles. It sounded hollow.

'It's—'

'It will be filled,' Kalish assured her, 'with a highly explosive chemical. That's what you want, don't you?'

'Yes.'

'Who will be driving it? It can be heavy. It needs some expertise.'

'We'll send the driver tomorrow. Will it be topped up by then?'

'Yes.'

'You are aware, these bikes and the tanker, they won't return intact.'

'Yes, our friend told me. For him, I'll burn down my dealership.'

'That's how we work.' Dalia smirked when she saw the sisters' bemused expressions.

'We know,' Beth replied crossly, as she seated herself in the taxi they flagged outside the dealership. 'All this,' she said, looking at Kalish's establishment. 'Your boss has more reasons to gloat now. How great Mossad is, and all that.'

'It is. There's nothing we can't do.'

'Don't start,' both twins groaned in unison.

Zeb was watching Rezghi as the women were returning from the dealership. Earlier, he had picked a few blind spots, but he wanted the Israeli women to check them out, too. *They'll be the ones at those spots.*

Tousi's man was parked outside his superior's office, which was walled. A security barrier manned by personnel restricted access to it. It was one of those gates where a steel beam ran from the guard's hut at one end of the wall to a harness at the other end. It lifted to allow vehicles to enter or depart. A side entrance by the hut allowed pedestrians to move in and out of the office.

Zeb was slumped in a cab, a cap pulled low over his head. The taxi's driver had been delighted to receive a wad of bills from him for its use and had made himself scarce.

Zeb watched the Sepah man in the distance. He had an idea of the man's routine by now. Before a lengthy engagement, the driver crawled beneath the vehicle and inspected it. He then paid a visit to the bathroom. Finally, he came outside the office complex and walked around, presumably to breathe some fresh air.

He then crossed the road to a street vendor and ordered a chai. The roadside stall didn't get many customers, and those few who patronized it were from Tousi's office. Zeb figured the chai seller made his money by inflating his prices.

Rezghi paid the man, drank from his cup and gave it back when it was empty. He stretched and walked a few paces towards the cab, turned his back to the road, unzipped and relieved himself.

That, too, was routine.

He sometimes chatted with the guards on his return, but more often, he didn't. He brushed past them and waited by his vehicle to drive Tousi to his destination.

Zeb didn't move a muscle. He hadn't twitched when the bodyguard had peed by the side of the street, close to his cab.

That tea vendor ... no one looks at him. He's insignificant to

Sepah. None of the guards watched Rezghi drink his beverage.

Seven minutes at the stall. That includes his toilet break.

Zeb had his window.

Zeb joined the women the next day as they visited Morsad Arik. The curtain seller's eyes flicked over him, but he didn't say a word as he took them deeper into his store, to the back, where a large cutting room was situated.

He had cleared a big space in its center, and on the floor was a drape of cloth. The sisters knelt over it and compared the fabric to the sample they had. It was a match. Dalia bent, too, and fingered it.

'It looks good,' she said. She searched, nodded a thanks when Carmen handed her a pair of scissors. The kidon cut the sample in half, picked up one piece, left the other on the floor and looked at Beth.

'You do the honors.'

The younger twin reached into her pocket and drew out a box of matches. She lit one and dropped it on the sample.

It *whooshed* into flame and burned brightly.

'Wow,' she breathed. 'That's silk?'

'Yes,' Kalish nodded. 'I used some dyes and additives to get it to burn faster. An electrical spark will be enough to set it alight.'

Zeb looked on as the fabric burned. 'That other piece?' he asked the women.

'We'll get it to Gol—' Carmen bit her lip. 'To our friend. He'll compare in person and let us know.'

At 6 pm, Carmen and Dalia went for a ride. They were dressed in dark leather, their hair tucked beneath their full-face helmets.

They carried licenses with them that identified them as men. Getting stopped by the police wasn't an option.

They rode out of Kalish's showroom, out of Niavaran, down to central Tehran and then to Azarbayjan Street, onto Farvardin Street, then Pasteur Street, circling the Supreme Leader's residence before taking the route to the university.

The in-line four-cylinder engines purred as they streaked past buses, cars and other two-wheeled vehicles. Tehran's traffic slowed them, but the kidon didn't accelerate needlessly.

They slowed when they arrived at the blind spots Zeb had identified. Sped up again, and when they reached the university, idled in a parking lot.

Carmen looked around cautiously. No one was watching them. From their previous recon, she knew there were no cameras. She removed her helmet and grinned at Dalia.

'Let her rip?'

'Carefully,' her partner agreed.

They throttled, loving the sound of German engineering at its finest, and then sped out of the lot. Both were trained in high-speed driving. That experience showed as they tunneled through slower-moving traffic, often brushing past the sides of buses and trucks with scant inches to spare. The trick with urban driving at that pace was to let the eyes blinker out everything except what lay ahead. And get a *feel* for the traffic. The way it breathed, moved, and sensed incoming vehicles.

'Police,' Dalia warned suddenly, spotting flashing lights far ahead. She cut her speed and took a left on Azin Alley, idling at the first blind spot Zeb had identified. Carmen joined her, and the two inspected the place.

Right on the junction was a dilapidated building half-demolished by a wrecking team, which left behind a few standing walls and lots of rubble.

A vehicle could be concealed in it, hidden from traffic on the main street. The alley itself had few vehicles passing through.

'This is a possibility,' Carmen grunted as she revved. 'Let's check the next one.'

They emerged cautiously, found no cops, and merged into traffic. They cut another left, this time on Nazari Street.

There, right on the junction with Daneshgah Street, was an overturned truck, its belly exposed for all to see, rusted metal and worn tires presenting themselves.

'This one is better,' Carmen said in satisfaction.

'Why?' Dalia asked.

'Look behind you.'

The second kidon turned and saw a hospital sign in the distance.

'There will be traffic on this street, to and from that hospital. No one will think much of a vehicle parked behind this truck. Especially one with Sepah markings.'

Dalia mulled it over and then nodded. 'Makes sense.' Her eyes brightened. 'Shall we surprise our friends?'

Zeb and the sisters got a surprise when they met the Israelis in Kalish's garage that night.

'I thought you were going to bring a sayanim. Someone who would drive the fuel tanker,' Beth said accusingly when the kidon arrived.

'We brought someone better.' Carmen whistled sharply.

A man emerged from the darkness. Lean, wiry, sporting a broad smile. He high-fived the Israeli women and chuckled when he saw the Americans' expressions.

'The boss,' Adir, a Mossad agent whom Zeb and the twins knew well, 'says there's nowhere that Mossad can't reach.'

'Yeah,' Zeb said in disgust. He hugged the operative and smiled in satisfaction. A kidon as the driver was a much better solution than a sayanim. 'He would say that.'

Golzar went to the university at 10 pm. He was in full uniform, and when he climbed out of his vehicle, soldiers sprang to attention.

'How're the preparations coming along?'

Lieutenant Colonel Javad Kianian ran down the steps and saluted him. 'They are coming along well, agha. Something wrong?'

'Why would it be?'

'It's late, agha,' Kianian said uneasily.

'That's the best time to conduct an inspection.'

'Of course, agha.'

He took the deputy head inside the building and walked him around. Golzar listened to him for several minutes and then cut him off with an imperious wave.

'I want to see everything for myself. I don't need to be escorted.'

'Of course, agha,' Kianian nodded and made himself scarce.

Golzar went to the control room and nodded in approval at the heads peering at screens. He waved the soldiers down when they attempted to stand and salute him.

He went to the private drive and made a show of looking around. He then went to the theater through the emergency passage. Soldiers were sprawled in chairs, snoring. Some workers were still on the stage, putting in the finishing touches. Adjusting the seats, cleaning the stage, checking the audio equipment.

He went to the dais and surveyed the auditorium. It was impressive. He went to a side curtain and casually felt it. Discreetly, he brought out Arik's sample and compared it.

It was a perfect match, visually.

He pocketed the piece, looked around carefully to see no one was watching, then brought out a knife and ripped the hanging curtain.

'Kianian,' he shouted angrily after heading outside. 'Come, see this,' he told the officer who approached at a trot.

'See,' he showed the tear. 'Some careless fool tore the curtain.' He swore and raged and saw that the colonel had turned pale.

'I'll find who was responsible,' the officer moistened his lips. 'I'll have him whipped.'

'You aren't listening,' Golzar raged. 'That won't help. We need to replace the curtain.'

'Replace, agha? Surely we can have it stitched.'

The Sepah man drew himself to his full height. 'Our boss is presenting for the first time at the university. Our image is at stake. You want him to stand amidst stitched curtains?'

'No … agha,' Kianian stammered.

'I'll personally supervise the fitting.'

'But agha, will we find a replacement so quickly?'

'We are Sepah. Don't forget that,' Golzar reminded him coldly. 'When we say jump, every Iranian says how high.'

He marched back to his vehicle and climbed into it.

When he was alone, he brought out his burner phone and made a call.

'Stage is set for replacement,' he told Meghan.

Chapter 57

Broker was watching a screen in their Columbus Avenue office while Zeb was watching Rezghi.

He had made a few calls and gotten what he wanted. Exclusive use of eyes in the sky. A geo-mapping cluster of satellites that collected data on weather and climate change markers, and passed on that information to various research organizations funded by one of their billionaire friends.

These birds had more punch than standard weather-mapping satellites. They were keyhole-class military birds. They had charged coupled devices, CCDs, to gather images and transmit them back to Earth from their perch two hundred miles in the sky.

The billionaire had outfitted them with the best imaging and mapping technology in existence, just because he could. He hadn't asked any awkward questions when Broker called.

'You want it? You got it,' was his standard response whenever Broker, Zeb or any of the warriors approached him. The Agency had rescued his family from a hostage situation in Africa. It had saved his own life from a Mexican cartel. Such debts could never be repaid.

Broker went to a secure web page, logged in with his credentials, spoke into his lapel mic to the satellite's control room in Arizona. He got handed over control. The cluster was his.

'It'll be stationary?'

'That isn't how it works.' The technician at the other end launched into a spiel on orbits, atmospheric drag and maneuverability.

Broker listened patiently for a few seconds and then cut in. 'I'll get real-time images of Tehran, whenever I want them?'

'Yes.'

'Cool.'

He got himself familiar with the controls. The technicians had conjured up a simple online system that allowed him to manipulate the cameras and view Tehran. He could zoom in and out and exploit the full power of the six-inch image resolution.

He had gotten Werner involved, to link the images to real-time traffic in the Iranian capital, and by overlapping the signals from Zeb and the twins' encrypted phones, he could track them.

Which he did.

Hollywood and popular media got it wrong when it came to spy satellites. Those birds couldn't identify individual human faces, nor could they read the time on someone's wristwatch. Those were myths that militaries and intelligence agencies all around the world allowed to perpetuate. Why correct falsehoods if they helped keep the bad guys in check?

But the birds were more than capable of zooming down to individual vehicles and tracking them. Or identifying individual buildings, like the hotel where Meghan, Beth and the Israelis were staying.

He checked his watch. New York was eight and a half hours behind Tehran. *Werner and those birds say they are in one room.*

'Ladies,' he drawled in their comms channel, 'I bet you're missing me!'

'Like a hole in the head,' Meghan snorted. 'What's up?'

'Where's our friend?'

'In his room.'

'Yeah, I can hear you,' Zeb replied. None of them were using names. Standard operating protocol. 'No need to shout. Did you get them?'

'Get them? Not only do I have them, I have eyes on you right now. The women are in someone's room, aren't they?' he chortled.

'That's creepy,' Meghan said in disgust. 'What exactly can you see?'

'Relax. I tagged your phone signals and overlaid—'

'We get the picture,' Zeb cut in. 'You can track vehicles? You know the ones I mean.'

'Yeah, hold on.' Broker toggled the control. 'Our friend's home. His vehicle is outside his house. The other one, too, the main man. These babies in the sky are worth every dollar our friend spent on them. I could—'

'We're going online. Check your screen.' Meghan rolled her eyes at Beth and the kidon, who were lounging on a bed. She had her screen in hand and had typed out a message on a secure app. It was more secure than voice calls.

Curtain's going up tomorrow. Tanker, vehicle and bikes secured. Distraction in place, she had typed.

What about final getaway ride? Zeb responded.

There's a highrise hotel on Noshirvan, Broker replied. *Rooftop helipad. Avichai's making arrangements.*

Do I need to talk to him?

No.

How will you replace? Meghan asked Zeb.

I'll need Adir, he replied and went on to explain his plan.

Golzar went to the university the night before the event. In his vehicle was the curtain that had been dispatched to his office anonymously.

'Kianian,' he told the officer on arrival. 'Put that up in place of the torn drape.'

'Yes, agha.' The colonel barked orders to soldiers who jumped at his command.

'Careful,' the Sepah deputy head warned. 'Don't tear it like the other one.'

He followed the men and watched as they positioned ladders into place, climbed, removed the damaged curtain, and put up the new one.

He went forward to inspect it when they had finished. Yes, it matched the others. He breathed discreetly. It didn't smell any different. It felt the same, too.

He didn't know what it was made of and didn't want to know.

I hope it works.

Panic grabbed him for a moment. What was he doing? If he was caught, he would be killed for sure. His wife … Tousi would rape her. His children …

'Agha, are you all right?' Kianian, asked, concerned. 'You look pale.'

'Yes,' he snapped. Weakness couldn't be shown. Not in Sepah. 'Nothing's wrong with me. I'll be back tomorrow for a final round of inspection.'

He reached home and checked his phone. There was a message.

The devices will be in your vehicle tomorrow.

Chapter 58

The day of the speech dawned. Hot, with clouds and smog obscuring the sun. The Alborz mountains peeked through the grey fog hanging over the city. Milad Tower loomed over the city majestically.

None of those sights, nor the weather, improved Tousi's mood. He rushed into the office building without waiting for Rezghi to open the door. He crashed into Golzar's office.

'Rostam, do you have those files for me?'

'Yes, agha,' his deputy replied, coming from behind his desk and handing over a thick bunch of folders.

'You know my schedule today?'

'Yes, agha. First, a meeting with the President. Then discussions with the defense minister. Lunch with the head of NAJA. Then an afternoon meeting with the Supreme Leader. Your speech in the evening, after which, a debriefing with the Supreme Leader. You have a long day ahead, agha.'

'Don't I know it. All missions are in here?' he flicked through the files.

'Not the Israel one or the G20 one.'

'Good,' Tousi looked relieved. 'Only the Supreme Leader

knows about those.' He grimaced. 'I don't know how I am going to last for the speech. My energy levels will be low. My uniform—'

He ducked out of the office and roared, 'Hassan? Where's my spare uniform?'

'Here, agha,' his driver came running, with his clothes neatly arranged on a hanger.

'Put those in my office. And then let's go. Rostam.'

'Yes, agha.'

'How are the preparations for tonight?'

'Security is tight, agha. All students have been checked. The venue is ready. I will be going shortly to inspect it again. Police and our soldiers will be lined up on the route to the university. Go for your meetings in peace, agha. Today is your day.'

Tousi clapped him on the shoulder. 'What would I do without you? Oh, I nearly forgot.' He brought out his cell and called his wife. 'I'll be on TV tonight. Record my speech.'

And he left.

Golzar waited till 11 am and then he, too, departed with his driver. To the university.

Kianian was there to greet him as usual. He followed the Sepah deputy, pointing out new posters and paintings that had been put up overnight. There were body scanners at the glass entrance, and uniformed soldiers.

'They will be here till the speech?'

'No, agha. We will have shifts. They will be replaced by others just before the event.'

They went to the private driveway at the rear. 'There should be no vehicles here,' Golzar warned. 'Only the boss and his security vehicle will park here.'

'Yes, agha.'

'Have you run a security check again?'

'Yes, agha. We will run a final one just after 3 pm. After that, the auditorium will be sealed and only our soldiers will be inside. It will be opened just before the students start arriving.'

The Sepah deputy head went into the theater. The curtains looked lustrous under spotlights in the ceiling. Chairs were arranged on the stage. A table in front of them, with an elaborate flower arrangement on it.

'Won't those wilt?'

'They will be replaced every three hours, agha. Last change will be when we conduct our final check.'

Golzar nodded. 'You have done well, Kianian.'

He went to his vehicle and climbed into it. 'Back to our office,' he told his driver.

He felt underneath the seat when they were en route. There was something there: a plastic bag. He drew it out cautiously, making sure his driver couldn't see him.

He opened it and saw some kind of electrical circuits inside. Four.

Those must be the igniters.

He didn't know how Carter had gotten them inside his vehicle, but by now he had stopped wondering. It seemed the American could achieve anything.

Let him pull tonight off as well. And he swiftly and discreetly made the sign of the cross.

Carmen and Dalia went to Niavaran, to Kalish's showroom. They inspected the bikes, which now sported police plates.

'We won't be coming back,' Carmen told the dealer.

'I know.'

They rode at a sedate pace and parked in the demolished building on Nazari Street. The NAJA markings on it would ensure they wouldn't be touched by citizens. Golzar would make sure that no police or Sepah soldiers handled or towed them away.

The kidon sat on their bikes, helmets on their heads. Fifteen minutes later, they heard the growling of an engine. A fuel truck nosed through the midday traffic, clumps of smoke swirling behind it.

The driver honked and waved angrily at a slow-moving car in front. He put on his flashers, and the vehicle shuddered to a halt next to their bikes. The driver jumped out and wiped his brow with his sleeve. He knelt next to the driver-side tire and pretended to inspect it.

'Is it full?' Dalia asked him in a low voice.

'Yes,' Adir, the driver, replied. 'Liquid petroleum gas. It will explode in an accident.'

'That's the plan.'

She and Carmen removed their helmets and clipped them to the handlebars of their bikes. They adjusted their headscarves and followed Adir onto the main street, where they flagged cabs and returned to their respective hotels.

Tousi returned at 3 pm, sweating and swearing. He flung his files on Golzar's desk and threw himself into a chair. His deputy brought him a glass of water to drink, which he gulped in two swallows.

'Our Supreme Leader,' he grated, 'Rostam, I hope you are right about his plans for me. Because the way he's behaving, it feels like he wants to sack me.'

'He's testing you, agha. He wants to see if you can take

the pressure. He was needling you about Khalili and the Israel mission?'

'Yes,' the Sepah boss brooded. 'Who do we have as prisoners?'

'There's the Italian journalist. An American nurse. An Israeli—'

'She's Mossad, isn't she?'

'She hasn't admitted it, agha. She says she isn't from that country.'

'Nonsense. She was speaking Hebrew and had photographs of the Supreme Leader's office on her cell phone. Give her to Rezghi. He'll rape her and get her to confess. Give him the American nurse, too.'

'Agha—'

'Enough.' Tousi heaved himself to his feet. He gathered some of the files and went to his office.

Golzar returned to his seat, but shot up again when his boss poked his head through the doors.

'Where are those women?'

'Our soldiers from Farur Island, agha?'

'Yes.'

'I will bring them before you leave.'

'Are they good-looking?'

'I think so, agha.'

'They will sit with me, in my vehicle.'

'Of course, agha. That's what I had planned. The second vehicle will have six guards.'

'Did you find anything about those missing dogs?'

'Abbas, Majid—'

'Yes.'

'I think they are deserters, agha. Or they have fled the

country and sought asylum in another.'

'No one else should know about their absence.'

'No one will, agha. I have made appropriate entries in their records. All four are visiting their families.'

'Where are you going?'

'One final check at the venue, agha.'

'You take good care of me, Rostam.'

'I try to, agha.'

Golzar hurried out and sent a text when he was in his vehicle.

Your friends will be sitting next to him.

He looked up to the sky. No sign, no miracle. He sent another message.

This cannot fail. He's planning to get Rezghi to rape and torture prisoners.

Chapter 59

Rostam Golzar hid the phone underneath his seat. He knew it would be found if anyone searched his vehicle, but there was no time for elaborate concealment.

He wasn't a praying man, not outside his home. But in the rear of his vehicle, hidden from the driver, he clasped his hands and bowed his head for a moment.

'University, agha?' his driver asked.

'Yes,' he put a snap in his voice. His life and his organization's future would change in a few hours. If everything went to plan. But till then, he still was the second most feared man in Sepah.

They arrived half an hour later, and Golzar waved Kianian away. 'I want to inspect myself.'

The colonel nodded, turned to his soldiers and occupied himself. The Sepah deputy boss walked the hallway to the drive. He inspected it. It was clean, not a speck of dirt on the concrete. No vehicles. He went to the control room. The soldiers looked alert. They didn't look up from their screens, even though there wasn't anything significant to watch.

The emergency exit was empty.

He went inside the auditorium. Soldiers and workers putting on finishing touches. Cleaning the rows of seats. Tidying up the stage.

He went up the dais and inspected the restroom at the back. The sink gleamed, the room smelled fresh. He went to the curtain and, using the long drapes as cover, brought out the circuits from his pocket. There were adhesive strips behind each. No instructions. He reached as high as he could and attached them to the replaced curtain. He pressed the black buttons on them, the way Carter had instructed in his brief message. A countdown began on their panels.

His heart was pounding and his forehead was damp when he finished. He adjusted the hang so that they wouldn't be visible to the naked eye and then went onto the stage, placed his hands on his hips, and looked around.

'Good,' he said to no one in particular.

'You did your security check?' he asked Kianian when he emerged.

'Yes, agha. Just before you arrived. We will seal the theater now.'

'Great work, Lieutenant Colonel,' Golzar said, congratulating him formally. 'I will make sure you get a commendation for this.'

'Thank you, agha.'

'I will let you know when the boss leaves our office.'

'Yes, agha.'

4 pm

'The Shah Palace,' Golzar ordered his driver.

It was a hotel on Enghelab Street that Sepah used to house its soldiers. He had passed its details to Carter and his companions.

I hope the women have moved to it.

'Yes, agha.'

The drive from the university was short. The siren and lights on his vehicle moved other traffic out of the way, and fifteen minutes later, they were at its entrance.

Golzar climbed the few stairs and entered its lobby. A manager recognized his uniform and rushed over.

'I don't need help.'

The Brigadier General cast his eyes about and stopped when he saw two women.

The American sisters, in full Sepah battle dress, all dark, black scarf over their heads, fully covering their hair. They gripped HK416s competently.

They approached him and saluted smartly.

Pouri Vakili, Akhtar Nassour, their nameplates read. Both first lieutenants, their epaulets said.

'You are ready?'

'Yes, agha,' they replied.

I was expecting four women.

He didn't ask them, however. There were too many eyes on them.

'He's going to sit with you,' he murmured as he strode to his vehicle. 'You'll have to manage that.'

He climbed into his ride, the twins getting inside and seating themselves on the last bench, which was when inspiration struck him.

Of course!

His vehicle was the same build as Tousi's.

It had three bench seats behind the driver.

I can split them up. I have just the reason.

5 pm

Adir went to the chai vendor opposite Tousi's office. He was dressed just like the man, and flashed a wad of notes before the stall owner spoke a word.

'I am Sepah. This is a covert operation. Take this and go away.'

'But—'

'You didn't hear what I said?' he growled, his eyes cold. 'I am Sepah. You can go to those guards,' he nodded in the direction of the security barrier, 'and ask them. However, you won't be treated well if you ask. Or if you refuse.'

The man mopped his face with a towel. 'What's this about, agha?'

'Fool!' Adir hissed. 'Does Sepah tell you or any civilian the reasons for its operations? I think I'll just shoot you.' He reached for his waist when the vendor broke.

'No, agha. I'll go,' he quavered. 'How long should I be away?'

'For the rest of the day. Here,' Adir slapped the notes in his palm. 'Take these. And don't tell anyone. Otherwise, I'll personally kill you.'

The man stumbled away while Adir took his place.

The guards hadn't looked in their direction. A chai vendor was just part of the landscape, of no interest to them.

Avichai Levin made two calls.

Seconds later, a chopper landed on the Noshirvan hotel's helipad.

Getaway in place, he messaged Zeb, when he got the pilot's confirmation.

5:30 pm

A cab rolled up to the chai vendor. Adir looked casually, saw Hasan Rezghi behind the wheel.

'In position,' Zeb's voice came over his earpiece.

He clicked his tongue in acknowledgment. Beth and Meghan, now on the concrete drive at Tousi's office, clicked.

Carmen and Dalia, seated in their Sepah lookalike vehicle near the university, clicked too.

'Yes,' Malbim said, in Nazi Abad.

'I have eyes on,' Broker rumbled from their New York office.

5:45 pm

Hassan Rezghi didn't look at Vakili or Nassour, who were standing on the side of the driveway. They were beneath him. He knew why his boss wanted the women soldiers, but he didn't agree with Tousi.

Women were only good for sex and rearing children.

He sneered contemptuously, before getting belly-down to inspcct the bottom of his ride.

All clear.

He got to his feet and walked down the drive. He went out of the office complex through the pedestrian gate, stretched and loosened his legs.

He looked right and left and then crossed the street.

'Chai,' he ordered.

'Yes, agha,' the vendor sprang to action.

'You are new.'

'Amjad is ill, agha. I am his brother.'

Rezghi drank the beverage swiftly, placed the cup on the counter, and walked a few feet to the right. There was a cab a short distance away. The sun was still out, but its rays were already fading. They glanced off the vehicle's windshield, making it difficult for him to see inside.

He shrugged. He had a schedule to keep.

He unzipped and relieved himself. It was something he did with pride. He was Sepah, bodyguard to the most important man in the organization. Who dared admonish him?

He zipped up and was walking back when the vendor stopped him.

'He's calling you, agha.'

'Who?' Rezghi spun on his heel.

The cab driver had his head half out of the window and was saying something, beckoning with one hand.

'What is it?' the Sepah man asked.

'I … something … tell … you,' the driver's voice faded.

'This had better be important.' Rezghi glowered and approached the vehicle.

His eyes sharpened when he made out the driver's face.

Was that …? Did he look …?

He heard a footstep behind him.

A firework exploded loudly in the sky.

He started turning.

More fireworks exploded.

And then something slammed into his shoulder. He felt a prick. At the same time, the driver, who looked just like him, flung the door open, catching him in the knees and belly, then reared out like a striking cobra. Before Hassan Rezghi could react, two hammer blows struck him, one in the belly and one in his throat, and then he felt, heard, and saw nothing more.

Zeb and Adir grabbed the dead weight between them and dragged the bodyguard to the back of the vehicle. The trunk popped open.

They shoved Rezghi inside and swiftly zip-tied his wrists and legs and taped his mouth.

Adir looked at the syringe in his hand. It was empty. The nerve agent it had contained turned a person into a puppet. Now it was in Rezghi's bloodstream, acting instantly to shut down his thinking and speech faculties. The bodyguard was theirs to control. He would move where they wanted, how they wanted, without protest, without uttering a word. To the unknowing eye, such a victim would seem to act normally, so long as he wasn't required to speak.

'You knocked him out,' Adir said. He bent over the bodyguard and felt for his breath.

'He's dead! That blow to his throat must have killed him.'

'No loss,' Zeb grunted. He recalled the message Golzar had sent. What Tousi had planned for Rezghi. He felt no remorse.

He removed Rezghi's HK, strapped it across his own chest, and slammed the trunk shut. Adir trotted to the driver's side and climbed in.

In the distance, Malbim's fireworks were still bursting in the sky, drawing the guards' attention. That had provided them with the cover they needed to take Rezghi down.

'How do I look?' Zeb asked the Mossad agent.

'Like Hassan Rezghi.'

And with that, Zeb went to Tousi's office.

Chapter 60

6 pm

Zeb walked up the drive. Spotted Beth and Meghan, who stared straight ahead, their hands clasped around their HKs.

The second security vehicle had driven up and was parked behind his. Six men in it. He knew their names but didn't approach them.

Rezghi didn't mingle with them. He was Tousi's bodyguard. His standing was higher.

Zeb went to the glass entrance and waited for the Sepah boss.

The twins saluted smartly at his approach.

'I'll cap you if you smirk,' Beth whispered without moving her lips.

6:15 pm

There was a flurry of movement from within the office, and then Tousi was outside. His uniform had razor-sharp creases. His medals gleamed in the light. His mustache and beard were neatly trimmed, and the white in them added to his gravitas. He looked like a man of importance, someone who had to be listened to. He looked like who he was, the head of Sepah.

'Agha,' Zeb sprang alert as Tousi brushed past him, his eyes on the cell phone in his hand. 'These are our soldiers. Lieutenants Pouri Vakili and Akhtar Nassour.'

The women snapped a crisp salute.

'Good, good, they will sit on either side of me.'

The Sepah head climbed inside the vehicle.

'Agha,' Golzar hurried up. 'They should sit in the back bench. Not with you.'

Tousi frowned, 'Why, Rostam?'

'Agha,' his number two looked horrified. 'Think of the optics. How it will look. Your sitting with them will make them look like your equal. We want to show the students that we are modern. We have female soldiers. But women still have their place. And that's not with you, agha.'

Tousi's brow cleared. He clasped Golzar's hand. 'That's a very good point. Hassan, I have changed my mind. They will sit in the back.'

'Yes, agha.'

'Rostam, aren't you coming?'

'No, agha. I checked the university a short while ago. Everything is ready for you. Tonight is your night. You alone should be there.'

'Rostam, you think of everything. Hassan, enough waiting. Let's go.'

Zeb adjusted the rearview mirror. He could see Tousi's head bent over his phone. Beth and Meghan met his eyes, both of them impassive.

He set out, the second vehicle falling behind. Ten minutes later, he turned on the siren to clear traffic.

The Sepah man's head snapped up.

'Hassan? What's wrong with you? We never use the siren. You know that. People know who I am. They know my vehicle and the security one.'

Zeb gripped the wheel tighter. Recon wasn't perfect. Impersonating another person required more time than they had. This was a slip-up.

He raised his eyes and saw Tousi's eyes boring into his. Beth and Meghan's, behind, were worried.

'Not tonight, agha,' he replied confidently. 'Tonight, we should make a show of who you are. Let all of Tehran know that Major General Zarab Tousi, head of Sepah, is on the move, heading to the university to give a major speech.'

The anger in the Iranian's eyes faded. He smiled. 'You fox, Hassan. You are like Rostam. You are always one step ahead.'

'Thank you, agha,' Zeb replied and caught the sisters' eyes. They were relieved.

6:45 pm

Zeb rolled into the private drive right on schedule.

He jumped out of the vehicle and opened the door for Tousi, who stepped out and waited for the twins to climb out.

The security vehicle arrived. Soldiers emerged.

'You,' Zeb tossed his vehicle's keys to one of them. 'Turn my vehicle around to face the exit. Let the key be inside. Your vehicle should be behind mine. There,' he pointed at the parking bays at the end.

'All of you,' he ordered, 'you will station yourselves in the hallway. You will not enter the auditorium. Only I, Vakili and Nassour will be with the boss.'

Will they protest? Did Rezghi have something else agreed with them?

The soldiers did not say a word.

Looks like they obey Rezghi blindly.

That was good. It would play to their advantage.

He moved fast, went to the doors and opened them. Tousi was behind him. The sisters a step behind the Iranian.

Down the hallway, moving quickly, not just to stick to their schedule, but also to make sure no one looked at him for too long.

'You all,' he turned back once at the security detail. 'Three of you on either side of the hallway. Don't move from there.'

The soldiers took their positions.

A uniformed soldier approached from the other end. Kianian. He saluted Tousi, looked at the women but didn't say a word.

'Colonel.' Zeb addressed him respectfully, but it was a command. 'No one enters the auditorium with the boss but me and these two soldiers. Where are the chancellor and the vice-chancellor?'

'Inside, waiting for the boss.'

Zeb took Tousi through the emergency passage, through the back, and when they came to the stage, he stood aside.

A burst of applause greeted them. Students stood and cheered. A few whistled. Two men on the stage, in suits, approached them, hands outstretched, smiling.

'Agha, I and the women will be on stage, but behind you,' Zeb whispered. 'Best of luck with your speech.'

Tousi nodded and went past him to greet the university staff, and the event began.

Chapter 61

7:15 pm

Zeb stood motionless at the back of the stage, right arm clasping his HK 416, eyes swiveling, taking everything in. Beth and Meghan were to his left, five steps away, similarly posed.

The Chancellor was winding down his lengthy speech. The audience was getting restless. It wanted to hear the main speaker: Tousi.

The university officer laughed when someone booed.

'Now, let me introduce our chief guest.' A roar of approval sounded. 'Major General Zarab Tousi, Head of the Islamic Revolutionary Guard Corps.'

Zeb remained impassive as thunderous ovation filled the air.

I didn't think Tousi was this popular with the young generation. Golzar must have paid students to applaud.

The Sepah head approached the lectern and gestured with his hands for the crowd to quieten.

'Honorable Chancellor, Vice-Chancellor, dear students,' he began, at which Zeb tuned out.

He ran through a checklist in his mind.

Chopper's in place. Dummy flight plan has been filed.

Adir's with the fuel truck.

Carmen and Dalia are in position.

My disguise, Beth and Meghan's are holding up.

That left the detonators.

I hope they work.

Plan B, if they failed, was to somehow get away from the security vehicle and get to the chopper.

Golzar won't be able to help anymore. He's done as much as he can. Any more intervention will implicate him.

All of which boiled down to: failure wasn't an option. Not if he wanted to get out of Iran alive, along with the sisters, the Israelis and Tousi.

7:40 pm

'President Morgan is trying to destroy our nation with his sanctions,' Tousi thundered. He paused to take a sip of water.

A sharp crack sounded from somewhere behind.

Zeb tensed. He dropped his left hand to his side. Three fingers shot out, a message to the sisters, who he knew were sensing his moves.

Three.

'We will not bow,' The Iranian boomed, ignoring the sound. He had Rezghi at his back. he wasn't worried.

Two.

'We will retaliate. America will know the might of our country.'

One.

The curtain to their right burst into flame. A shocked gasp

ripped through the crowd. Tousi turned to look, just as the neighboring drapes caught fire and began burning brightly.

Zeb leaped forward, 'AGHA!' he yelled at the Iranian, who was frozen, staring at the blaze.

He grabbed the man, one hand around his left shoulder, the next around his neck.

'We need to get away. Vasili, Nassour, one of you in front, one of you behind. Shoot down anyone with a weapon.'

Tousi said something, but his voice was drowned in the panicked screams and yelling of the crowd. The gathered students rushed towards the exits. Smoke billowed from the curtains. A beam fell and accelerated the stampede.

Zeb pushed the Iranian towards the emergency passage, Meghan ahead of him.

'Run faster, agha,' he snapped, as he let go of the man's neck and glanced swiftly behind him. Beth, running behind them. No one else following.

'Hassan,' Tousi began, shrieking when Zeb jabbed him with a syringe and emptied the nerve agent into him.

The syringe went back into his pocket.

Meghan opened the doors ahead.

'YOU!' Zeb slowed for a moment, commanding the security officers who were running to join them. 'Get back into the auditorium. Find who's responsible. Arrest them.'

'But, the boss,' the nearest soldier protested.

'DO AS I SAY OR YOU'LL ANSWER TO ME LATER. I HAVE THE BOSS. I'LL TAKE HIM TO SAFETY. WE NEED TO FIND THE DOGS WHO STARTED THAT FIRE.'

The soldiers hesitated. The control room opened, heads peered out. The sounds of a panicked crowd from inside the theater reached them.

I have to divert the protection detail, send it to the fire. Quickly. We're losing time.

'GET BACK INSIDE, YOU FOOLS,' Zeb bellowed at the control room soldiers. 'MONITOR YOUR SCREENS. YOU,' he barked at the security personnel, 'GO TO THE THEATER. THAT'S AN ORDER.'

They slunk away. Zeb shoved Tousi forward and broke into a run. He glanced at the Iranian. He was glassy-eyed, sweat was on his forehead, a frozen expression on his face.

Good. Anyone who sees him will think he's scared, unable to talk.

The Sepah man's legs were pumping, his body working automatically to keep up with Zeb's run.

7:45 pm

They reached the drive. Cool air hit them. Zeb and Beth maneuvered Tousi onto the second bench. Meghan climbed into the driver's seat, keyed the ignition, looked back to check they were seated, and floored the vehicle.

Tires squealed. Rubber burnt and bit, and the vehicle shot out.

Beth climbed awkwardly into the front seat, next to her sister.

'Any cops, any Sepah vehicle shows up,' Zeb said tersely, 'shoot at their tires. If that doesn't stop them, shoot into them.'

'Gotcha. We're on the move,' she said, sending an alert on her mic.

Meghan raced out of the university campus, joined Tale-qani Street and lit up the lights and siren.

Cars and trucks got out of the way. Pedestrians looked on curiously, trying to figure out who was behind the darkened windows.

A right turn on Qods Street. Pedal to metal. Storefronts flashed past, their lights a river of colors. Sounds reached them dimly through the soundproofed sides of the vehicle. A honk here. A fading shout there.

Zeb checked on Tousi. He was breathing normally. His eyes staring ahead. His throat working now and then as he swallowed.

7:53 pm

Broker's voice in their headsets.

'Bad news. Those soldiers? His protection men? They have set out of the university in pursuit.'

Zeb craned his head back instinctively. He couldn't make out the Sepah vehicle in the dark.

'How far behind?' he snapped.

'Eight minutes.'

'How come we haven't heard anything on their comms channel?'

'I turned it off,' Meghan replied grimly. She turned a knob and the vehicle was immediately filled with voices.

'Rezghi? Where are you?'

'Where's the boss?'

'Kianian.' Zeb recognized Golzar's voice. *He must have taken charge from his office.* 'How could a fire break out there? Where's our boss?'

'Rezghi's taken him, agha.'

'Where?'

'He isn't answering. We're trying to follow him.'

'Go after him. Hassan Rezghi, if you are listening, bring the boss to the office immediately.'

A car swerved in front. Meghan turned the wheel hard and got out of its way, overtook it and sped. Beth turned down the comms. Quiet returned.

'Six minutes now. They're catching up. They should be able to track your vehicle.'

7:55 pm

In Azin Alley, Carmen fired up her vehicle, the Sepah look-alike.

'We'll take it from here,' she said calmly, as if discussing the weather.

She nosed out of the street, joined Qods Street and hit her light bar and sirens. Vehicles got out of the way.

'Now four minutes behind you,' Broker announced.

Dalia fingered her HK. Shooting wasn't on the agenda, but any plan got bent out of shape when it met reality.

Carmen was driving slowly, waiting for the pursuing security team to catch up.

'Police? Other soldiers?' she asked.

'Lots of them,' Broker answered, 'but everyone's going to the university. It looks like they're still trusting Rezghi.' He chuckled. 'Golzar's helping with that. He's asking Sepah men to set up a perimeter around the venue. Stop all the students, search them again.' His voice sharpened. 'Now a minute behind you. You should see them.'

'Yes, got them,' Dalia replied, watching the incoming vehicle in her side mirror.

She counted down softly, waiting for it to come close, its siren wailing too, its lights flashing.

'NOW!'

8:10 pm

Carmen hit the gas. Their Mercedes leaped forward. The Sepah vehicle was close, so close that they could see soldiers in the rear mirror, hands waving, gesticulating furiously at them.

She didn't get out of the way.

She matched the pursuit ride's speed. The idea was to slow it down. Let Zeb get away. So far, it seemed to be working.

Until the Sepah soldiers rammed the Merc. Carmen fought for control. She looked at Dalia, who was fingering her weapon.

'Not yet,' she replied. No panic in her voice. 'They won't be able to overtake.'

The Sepah ride tried to pass from the left. She cut it off. Both vehicles going at breakneck speeds on the streets of Tehran.

Bozorgmehr Street flashed past. An ambulance raced in the opposite direction.

'You won't hold them off for long. They'll soon know your vehicle is fake,' Broker warned. 'Other Sepah vehicles will come to surround you.'

'Yes. Meg, how far ahead are you?'

'We've crossed Nazari Street. No one's pursuing us. Go for your act.'

Carmen opened up just as a warning shot flew over their Merc. The three-liter engine under the hood responded. A widening gap appeared between them and the pursuit.

Enghelab Street appeared. Heavy traffic on the cross street. Dalia reached over and pressed the horn, adding its sound to the siren's.

They flew through holes in traffic, Carmen weaving in and out expertly, and then saw clear road ahead. Just as if it had been made to order for them.

'Adir?' Dalia asked.

'Ready.'

The kidon looked in the mirrors. The soldiers had fallen behind but were catching up fast. Carmen eased up on the gas, fractionally. The Sepah ride came closer.

'Go,' she told Adir as Zhandarmeri Street fell behind.

8:17 pm

Open road ahead of them, still.

And then movement.

A fuel truck lumbered through Nazari Street. Going to the right. Crossing right ahead of them.

Carmen timed it.

The Sepah vehicle was close. So close that the Merc would have obscured a lot of the view ahead. Rounds hit their rear window.

She and Dalia ignored them.

The truck was gathering speed. Thirty feet in front of them.

Now twenty.

She unsnapped her belt.

Dalia unsnapped hers too.

'Ready?'

Her partner nodded.

Ten feet to the truck, which was right in front of them.

A look in the mirror.

Sepah soldiers close enough for them to see mouths opening in panic. But the pursuers were too close to maneuver out of the way.

'Go.'

She and Dalia flung open their doors and leaped out of the vehicle.

They hit the road hard, breath escaping them in a grunt. They rolled with the momentum, and then the ground shuddered as an enormous blast tore through the night sky when their Merc slammed into the fuel truck and the petroleum gas exploded.

Carmen didn't stop to watch. She ducked low, ran across the street, heaved Dalia to her feet. They hustled to the ruined building on Nazari Street.

'Good work,' Broker, in their headsets. 'The Sepah soldiers got caught in the accident.'

The kidon went to their waiting BMWs. A figure moved and came to them. They didn't react in alarm.

It was Adir.

He climbed behind Dalia, the bikes came to life, and the three kidon shot out into the night.

8:28 pm

They caught up with Meghan's ride just as it was turning into the Noshirvan hotel's drive.

Zeb clambered out, got hold of Tousi and helped him out.

The sisters and Carmen and Dalia fanned out in front, leading the way. Adir brought up the back.

'Chopper's ready. No pursuit so far. But y'all will have to

hurry.' Broker, guiding them.

They entered the lobby, moving fast.

'Stay back,' Zeb thundered when the suited manager looked up. 'This is Sepah business.'

Two women behind a counter. A guest checking in. All of them looking their way.

The hotel owner was a sayanim, but its employees were Iranian. They weren't involved.

Another thought occurred to him.

They could call the police and report Tousi's presence.

He waited, holding onto the Sepah boss, as Beth jabbed the elevator button.

It arrived. All of them crammed in.

They could have taken the stairs, but the hotel was eighteen floors high.

'Uh-oh,' Broker commented. 'An outgoing call from the lobby to the police.'

The elevator was a highspeed model. It moved silently, fast.

'I have overridden its controls. No one on any floor will stop it. I can see three vehicles peeling off Daneshgah Street, coming towards Noshirvan.'

The fourteenth floor flashed past.

The elevator slowed and stopped at the eighteenth.

A second for the doors to open.

They rushed out, went to the door on the landing, stairs that went to the roof.

'Those vehicles are close, now entering the hotel's drive.'

Another door, to the roof.

It was locked.

8:35 pm

Meghan and Beth kicked it.

It shuddered.

'Stand back,' Carmen snapped and fired around the lock.

The door was wooden. It finally splintered and gave way when the kidon smashed her shoulder against it.

They ran onto the roof.

The chopper was ahead, its blades swirling, lights at its tail. The pilot pointed a gun at them.

'Put that away, Harel,' Adir shouted, 'and get us off the ground.'

The women climbed in first. Grabbed Tousi and hauled him inside. Zeb followed, then Adir.

The chopper's blades whirled. Its engine whined.

'Cops and soldiers entering the lobby,' Broker announced.

And then they were lifting, and in eight minutes had cleared Iran's airspace.

Chapter 62

Tousi woke up when something shook him. He raised his head. He felt woozy. He blinked and licked his parched lips. Tried to move and found that his hands were tied, as were his legs.

And then he noticed where he was.

In a chopper, whose landing had woken him up.

And next to him was Hassan.

'Hassan?' he croaked and then his eyes fell on Vasili and Nassour, their nameplates close enough for him to read. He noticed the two women and the man next to them. Strangers, all of them wearing Sepah uniform.

'Hassan?' his voice strengthened. 'What is this? Where are we?'

The chopper's door opened. Rezghi climbed out, grabbed him and pulled him out.

Tousi stumbled. Regained his balance.

'HASSAN REZGHI! WHAT ARE YOU DOING? ANSWER ME,' he roared.

'WHY HAVE YOU TIED ME—'

Shock flooded through him. 'You have turned traitor. All

of you. You don't know what you have done. You can never escape …'

He trailed off, watching dumbfounded when his bodyguard and the two Farur Island soldiers did something to their faces.

'You!' he gasped, staggering back. 'Carter! You!'

He recognized the women next to the American. Twins. Their names escaped him.

'How … What have you done to Hassan?'

Carter didn't answer. He was looking into the distance.

Tousi followed his eyes and only then realized they were at some airport. In some secluded area, far away from the main building. He couldn't see any names, any way to identify where they were. A Gulfstream was parked close, another private jet next to it. He couldn't read their tails.

He shivered as a cold blast of air hit them.

It was night. His last recollection was that of the fire in the auditorium. Was it the same night?

He glanced at his watch. Yes, it was. Five hours ago.

He gathered his courage. He was Sepah's head. He had run agents all over the world. His people had carried out audacious missions. He had grabbed prisoners and tortured them. He had the Supreme Leader's ear.

'Carter,' he scoffed. 'Do you think you can get away with this? My people will piece everything together. Golzar is a highly competent man. He will be searching for me, even as we speak. Where are we? Kish? Tabriz? Shiraz? You might have captured me, but you cannot escape from my country.'

'And anyway, what are you going to do with me? Your President Morgan does not believe in torture. He wants to close down Gitmo. He does not believe in rendition. He's weak. How will you extract everything I know? By offering me money?'

He laughed. 'Whatever you offer won't be enough. I won't cooperate. I might be your hostage, but I am untouchable.'

'That's what you think,' said a man as he came from behind the second aircraft and approached them.

Tousi recognized him immediately, and cold terror flooded him.

'Zarah Tousi.' Avichai Levin pierced him with hawk-like eyes. 'Welcome to Israel. Your days of attacking my country, the USA, our allies, are over. You won't see daylight again. Your life will be one long night.'

'You can't get away with this,' Tousi blustered.

'We just did. We are in Tel Aviv. Take him away.'

The man in the chopper, the stranger, grabbed him and led him away.

'My country will retaliate! We'll start a war!' Tousi shouted.

No one paid him any attention.

'That was close.' Levin watched along with Zeb and the others as Adir took Tousi to a vehicle and drove him away.

'I didn't think it would work,' he confessed.

'Neither did I,' Zeb said, breaking into a rare grin. 'Your support, Carmen and Dalia, a lot of luck, and Golzar made the difference.'

'Golzar. We own him now.'

'He's a good man, Avichai. I am sure he will turn Sepah around. Let him be.'

'We'll watch him closely,' Levin replied, unimpressed by Zeb's endorsement. There was too much history between

Sepah and Mossad for him to trust a new boss that easily.

'Watch, but don't do anything. He will stick to his promises.'

The two men stood silently in the night as the sisters spoke softly to the kidon.

Dawn would break in a few hours. It would light up Israel, a country that had embarked on a new journey with Palestine. There was hope. There was optimism. The threats of war had receded.

It won't be easy, Zeb mused. *Iran won't change its ways just because Tousi's captured. But it's a step.*

'Your plan had to work, didn't it?' Levin gazed at him keenly.

'Yes,' Zeb admitted. 'We didn't have time for trial runs. Those igniters? Broker had arranged for those. He had tested them and they worked. But we never got to see if they would work with the curtains. Luckily, they did.'

'What about Rezghi?'

'Adir parked the car near Tousi's office. It will be discovered soon, if it hasn't been already. The Iranian government will put two and two together.'

Meghan's brow cleared. She had been listening to them. 'I was wondering why you waited so long to move him when the fire started. You wanted the TV cameras to focus on him and you.'

'Yeah. Tousi attacked Israel. He was behind Khalili. The Iranians will work out that it wasn't Rezghi on the stage with him. The Supreme Leader, if he's smart, will figure out the message. That despite all their security, we can reach out and strike them. None of them are safe.'

'If you had failed?' Levin asked.

'Then we would have died, eventually. Tousi would have captured us, tortured us and would have paraded us in front of the media.'

Death had no meaning for him, but that of the sisters and the Israelis would have been on him.

A hand gripped his shoulder. Carmen, her eyes twinkling.

'There's no way we would have failed. You see, Mossad was involved.'

They broke up half an hour later.

Zeb hugged Levin and patted him on the back, 'Shalom Avichai.'

'Shalom, achi.' *Achi*, brother. It was how the Mossad director regarded him.

Zeb watched as his friend left, along with the kidon. He felt a hand around his waist. Beth's. Meghan's arm encircled him, too.

He looked at them.

'Home?' the elder sister asked.

Tehran was where his world had collapsed. It was where life had lost any meaning for him.

It wasn't all dark and bleak, however. He had a team. It had become his family.

'Home,' he confirmed and the three of them went to their Gulfstream.

Bonus Chapter from The Peace Killers

Jerusalem, Israel

Eliel Magal woke up when the city was still dark.

No, he corrected himself, when he cracked open the window and peered out at the quiet neighborhood. It was grey. Dawn was approaching fast.

Five-thirty am. He didn't have to look at the bedside clock to know what time it was. He always woke up at that hour, a deeply ingrained habit.

He padded to the small bathroom and, when he emerged, knocked on the door down the hallway. Navon Shiri opened it instantly, eyes alert, hair brushed neatly, dressed in plain white.

The two men went to the kitchen and prepared breakfast. Warm milk for Magal, cereal and a banana for Shiri, who took his bowl to the living room and turned on the TV, to the Palestinian Broadcasting Corporation, PBC, channel. The programming wasn't available in Israel, but the two men had piggybacked on an illegal feed and were able to watch the content.

Magal joined him on the couch, and the two watched the news in silence.

The two men could have been brothers. They weren't. They were lightly tanned, with dark eyes, short cropped hair, clean-shaven. Five feet, six inches tall. No distinguishing features. Nothing about them stood out.

Magal's glass clinked when he placed it on the table as he watched the screen.

Gaza was burning, as was the West Bank.

The United States had opened its embassy in Jerusalem, and that had triggered intense outrage and violent protests in Palestine.

Thousands of Palestinian protesters had gathered at the border fence and had thrown Molotov cocktails, burning tires, stones, whatever missiles they could find, at the Israeli Defense Forces, IDF, on the other side of the fence. The IDF had fired in return, and dozens of people had been killed.

Shiri peeled his banana and flicked to another news channel. Different reporter, same coverage. He went back to the previous one and bit into his fruit.

The two of them didn't need to discuss the riots. They knew what had happened. Every person in Israel and Palestine knew of the region's history and that of Jerusalem in particular.

Palestinians believed they were an oppressed people, Israel the oppressor. The majority of Israelis believed they were defending their country and their land.

Nabil and Shiri didn't look at the screen when the reporter brought up a map and went through a history recap.

In 1948, Israel declared itself an independent state. The next day, war broke out between a coalition of Arab nations and the newly formed country. Jordan occupied West Bank and East Jerusalem. Egypt took over Gaza at the end of the war.

In 1967, there was another war, at the end of which Israel occupied East Jerusalem, Gaza, Golan Heights and Sinai. In 1979, Israel and Egypt signed a historic peace treaty and Sinai was returned to Egypt.

That eventually led to what the Palestine state currently was, a country in two geographical parts. West Bank, bordered by Jordan to the east and Israel in all other directions, and the Gaza Strip, which had the Mediterranean Sea behind it, Egypt to the south and Israel at the north and west. Palestine's two regions did not share a border between them.

The politics and governance of the state were divided, too. The West Bank was administered by the Palestinian National Authority, while Gaza was ruled by Hamas, which, Israel, the United States and the European Union regarded as a terrorist organization.

The reporter droned on about the status of Jerusalem, that East Jerusalem was claimed by Palestine but was controlled by Israel. Shiri tuned to Kan TV, the Israeli channel. Similar news, with an Israeli slant. He grunted in disgust and was about to turn off the TV when Magal raised his hand.

The reporter went into breathless excitement mode.

'There are several rumors,' she said, leaning forward, her eyes sparkling, 'that Israeli and Palestinian negotiators are meeting in secret to work out a historic peace accord. Government officials on both sides have declined to comment on this.'

She went on about the significance of the development, if true, and at that point Shiri turned off the TV. He finished his cereal and went to the kitchen, where he washed and rinsed his bowl.

Magal yawned and stretched. 'I'll get ready,' he said.

Shiri grunted and peered out of the kitchen window. It was

seven am. Light traffic outside in German Colony, the Jerusalem neighborhood they were in. He went to his room and changed into white shirt and khaki trousers. Walking shoes over his feet. A Glock 17 went into a holster attached to his belt. He adjusted his loose shirt to ensure the gun wasn't visible to the casual eye. In his trouser pockets went several spare magazines.

He emerged from his room to see an old woman in the hallway. She was in a patterned dress that fell below her knees. Hunched over, her white hair tied in a neat bun. Glasses on her wrinkled face. Left hand trembling as she held a walking stick. Right hand clutching a large bag, which seemed heavy.

Magal, the woman in disguise, placed the bag on the floor and flexed his fingers. Shiri toed it and felt something hard inside it. He peered down and nodded in satisfaction when he saw the shape of a Galil MAR, an Israeli automatic rifle.

'Ready?' he asked in Hebrew.

'Let's go,' Magal replied.

Author's Message

Thank you for taking the time to read *Burn Rate.* If you enjoyed it, please consider telling your friends and posting a short review.

Sign up to Ty Patterson's mailing list (www.typatterson.com/subscribe) and get *The Watcher*, a Zeb Carter novella, exclusive to newsletter subscribers. Join Ty Patterson's Facebook Readers Group, at www.facebook.com/groups/324440917903074.

Check out Ty on Amazon, iTunes, Kobo, Nook, and on his website www.typatterson.com.

Books by Ty Patterson

Warriors Series Shorts

This is a series of novellas that link to the Warriors Series thrillers

Zulu Hour, Book 1
The Shadow, Book 2
The Man From Congo, Book 3
The Texan, Book 4
The Heavies, Book 5
The Cab Driver, Book 6
Warriors Series Shorts, Boxset I, Books 1-3
Warriors Series Shorts, Boxset II, Books 4-6

Gemini Series

Dividing Zero, Book 1
Defending Cain, Book 2
I Am Missing, Book 3
Wrecking Team, Book 4

Zeb Carter Series

Zeb Carter, Book 1
The Peace Killers, Book 2
Burn Rate, Book 3

Warriors Series

The Warrior, Book 1
The Reluctant Warrior, Book 2
The Warrior Code, Book 3
The Warrior's Debt, Book 4
Flay, Book 5
Behind You, Book 6
Hunting You, Book 7
Zero, Book 8
Death Club, Book 9
Trigger Break, Book 10
Scorched Earth, Book 11
RUN!, Book 12
Warriors series Boxset, Books 1-4
Warriors series Boxset II, Books 5-8
Warriors series Boxset III, Books 1-8

Cade Stryker Series

The Last Gunfighter of Space, Book 1
The Thief Who Stole A Planet, Book 2

Sign up to Ty Patterson's mailing list and get *The Watcher*, a Zeb Carter novella, exclusive to newsletter subscribers. Join Ty Patterson's Facebook group of readers, at www.facebook.com/groups/324440917903074.

Check out Ty on Amazon, iTunes, Kobo, Nook and on his website www.typatterson.com.

About the Author

Ty has been a trench digger, loose tea vendor, leather goods salesman, marine lubricants salesman, diesel engine mechanic, and is now an action thriller author.

Ty is privileged that thriller readers love his books. 'Unputdownable,' 'Turbocharged,' 'Ty sets the standard in thriller writing,' are some of the reviews for his books.

Ty lives with his wife and son, who humor his ridiculous belief that he's in charge.

Connect with Ty:

Twitter: @pattersonty67
Facebook: www.facebook.com/AuthorTyPatterson
Website: www.typatterson.com
Mailing list: www.typatterson.com/subscribe